Jihad at Sea

The Barbary War, America's First Encounter with Radical Islam

Winter Island Press
Salem, Massachusetts

RICHARD SCOTT

JIHAD AT SEA

For Jeanne

I

Copyright © 2016
Winter Island Press
Contact the author at richard.scott2000@comcast.net

Books by Richard Scott

Tony Dantry Thrillers
The Reluctant Assassin: Paper and ebook
The Eager Assassin: Paper and ebook
The Assassin Chip: Paper and ebook
Closer Than You Think: Paper and ebook

Other books by Richard Scott
Murder on Third Avenue: Paper and ebook
The Second Assassination (Historical Novel): Paper and ebook
Salem, the Novel (Historical Novel: Paper and ebook
Mission in Time (Historical Sci-Fi Novel): Paper and ebook

JIHAD AT SEA

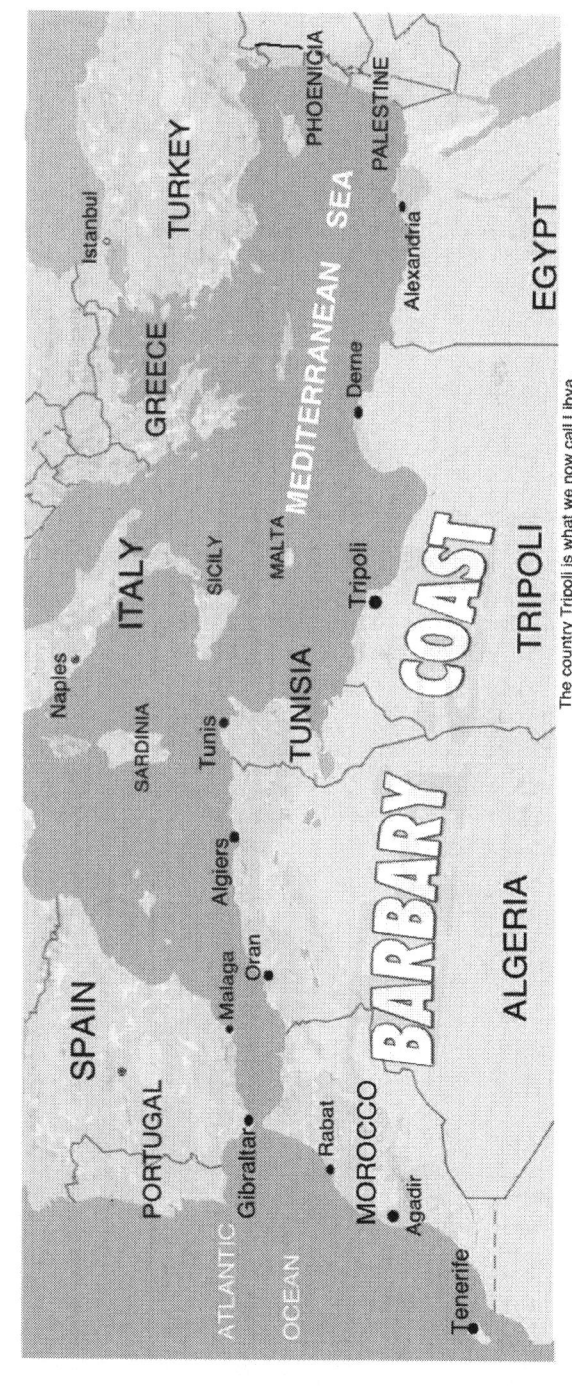

The country Tripoli is what we now call Libya.

Cast of Characters

Abdallah, Mohammed Ben (Mohammed III): Sultan of Morocco 1784 *Real*
Adams, John: President of the United States 1797-1801 *Real*
Adja, Sidi Haji Abdul Rahman: Tripoli's ambassador to Britain in 1786 *Real*
Ahmad: Footman to Sultan Mohammed Ben Abdallah 1784.*Fictional*
Bainbridge, William: Captain of the *Philadelphia*. *Real*
Barron, Samuel: Commodore in U.S. Navy. *Real*
Beveridge, Captain: Captain of lead ransom ship. *Fictional*
Billings, Josiah: First mate replacing Will Proctor in 1780s on the *Betsey*.*Fictional*
Blount, William, Delegate to Continental Congress from North Carolina. *Real*
Carlisle, Robert: Owner of the shipping company that owned the *Betsey*.*Fictional*
Carrington, Edward: Delegate to Continental Congress from Virginia. *Re*
Cathcart, James: Bosun on the merchant ship *Betsey* .*Fictional*
Chase, Jeremiah: Former mayor of Annapolis, Md., Delegate to Continental Congress *Real*
Dale, Richard: Commodore in U.S. Navy. *Real*
Fitzhugh, James: Prisoner killed by guard at grave-digging site and identified by Lisle. *Fictional*
Gerry, Elbridge: American statesman, Vice President under James Madison. *Real*
Gorham, Nathaniel: Massachusetts delegate to Continental Congress in 1786 – 1787.*Real*
Habib, Captain: Pirate captain of the *Jabbar* .*Fictional*
Hardy, Richard: First mate for Proctor in 1801 on the *Trenton* *Fictional*
Hopkins, Stephen: Delegate to Continental Congress from Rhode Island.*Real*
Hussein: Chief Advisor to Suleiman 1782.*Fictional*
Jefferson, Thomas: President of the United States 1801-1809.*Real*.
Karamanli, Hamet: Older brother of Yusuf. *Real*
Karamanli, Yusuf: Pasha or Bashaw of Tripoli. *Real*
King, Rufus: Delegate from Massachusetts to Continental Congress. *Real*
Lee, Richard Henry: President of Continental Congress in 1786. From Virginia. Famous for calling for American independence from Britain. *Real*
Lisle, Peter: Scottish deckhand who converted to Islam. Became pirate and took the name of an earlier pirate, Murad Rais.
Madison, James: Secretary of State under Jefferson. President of the United States 1809-1817 -

JIHAD AT SEA

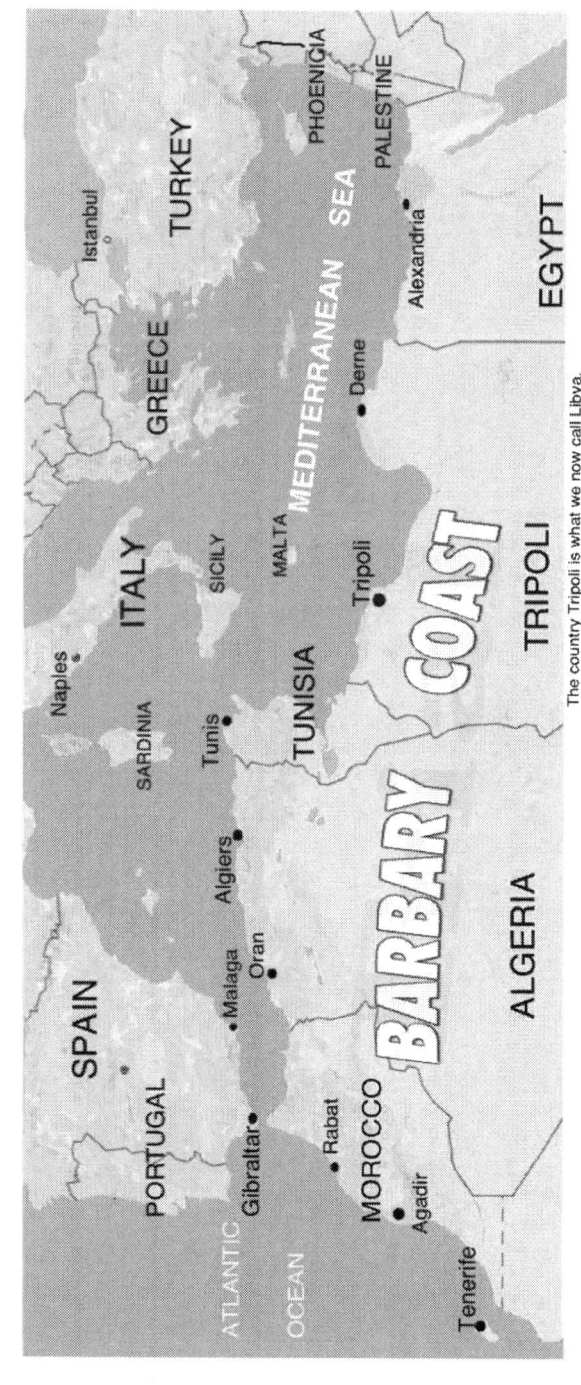

Cast of Characters

Abdallah, Mohammed Ben (Mohammed III): Sultan of Morocco 1784 *Real*
Adams, John: President of the United States 1797-1801 *Real*
Adja, Sidi Haji Abdul Rahman: Tripoli's ambassador to Britain in 1786 *Real*
Ahmad: Footman to Sultan Mohammed Ben Abdallah 1784.*Fictional*
Bainbridge, William: Captain of the *Philadelphia*. *Real*
Barron, Samuel: Commodore in U.S. Navy. *Real*
Beveridge, Captain: Captain of lead ransom ship. *Fictional*
Billings, Josiah: First mate replacing Will Proctor in 1780s on the *Betsey.Fictional*
Blount, William, Delegate to Continental Congress from North Carolina. *Real*
Carlisle, Robert: Owner of the shipping company that owned the *Betsey.Fictional*
Carrington, Edward: Delegate to Continental Congress from Virginia. *Re*
Cathcart, James: Bosun on the merchant ship *Betsey* .*Fictional*
Chase, Jeremiah: Former mayor of Annapolis, Md., Delegate to Continental Congress *Real*
Dale, Richard: Commodore in U.S. Navy. *Real*
Fitzhugh, James: Prisoner killed by guard at grave-digging site and identified by Lisle. *Fictional*
Gerry, Elbridge: American statesman, Vice President under James Madison. *Real*
Gorham, Nathaniel: Massachusetts delegate to Continental Congress in 1786 – 1787.*Real*
Habib, Captain: Pirate captain of the *Jabbar* .*Fictional*
Hardy, Richard: First mate for Proctor in 1801 on the *Trenton* *Fictional*
Hopkins, Stephen: Delegate to Continental Congress from Rhode Island.*Real*
Hussein: Chief Advisor to Suleiman 1782.*Fictional*
Jefferson, Thomas: President of the United States 1801-1809.*Real*.
Karamanli, Hamet: Older brother of Yusuf. *Real*
Karamanli, Yusuf: Pasha or Bashaw of Tripoli. *Real*
King, Rufus: Delegate from Massachusetts to Continental Congress. *Real*
Lee, Richard Henry: President of Continental Congress in 1786. From Virginia. Famous for calling for American independence from Britain. *Real*
Lisle, Peter: Scottish deckhand who converted to Islam. Became pirate and took the name of an earlier pirate, Murad Rais.
Madison, James: Secretary of State under Jefferson. President of the United States 1809-1817 -

Masad, Salma: Chief aide to Sultan Abdullah 1784 *Fictional*
Mason, Jonathan: Massachusetts Federalist delegate to U.S. Senate 1800-1803, College of New Jersey (Now Princeton University) *Rea*
Mifflin, Thomas: Of Pennsylvania, President of Continental Congress Nov 4, 1783- Nov 29, 1784 *Real*
Mohammed III: See Abdallah, Mohammed Ben above, Sultan of Morocco 1784 *Real*
Morris, Richard: Commodore in U.S. Navy *Real*
Orne, Henry: Captain of the *Betsey*. *Fictional*
Perry, Elias: Dale's first mate. *Fictional*
Pickering, Timothy: Secretary of State under Washington and Adams (Harvard University) *Real*
Pierce, Daniel: Seaman on Betsey. *Fictional*
Platt, Zephaniah: Delegate to Continental Congress from New York. *Real*
Preble, Edward: Commodore in U.S. Navy. *Real*
Proctor, William: Salem seaman and ultimately officer in U.S. Navy. *Fictional*
Rahim, First mate to Rais *Fictional*
Rais, Murad: See Lisle, Peter above
Sharif: Old, Wizened advisor of Yusuf Karamanli. *Fictional*
Strong, Caleb: Massachusetts delegate to Constitutional Convention *Real*
Suleiman: Sultan of Morocco, son of Mohammed III and brother of
Washington, George: First president of the United States 1789 – 1797 *Real*
Yazid: Sultan of Morocco, son of Mohammed III and brother of Suleiman 1790 -1792 *Real*

Ships

USS Baltimore, *S*hip commanded by William Proctor in Preble's squadron 1803
Betsey, American merchant ship
USS Constitution, flagship of Commodore Preble's squadron 1803
da Gama, Tripolitan pirate ship
USS Enterprise, Ship sent from Dale's squadron to Malta for supplies
Jabbar, Moroccan pirate ship
HMS Maidstone, British ship. Sir Richard Strachan in command. 1803
Mastico, Tripolitan pirate ship, later renamed ***USS Intrepid*** when captured
Mirboha, Moroccan pirate ship
President, Flagship of Commodore Dale's squadron 1801
Sabha, Tripolitan pirate ship commanded by Rais against U.S. in 1801
Tocra, Tripolitan pirate ship
USS Trenton, Frigate under the command of Proctor 1801

Jihad at Sea

The Barbary War, America's First Encounter with Radical Islam

Part 1

Chapter 1
The Atlantic, May 1784

The 300-ton merchant ship *Betsey* was within sighting distance of Tenerife, the capital of the Canary Islands. The Canaries, an archipelago conquered by Spain in the 15th century and roughly 100 miles west of Morocco's Atlantic coast, had been a profitable port of call for British North American merchant ships for decades. The *Betsey* was one of the first vessels to fly under the flag of the United States.

Up to this point the *Betsey* had enjoyed a swift and uneventful crossing, having left Boston just 28 days earlier. One of the ship's crew pointed to another ship less than a mile off to their starboard. The vessel appeared to be minding its own business, as they were. It was not unusual to see ships as you neared land.

William Proctor, the *Betsey*'s first mate, was looking forward to arriving in the colorful island capital. This was his first voyage as a first mate, having been promoted just two months ago at the age of 19. As far as he knew, he was one of the youngest first mates out of Boston. He'd been a seaman for two years and had distinguished himself with competence and maturity beyond his years.

As a seaman, William Proctor had had very little time or money to spend pursuing his own interests when arriving at a foreign port. This time, as first mate, he hoped to enjoy Tenerife more. He'd been there on a previous trip and found it to be a pleasant, welcoming place. He couldn't wait to explore it.

Captain Henry Orne, a man in his early forties, balding and of average height, looked more like a school teacher than a veteran sea captain. Proctor knew from personal observation that Orne's stern, scholarly manner and less than robust appearance was deceptive. The man was strong, forceful and commanding when the occasion called for it.

Orne stood at the helm watching carefully for reefs, shoals and other hazards that can turn a successful crossing into a nightmare. Proctor, several inches taller than the captain, with long, blond, slightly unkempt hair, was at Orne's side. He'd learned on the trip over that the captain only appeared stern at first glance. He soon saw that the man made an effort to understand his crew and treat them with respect. Proctor, in turn, found himself respecting Orne. He looked to the captain as a mentor.

Now, at the helm with the captain, he was keeping a watchful eye out for things that Orne might miss. So far, everything had gone more smoothly than any seafarer could have hoped for. Even the weather had cooperated. The captain appeared relaxed and even exchanged a joke or two with young Proctor.

A few minutes later Proctor called his attention to the ship off in the distance.

"Looks like a Mediterranean sloop," said the captain. "Probably Spanish or Portuguese. Seems to be heading our way."

"You think she's on her way to America?"

"Doubt it. These cargo sloops tend to run up and down the coast of Africa or along the northern coast of the Med. Mostly trade in sugar, coffee, bananas and other fruit."

Proctor nodded his understanding, but something didn't make sense to him.

"Doesn't it seem a bit strange, captain, that she'd be heading our way if she was plying the coastal trade? She's heading almost due west."

"Aye, I see your point, William. 'Tis a bit strange. If they come close enough we'll ask 'em where they're off to. In the meantime best you talk to Cathcart about landing."

William left the helm and met with James Cathcart, bosun of the

Betsey, and told him it was time to ready the crew for landing in Tenerife.

"Aye, sir," said Cathcart, who was five years Proctor's senior. At first he'd found it difficult to take orders from someone so much younger. Gradually, though, Proctor had won him over as he demonstrated a competence beyond his years. "What do we do about that sloop approaching us?"

"Probably nothing but say hello as she passes us. Looks innocent enough."

"I suppose so, sir, but why do you thinks she's heading our way?"

"She must be on her way to America, though the captain says most of these sloops stay on this side of the Atlantic. She's not that big for a crossing, so it would be strange if she really was on her way to the New World. We'll know soon enough when she's closer."

"I can see her flag now, sir," said Cathcart. "Spanish, I think?"

"She's heading directly toward us, so we should be able to hail her and find out her destination. Continue on, James. I'd best be getting back to the helm with the captain."

Cathcart nodded.

Back at the helm Captain Orne said, "Fast-moving vessel. We'll be able to talk to them in a minute or two. Take in some sail, William, and be prepared to hail them as they pull close. I'm assuming they'll trim a sail or two so we can exchange a few words."

"Aye, sir," said Proctor. "They should pass our port side. I'll go down there to hail them. Will you be joining me?"

"If they want to come aboard, I'll be glad to welcome their captain so we can chat."

As the trim ship neared the *Betsey* someone aboard the sloop waved, and Proctor waved back. Now the sloop was within 50 yards and parallel to the *Betsey*. She obviously intended to come alongside. Proctor smiled. He hadn't seen anyone but the crew in 28 days. He always enjoyed meeting folks from other parts of the world.

What he saw next made his heart stop. The Spanish flag was being lowered. As soon as it was down a new flag was raised—yellow crescent with a yellow star on a red background—one of the many flags used by the Barbary pirates. The Barbary pirates were known maritime predators based in four North African countries: Morocco, Algeria, Tunisia and Tripoli. The four countries were known as the Barbary Coast.

"Alert the crew!," yelled the captain. "Raise sail for as much speed as we can muster. We'll see if we can outrun them, but I'm not optimistic. If they come alongside, we'll have to deal with 'em. In that event tell the lads not to resist, as these bastards can be ruthless, and we're mostly unarmed."

Minutes later Proctor said, "They're gaining on us, cap'n. Should be abreast shortly. Nothing we can do. They're faster, and they maneuver better."

As he said this one of the pirates on the attacking ship raised what appeared to be a cutlass and bellowed in a heavily accented English, "I'm Captain Habib of the *Jabbar*. We are coming aboard to claim your cargo. Do not try to stop us, or you will not survive." Habib's jet black facial hair and piercing fiery black eyes lent a fierceness to his appearance that couldn't be ignored. Orne had no doubt that the man meant business. Still, he was not about to roll over without a show of resistance.

"You have no business on this ship," roared Captain Orne. "We are in international waters."

"You are in Moroccan waters, captain, and subject to the authority of Mohammed Ben Abdallah, Sultan of Morocco. As such, you must submit to our demands. We demand your cargo." The Barbary corsair paused to let that sink in before continuing. "If you resist, you will perish."

Captain Orne turned to Proctor with a look of desperation on his face. "Do we have any choice, William? Most of our men are unarmed. If we resist we are all doomed." It was not as if Orne was afraid to fight. He'd fought nobly as a foot soldier in the war of independence, but now he was captain of a merchant vessel. His crew were not soldiers or naval seamen. They were not trained or equipped to fight.

"No, Captain, I don't think we have any choice. We will lose the cargo, but at least we shall have our ship and our lives."

"Aye, lad, go ahead and tell them. 'Tis a terrible choice, but what else can we do? Hopefully it will be quick so we can be done with them."

"Yes, Cap'n. God willing we can at least pick up a cargo in Tenerife so our trip won't be a total loss."

"Won't be much lad, as we won't have the coin from the sale of this cargo."

They were interrupted by a cry from the pirate on the Moroccan sloop. "What's your decision? Will you comply or do you wish to die? This is the last time I ask."

Captain Orne, looking pale and beaten, said, "Tell him to come aboard, Will. Let's get this over with."

Proctor walked to the rail of the ship and yelled, "The captain says to come aboard. We will hold you to your word that you will not harm the crew or take the ship."

"Yes, yes. We're coming aboard."

As the sloop pulled alongside the *Betsey*, two pirate sailors threw lines around the *Betsey's* bollards, securing the two ships so that there was no space between them. With that, a dozen or more pirates with cutlasses raised, led by Captain Habib, scrambled over the gunwales of the two ships, landing on the deck of the *Betsey*. As they landed they pushed several of the *Betsey's* crew members aside brusquely. Captain Habib cried, "Take me to your hold. The rest of you stay clear."

Will Proctor noted that he could barely understand the man as his English was heavily accented with what Will assumed was Arabic.

No one stood forward to lead the pirates to the hold. Will realized that no one wanted to be the person who cooperated with the attackers.

"I said take me to your cargo hold," roared the pirate leader. "Show me, or we will start throwing men overboard. Do not make me wait."

With this, Will stepped forward. He was not going to sacrifice lives to save cargo. Before he'd gone more than one step, bosun Cathcart strode forward, saying, "I'll take you there. Follow me."

With that the pirate captain said, "That's better. Show us the way."

As Cathcart started toward the hold, one of the pirates accompanying the pirate captain shoved Cathcart forward impatiently, forcing him to struggle to maintain his balance. In a rage Cathcart roared, "You bloody bastard!" and struck the pirate on the chin, stunning him and nearly knocking him to the deck.

On seeing this, Captain Habib drew his cutlass, and with a forward thrust, ran it through Cathcart's abdomen just below the sternum. As he withdrew the bloody sword he smiled and said, "Now I expect your cooperation, or the rest of you infidels will enjoy a watery grave."

"My God!" cried Captain Orne. "You've killed him."

Habib motioned to two of his men and said, "Throw his body overboard." Then he turned to Orne and said, "That is the fate of you and your crew if you defy me again. Do you understand?"

Orne swallowed and said, "Yes, we understand." Then he shouted to his crew, "Stand down men. Do as the captain says."

Habib told his crew that he was going below to inspect the cargo. While he was down there he expected them to keep an eye on the *Betsey's* crew. If they gave them any trouble, kill them all.

Minutes later the pirate captain emerged from the dark hold and spoke to Captain Orne. "I see that you have a much larger cargo than I expected. It is far too much to bring aboard my smaller vessel. I have decided that we shall take the cargo and the ship."

"But how will my crew and I return to America?"

Habib grinned cruelly. "You will not be returning to America. At least not now. I declare you my slaves. During the trip to Agadir, you and your crew shall be secured so that you cannot create any more mischief. I haven't decided yet whether to hold you hostage or to sell you at the slave market. Either way this encounter should be profitable for me and my crew and for His Royal Majesty, the Sultan of Morocco."

"Is there nothing we can do to persuade you otherwise?" pleaded Orne. "Morocco was the first country to recognize the United States back in 1777. At that time your country opened its ports to American ships. Why are you treating us so disrespectfully today? We are not your enemies. Why do you not let us go about our business? Would you and Morocco not be better off if we could trade with you?"

"Very nice words, captain. Very nice, but apparently you are misinformed. That agreement seven years ago quickly came to an end when your man in Paris failed to thank the Sultan for recognizing your little country." He was referring to Benjamin Franklin, one of the five American commissioners sent to Paris to negotiate the treaty officially ending the war of independence against Great Britain.

"There must be some mistake."

"There is no mistake, Captain. The Sultan informed all Moroccan ships of this insult, and because of it, authorized our ships at sea to treat American infidels as enemies. Enough of this, though. We must set sail for Agadir."

Chapter 2

Agadir, Morocco 1784

After five days at sea, the *Jabbar* sailed into the small Moroccan port of Agadir.

Will Proctor was glad to soon be on land, for the voyage from the Canary Islands had been wretched. They hadn't starved, as Captain Habib had said they would always be fed because that would make them more attractive on the slave market. He pointed out that, if he decided to hold them as hostages, he would still need them to be somewhat healthy in order to bring a decent ransom.

The diet was barely edible, but sustaining. The men could handle that, but they were miserable because each of them had been tied or shackled to prevent them from interfering with the pirates, or worse, from attempting a reckless attempt at mutiny. While shackled in the dark hold of the ship, each man had been allowed one trip each day to relieve himself. If they could not control themselves beyond that they were forced to defecate or urinate in place where they were tied down. By the end of five days the ship's hold was a stinking, festering cesspool.

At first sight, Will thought that Agadir was a ghost town. Habib's crew pushed the shackled members of the *Betsey* crew through the streets of the dismal town. It looked to Will as if it had once been a thriving small city, but now many of the aging adobe brick dwellings seemed unoccupied. Dust was swirling in the air, and only a few dirty, bedraggled souls could be seen on the town's grimly depressing unpaved streets. Many of the these souls looked as if they could barely move. Those who could move approached the shackled Americans hesitantly, but with obvious curiosity. A small, motionless boy garbed in tattered rags was leaning against a crumbling building with flies crawling all over his face, neck and arms. Will wondered why Habib had brought them here to Agadir if he intended to put them in a slave market. Will couldn't believe that there were people in Agadir wealthy enough to own slaves.

As they were prodded stumbling through the town's streets, Will noticed that they were beginning to attract a crowd of jeering, taunting townspeople. Soon the crowd was quite large and menacing. Obviously, realized Will, Agadir was not quite the ghost town he'd thought it was. As the crowd became more threatening, he almost wished it were a ghost town.

"Where are you taking us?" demanded Orne.

"A place where you will be safe until I decide what to do with you, Captain. As you can see, the local residents do not think kindly of Christian infidels. You will be much safer under my protection."

"We would be much safer back on our ship."

"That's not going to happen, Captain Orne. That's not going to happen."

It was an ancient building of weather-beaten adobe construction. It might have been 100 years old or a thousand. Will had learned in his short career as a seaman that buildings in North African cities, no matter what their age, tended to be quite similar in appearance and construction. The forbidding structure was two stories high with tiny slits for windows. Small turrets on each of the four corners of the building set it apart from most of the neighboring structures. Will and his fellow crew members soon saw that the grim-looking building was an old jail. Will realized that this was to be their home for the next few months—or more. The full impact of it hit him now. He had no idea how long he and the others would be confined in this dreary structure. It could be a month, or it could be forever. Whatever it was, their future looked grim.

The inside of the jail was far more forbidding than the exterior. There was a dank smell that suggested decay and death. Will saw that the dark, gloomy interior of the building consisted of one large room lined with cells on three walls of the periphery. The cells were about six by eight feet, and none of them was occupied.

Captain Habib sensed their reaction and said, "You are our honored guests," he sneered contemptuously. "We have saved these quarters for you. We have not had any infidel guests in almost a year. The last ones were sold at auction on the slave market. Their country failed to offer a fair value for the return of their sailors. But that was the French. Let us hope that your young country places a higher value on your lives, else you, too, will find yourselves on the slave market. You should hope for a generous ransom."

Within minutes the 21 crew members had been herded into cells. Each tiny cell was occupied by three crew members. Captain Habib then looked at Captain Orne, "Captain, out of respect for your rank you will have your own cell."

"I don't need anything special. Let me share a cell with my crew."

"I wouldn't hear of it, Captain. Here, I have selected this somewhat larger cell for you alone since, as captain, you deserve better than your lowly crew members."

Chapter 3
Agadir Jail 1784

Within hours the crew of the *Betsey* had bravely reconciled themselves to their fate. Several of the men had spoken confidently about not letting their confinement get to them. It was only temporary, they said. As soon as Robert Carlisle, the ship's owner back in Boston, learned of their fate he would contact the American government, which would in turn pay a ransom, and they would be freed.

"How can we be sure of that?" questioned a seaman from one of the cells.

"We cannot be certain, of course," said Captain Orne, "but I would expect no less from the United States. What these pirates have done is an insult to our country and a threat to merchant shipping. When our government sends the ransom money and demands our return, the sultan will have no alternative but to free us."

"Yes," said Will Proctor, "but can we be sure, Captain, that these Moroccan pirates have any respect for our country? After all, we are new and not nearly as powerful as the European countries. From their perspective they have no reason to fear the United States. They can demand an unreasonably large ransom, and the United States will not be able to challenge it."

"You may be right, Will. We shall see. I would think they would accept money from a weak nation as certainly as from a powerful one."

"How long do you think this will take, Captain?" asked an able seaman from a cell across the room. He sounded desperate. "I've already seen two rats, and the stink of urine is enough to make you gag. There's moss growing on the walls of the cell and small pools of water on the filthy floor. There's a constant drip from somewhere up above. As if all this weren't bad enough, sir, some of the slop buckets must have overflowed in the past. There's dried shit on the floor between our two beds—if you can call two wide planks a bed. I don't know how the rats survive in here, much less human beings."

"I'm afraid it won't be soon, Jonas. We must all face the fact that this dungeon will be our home for a goodly time. We're going to have to learn to adjust to these foul conditions. Let's not lose heart, lads. It's a foul thing, but it won't last forever. Realistically, though, nothing will happen back in Boston until they learn about our fate. We must find some way to communicate with our people back home. Right now I confess, I don't know how we'll do that."

"Yes, you are right about that. If they do not know you have been captured, they cannot even consider a ransom." It was the strongly accented voice of Captain Habib. "I thought I would visit you to see how you are getting along. I see that I came at the right time to allay your fears. You are wondering how you will get a message to your people back in America. The answer is simple. I have no reason to restrict your ability to correspond with the outside world. Since it is clearly important that you reach your people back in your pitiful little country, you may send whatever messages you choose. You see, it is in my interest as much as it is in yours. How can I receive compensation for your release if no one knows you are missing? And if I were to send a letter from myself, how would the American authorities know that you and your ship had actually been captured? If you correspond with them, they will know you are truly in my custody and not dismiss your request. So feel free to compose whatever letters you wish to write, and I will see that they are sent to America."

"I still do not see why you have taken us," said Orne. "I understand that Mr. Franklin somehow failed to show his appreciation for your sultan's recognizing our country. I am sure there must have been some misunderstanding or miscommunication, for I know all Americans are grateful for the kind act of the sultan. It was very important to us. If you release us now I will make it my duty and first act to convey the sultan's feelings to the American authorities. I'm sure once they realize what has happened they will rectify this terrible injustice."

"I suggest you communicate that in your letters, Captain. If the United States is truly remorseful they will correct their oversight by paying ransom for your release."

"Respectfully, Captain Habib, by demanding a ransom are you not punishing this innocent crew rather than our government for its oversight?"

"Perhaps, but it is the only way we have of getting the attention of your government." Then, with a contemptuous smile, he added, "It is also the best way to add to my personal coffers."

"Then it is really not the sultan's feelings that concern you. What you have done is really for your personal gain?" As he said this, Orne realized that he might have gone too far. He'd seen what Habib had done to Bosun Cathcart back on the *Betsey*.

"You are an impertinent one, Captain Orne. I'm in good humor today, or I would teach you to be more respectful. Since you insist on pursuing this matter, there is another way your government could secure your release. They could offer a monetary tribute to His Imperial Majesty and you and your merchant ships would be granted free passage in Moroccan waters. This essentially is what many of the European powers do, and they are able to conduct free trade with no difficulty."

"But you will probably not propose this to His Majesty," challenged Orne recklessly. "If the sultan receives a tribute, it will not add to your personal coffers."

"You are indeed a bold one, Captain. You are wrong, though. The sultan would show his appreciation for my apprehending you and your cargo. So, as I said, there are two ways this could go. It matters little to me which. The sultan will decide. In the meantime, enjoy your stay here in Agadir. You will not be here long."

Chapter 4
Agadir Jail: One week later 1784

The crew, under Captain Orne's leadership, had agreed that each of them would send letters to their families explaining their plight and urging them to ask for help from their local officials back in Boston and the surrounding towns. The captain, in addition to writing a letter to his family, would send missives to Elbridge Gerry, Nathaniel Gorham, Rufus King and Caleb Strong, the four Massachusetts delegates to the Confederation Congress or Continental Congress as it was more commonly called. Captain Orne had said that between all these efforts they should expect someone to set things in motion to secure their freedom.

One of the guards had furnished them with paper, ink and quill pens with no hesitation. There had been no argument. It was as if Habib, the pirate captain, had a system in place to facilitate the writing of letters in order to expedite a payment of ransom or tribute as soon as possible.

Speaking the obvious, Will Proctor sighed and said to his fellow cellmates, "Now that we have sent off our letters, we can expect to languish in this dismal place for at the very least two months. Most likely, more."

Captain Orne said, "Almost certainly three or four months, lad. Knowing what little I do about government I wouldn't expect them to take action quickly when they hear about our capture. Between sailing delays to and from America and haggling over details once it reaches the halls of government, it will take a few months. I can imagine lengthy discussions over whether to pay ransom or pay tribute. I don't think our government has paid either in the few years since the war against Britain. They may hesitate about either of these payments. They may believe they would set a bad precedent by paying ransom or tribute. No, my good men, I would be lying to you if I said that this will be over in two months. We must plan for the worst and pray for the best."

Orne had barely uttered these words when Captain Habib

entered the room silently and barked out a demand. "I need six strong men to work down at the waterfront. We're fitting out the *Betsey* with armaments, and I need people who know the vessel."

"You're turning a merchant ship into a pirate ship?" snapped Orne. "It was not designed as an attack vessel."

Habib smiled. "We prefer to call it a warship. The term pirate implies that we are thieves."

An angry Orne could barely contain himself. "Isn't that exactly what you are—thieves?"

"To the contrary, Captain. We are warriors against nonbelievers who reject Islam and defy our laws. What we do is in the service of Allah."

"As Christians, we are not nonbelievers, Captain Habib. Perhaps we do not believe in the Muslim faith, but we do follow the Christian faith. As Americans, we think all faiths have a right to exist, so we do not reject Islam."

"Clearly you do, Captain Orne, or you would convert to the one true religion. As a Muslim it is my duty to wage jihad against all nonbelievers. If you and your crew choose to convert to Islam, you will no longer be our enemies."

"Then our capture is based on religious, not material matters? I find it hard to believe that you are not motivated by profit."

"There is nothing in the *Koran* that says good Muslims cannot profit in their jihad against nonbelievers. If anything it makes our struggle all the more commendable when we win against infidels in more than one way."

"Then you believe that Islam is superior to all other faiths?"

"There is no question. I not only believe it; I know it. As the Prophet Muhammad said, Islam is the way, the only way. The *Holy Koran* says that '*the only true faith in God's sight is Islam*'."

"Then there is nothing we can do to convince you that we are people of God also?"

"I have already said that you can convert."

"And if we do not, you will then feel justified in treating us badly?"

"Frankly, Captain, the *Koran* says that it is our duty to kill kafirs. That is the term we use for nonbelievers. So if your government does not respond to our satisfaction, then you will either be our slaves or put to death."

No one said anything as the impact of what Habib had said sank in. After a minute or so, Captain Habib said, "Now do I have six volunteers or shall I select them?"

Again silence reigned. No one volunteered.

"All right then. I shall pick the six. Without further hesitation Habib went to the cell occupied by Will Proctor and two other sailors. "The three of you shall join me." Then he moved to the next cell and selected its three occupants, saying, "When I release the six of you from your cells, do not do anything foolish. I have armed men waiting outside this room, and they will not hesitate to kill anyone who does not follow my orders."

Over the next few weeks the six American crewmen labored in sweltering conditions under the merciless rays of the Moroccan sun. The sky was rarely obscured by clouds that might have afforded even a moment's relief from the burning rays. As time went on the men suffered from extreme sunburn that never healed. As if this weren't enough, their days began at seven each morning and went on until sundown. The workday was interrupted only briefly for sips of water and to bolt down pieces of stale bread. On good days the bread was covered with a ground chickpea mixture, which often provided their only protein for the day. Once a week each man was given a piece of fruit.

Will almost lost control of himself when he and his fellow sailors were told to help load guns onto their merchant ship. There were 24-pounders, 18-pounders and 8-pounders. Finally there was a single 9-pounder long-barrel cannon that was mounted in the stern of the ship. The long-barrel cannon was designed to be aimed at ships as you passed them on the high seas. Will and his fellow prisoners couldn't bear to see their ship turned into a pirate warship that very likely would be used against other peaceful American ships in the near future. Could there be a more outrageous example of adding insult to injury.

Because of the physical work, Will knew he was getting stronger. At the same time he knew he was losing weight, and sensed that his newfound strength would gradually diminish as his weight continued to decrease.

The Moroccan overseers who directed their efforts seemed unconcerned about the discomfort of the American kafirs, yet they did not treat them as badly as Will had expected. It soon became obvious that the Moroccans understood that if they mistreated their slaves too much, they would become ineffective as laborers.

The six men assigned to work on the refitting of the *Betsey* were not the only prisoners assigned to slave duty. One man was ordered to empty slop buckets from the cells. The Americans quickly agreed to alternate this duty so that one man was not forced to deal with this onerous task every day.

Others were assigned to latrine duty, meaning they had to shovel soil over waste each day to contain the odor, which could be unbearable in the Moroccan heat. Still others were assigned to digging new latrines and to digging graves for the deceased in the town of Agadir. A few men were given miscellaneous tasks such as pulling two-wheeled carts heavily laden with various types of goods and carrying water for Habib's mercenaries.

Perhaps the most interesting assignment was for Captain Orne. One day after a week of confinement in his cell, Orne was summoned by Captain Habib.

"I have just received word from Rabat that the sultan would like to meet you, Captain."

"What does he want?"

"That I cannot tell you. We are going to Rabat, and you will find out for yourself. Your crew will be going, too. I will take you there myself." Orne knew that Rabat, the capital, was three or four hundred miles up the coast to the east. He couldn't imagine why the sultan would want to see him. Whatever the reason, he thought, it didn't augur well for him and his beleaguered crew.

Chapter 5

Annapolis, Maryland: Two months later 1784

The Continental Congress had been in its current session for less than a week. They had been meeting in the Maryland State House in Annapolis since fleeing Philadelphia eight months ago because of the growing protests by Revolutionary War veterans demanding back pay. It was no longer safe in Philadelphia for the delegates. Paying soldiers had been a problem from the very beginning of the war, as it had been close to impossible to raise sufficient funds under the loosely structured new government that gave most of its authority and taxing power to the individual states. Few of the states were willing to do their part to support the war effort, so the Continental Congress had to promise to pay soldiers when it could. In 1781, the formation of the Articles of Confederation, America's first constitution, only formalized the granting of most taxing powers to the individual states, so the Continental Congress remained incapable of honoring its promises to veterans. The protests grew so loud that the protesters armed themselves, and the members of the Congress felt threatened.

Now, in July of 1784, the members of the Congress found themselves facing a new problem. They had received a number of letters and several direct pleas from delegates and citizens concerning the confiscation of the American merchant vessel *Betsey* and the abduction of her crew. These reports said that the crew had been imprisoned and forced into slavery by the Sultan of Morocco.

Thomas Mifflin of Pennsylvania and the current president of the Continental Congress had asked a few of his most trusted members of the congress to join him in his office to discuss this latest problem confronting the nascent government. Mifflin, formerly the first governor of Pennsylvania, had served as General Washington's first quartermaster general. While effective in obtaining supplies for the war effort, he preferred being in the front lines and made a name for himself in action on Long Island. He'd been born a Quaker, but was excluded from their meetings because of his involvement in the military. He was known for his charm, winning personality and effectiveness as a speaker, all of which made him a popular figure in both state and national government.

With him now were Elbridge Gerry of Massachusetts, Jeremiah Chase of Maryland and Thomas Jefferson of Virginia.

Mifflin was known as one who liked to get right down to business, so it was no surprise to his colleagues that he launched right into the matter at hand.

"As I think you know, the merchant ship *Betsey* out of Boston has been the victim of a pirate attack off the coast of Morocco. The ship has been taken by these pirates and the crew under Captain Henry Orne has been thrown into slavery by the Sultan of Morocco. When the men are not working at their assigned, menial tasks, they are returned to cells in a Moroccan prison in the coastal town of Agadir.

"We and other state and local officials in the various states have received letters asking that the U.S government either pay ransom for their release or pay a tribute to the sultan. Payment of a tribute would apparently allow for the releasee of the crew and permit free commerce for American ships in the Mediterranean in and around Morocco. The question before us is do we succumb to these criminal demands in order to free our citizens?"

Eldridge Gerry said, "I think we have been fortunate up to now that we haven't been confronted by such acts of piracy before this. The Barbary States are known for this. Most of the European nations have found that the best way to deal with these threats is to pay a tribute to these criminal states in order to guarantee the safety of their merchant ships. It is expensive, but not as expensive as losing ships, thousands of tons of merchandise and the freedom of countless good seamen."

When Gerry spoke people listened, as he was respected as a man of accomplishment at an early age. He had attended Harvard College at the age of 14 and then gone into his father's successful shipping business. He had soon turned to politics, being elected to the Continental Congress, and signing the Declaration of Independence and the Articles of Confederation.

"Are you recommending the payment of tribute?" asked Mifflin.

"I would consider it. After all, we have a very small navy so I can't see us threatening Morocco and the other Barbary states with a show of warships. We certainly can't continue the way we are, or the *Betsey* will be the first of many ships to fall into pirate hands. American merchant ships will not be safe when they enter the Mediterranean."

"I understand your position, Elbridge, but if we pay tribute or ransom, we will be rewarding these renegade states for their inexcusable behavior. This will only encourage more such criminal behavior." It was Thomas Jefferson, the soft-spoken delegate from Virginia. Jefferson was known for being a more persuasive speaker in one-on-one situations or small groups than he was addressing a large audience. This was his kind of setting.

"Regrettably true," agreed Mifflin, "but I think all of us want to bring this crew home. How do we do that if we do not succumb to the sultan's demands?"

Jeremiah Chase the former Mayor of Annapolis, said, "Perhaps we should try diplomacy first. We could send Franklin or someone of his standing to negotiate with the sultan. We may find that he is quite reasonable." Chase did not know that Franklin was the last person the sultan would welcome into discussions.

Jefferson said, "Based on the sultan's authorizing and apparently encouraging brutal piracy, I would surmise that he will not be reasonable, but I suppose it is worth a try. He is old and has been sultan for more than two decades, so we cannot hope for a modern or fresh attitude. Hopefully he is a more reasonable and conciliatory monarch than we think, but based on what has happened to the *Betsey*, it would appear that he believes as his predecessors have believed for centuries—that it is their right as Muslims to wage jihad against Christians and other infidels. Nevertheless it is worth a serious effort at the very least."

"What could we offer that would satisfy him, if we are unwilling to pay ransom or tribute?" asked Mifflin. "I fear that we do not have a strong position from which to bargain."

"We could offer a preferred trade status. Better prices on goods. First access to desirable goods. Things of that sort," said Jefferson. "I am not overly optimistic, but I think we should at least give it a try."

"You realize," said Gerry, "that this means that the crew and Captain Orne will remain enslaved while our negotiations are going on. They might not see the light of day for months."

"I'm afraid, gentlemen, that there is no alternative," said Mifflin.

"And what if our negotiations come to naught?" queried Chase. "What do we do then?"

Chapter 6
Sultan's Palace: Rabat 1784

The voyage up the coast to Rabat was warm, but unpleasant. The Americans were fed scraps left over from the pirate meals. The pirates poked and prodded the American sailors whenever they passed by one of the seamen. Clearly they were trying to provoke a response that could justify a violent reaction, but Orne admonished his men not to take the bait.

Upon landing in Rabat, Captain Habib led Captain Orne through the hot, dusty streets of Rabat. Habib set a brisk pace. It seemed to Orne that the bold pirate captain, who could be so commanding and assertive himself, did not want to incur the wrath of the sultan by keeping him waiting any longer than necessary. As they hastened through the winding streets they were confronted by curiosity seekers who stared at the American. Some yelled questions in Arabic. Others just stared. Occasionally they were confronted by beggars who were brusquely brushed aside by Captain Habib with abrupt disdain.

Finally, Habib led Orne up a set of wide brick and mortar stairs leading to a grand adobe brick building that almost certainly must have been the finest structure in all of Rabat. Two unsmiling guards framed the entrance to the building. Habib nodded to each of them as he and Orne entered the building. Obviously Habib was known at the royal palace.

Inside they found themselves standing in a large, high-ceilinged room. It was pleasantly cooler than outside. The lighting was not good though, and it was difficult to see much beyond a few yards. Habib led Orne toward the rear of the room where the American ship captain made out the outline of a man sitting comfortably in what appeared to be a throne. There were no other chairs in the room. As he neared the throne, Orne could finally see the sultan. The man was not young, though Orne found it hard to guess his age. He wore a full black beard and a kind of headdress that appeared to be made of a rich magenta silken fabric. He was dressed in a gown-like garment of magenta that was trimmed with golden thread.

Captain Habib introduced Orne to the sultan. "Your Royal Majesty, this is Captain Orne, the American shipmaster I told you about. Captain Orne, this is Mohammed Ben Abdallah, Sultan of Morocco."

The sultan smiled, but his eyes were cold. "Indeed. Captain Habib tells me that you are an interesting man."

"That is very kind of Captain Habib." Orne did not enjoy kowtowing to Habib after the way he and his men had been treated, but he figured that if he appealed to the pirate's ego and showed a cooperative attitude to the sultan, he and his crew had a better chance of surviving.

"I suspect that you do not really feel that way, Captain. I would imagine that being captured and thrown into confinement would not make you feel kindness for the one who captured you. If we are to get on, Captain, it will be best that you speak your true feelings and not lie to me. I do not appreciate lying."

Orne studied the Moroccan sultan. "I'm not certain you want to know my true feelings, Your Majesty."

Now, close up, the monarch appeared to be well into his seventh decade. He was leaning back comfortably in his padded throne. He appeared to be extremely overweight, no doubt because he was granted his every wish and did not need to lift a finger to secure those wishes. Clearly he enjoyed more than enough fine food, a stark contrast to the meager diet of most of his Moroccan subjects. He seemed completely comfortable in his role as monarch, confident in the supreme authority of his position. He exhibited the sort of presence that proclaimed to the world that even his closest associates would dare not challenge him. This was the bigger-than-life figure Orne now faced.

Orne was accustomed to giving orders. First it was Habib. Now the sultan. Until recently, he had never been in a situation where he felt threatened or uncomfortable by the presence of other men, even his superiors. But this was different. He felt threatened for his very his life as he stood facing the sultan.

The sultan remained silent for what seemed an eternity before saying, "I see, Captain Orne, that you are not easily intimidated. That is good, for I am looking for a man who does not quake in my presence. I am looking for a man who has the courage to tell me things as they are and not what a man thinks I want to hear. You see, Captain, being sultan has many obvious advantages. I have great power, great wealth and considerable comfort. However, there are a few disadvantages, not the least of which is that not many people have the courage to tell me the truth. In fact, not many people have the courage or the wit to tell me anything other than brief responses to my questions.

"Make no mistake, it is good to be feared. It keeps people in line. But when you are feared too much, there is the danger that you lose touch with the outside world. I am hoping, Captain Orne, that you can help me stay in touch with the outside world. Perhaps we can even have good conversation from time to time. Very few of my subjects are educated. When I was young my father sent me to Cairo to be educated. Unfortunately, not many of my subjects have been so fortunate. There are few people with whom I can have an intelligent conversation. I am hoping that I can depend on you to make my life more interesting, Captain?"

Orne considered his answer before responding. The last thing he wanted to do was make life more interesting for the man responsible for the enslavement and imprisonment of his crew. On the other hand, he and his crew would gain nothing by provoking the monarch. Hopefully, if he cooperated, the sultan might decide to treat them better. Maybe even release them. Finally, he said, "Your Majesty, since you want my true feelings, you should know that by helping you, you put me in a difficult situation with my crew if they think I am accepting preferential treatment at their expense."

The sultan smiled. "Captain Orne, if it will make it easier for you, you can tell them that I have ordered you to meet with me—that I gave you no choice."

"Also..." Orne hesitated, fearing he might be going too far.

"Yes, Captain. What else?"

"Since you want total honesty you should know that by requesting my help to make your life more interesting, you appear to have no concern for me or my life."

"Let us not forget, Captain, that you are my prisoner of war. Under the circumstances, I think you and your men are being treated fairly. In Algeria or Tripoli, you might have all been killed."

"Yes, but in most countries we would be free and able to do as we wanted. We would not be taken as prisoners."

"I think this is going to be fun, Captain. I shall enjoy verbal fencing with you. First, though, we must make you comfortable. We need a chair for you to sit in." He snapped his fingers and a footman who'd been standing at the far end of the large room snapped to attention. "Ahmad, Bring us a chair. Quick. Quick."

When the chair was positioned facing the throne, the sultan dismissed the servant and addressed Orne. "Sit. Sit. We shall talk.

Tell me about your new country. How did you defeat the mighty British Empire? It is almost too hard to believe. The whole world fears them; yet your little colony rebelled successfully against them. How is that possible?"

"It helped that we were 3,000 miles away from them. They had to transport their soldiers, guns and ammunition across the sea just to get to us. Then, when they got to America, they needed foodstuffs to sustain them, and they had to get them from a disgruntled colonial population. It wasn't easy for His Majesty's army."

"Yes," said the sultan. "I can see that that would be difficult, but not impossible. There must be more than that to your victory over such a power."

"As I look back, Your Majesty, I think another advantage we had was that we were underestimated. The Crown thought that we would be easy and that we would quickly surrender and do their bidding. The Crown misjudged our determination and our belief in freedom."

"Freedom is a dangerous thing. You allow your subjects too much freedom and they will overthrow you. It is best that subjects be kept in hand. It makes for an orderly and controllable state of affairs that is best for all concerned."

"If I may, Your Majesty, that is what the British Crown believed and look what happened with their American colonies. The colonists were not content to be controlled by a government they had not elected and in which they had no representation."

The sultan sneered. "In my opinion you colonists should have been grateful to be part of the most important world power since the Roman Empire. Think of the prestige. Think of the protection it granted you. No one dared to challenge you. Think of the doors it opened for you. And you threw it all away for an immature colonial tantrum. If I were to guess, I'd say that you are still dependent on Britain even now, but that you no longer enjoy the protection offered by being a part of this great empire."

It was true. Before the American colonies declared their independence from Britain, American ships could sail the Mediterranean with impunity, as Great Britain had paid its tribute or subsidy to the Barbary States in order to gain treaties of peace with these Islamic states. The Islamic states dared not violate these agreements for fear of retribution by the largest and most formidable navy in the world. After 1776 Britain withdrew this protection. Fortunately, America's ally France immediately provided a renewed umbrella of protection that lasted until the Treaty of Paris in 1783 officially ending the war. Now a new and independent nation, America had to fend for itself and became vulnerable to the attacks of the Barbary pirates.

Orne was uncomfortable with the way the conversation was going. The sultan was better informed than he imagined he'd be, and he, Orne, found himself actually enjoying the mental challenges and stimulation after being confined to a cell. The sultan had a seductive way about him that made you forget that he was a ruthless dictator. Orne had to resist being charmed by this tyrannical despot. Still, he could not provoke the man to the point where he took it out on his crew.

Before he could respond the sultan said, "Captain Orne, I have enjoyed our conversation. We shall do this again soon. I will let my footman, Ahmad, escort you back to your cell."

After Orne had been led away, the sultan summoned his chief aide, Salman Masad. The sultan had known Masad for more than 30 years. Masad came from one of the ranking families in Morocco and himself had a significant following among the populace. This alone was reason enough for the sultan to consult him for his advice on important matters. The sultan knew well enough that Moroccan leaders were vulnerable to coups and violent seizures of power. He was well aware that sultans had been deposed in the past. It was important to maintain as much support as possible at all times. This pragmatic reason aside, the sultan considered Masad a friend and enjoyed both his company and his advice.

"It went well with the American ship captain, Salman. He is intelligent, well informed and, for a Christian infidel, somewhat courageous. While I suspect that he doesn't question my authority, he has enough of a backbone to disagree with me to my face. Very few Moroccans dare do that. Still, it is obvious that he is more deferential to me than he would like to be. Clearly he knows that if he is too direct with me it will not serve him or his crew well. A very disciplined, quick witted man, our Captain Orne."

"If the American government is not forthcoming with a reasonable tribute or ransom, do you think your Captain Orne can be persuaded to help us with our dealings with other infidel states? I know you can order him to, but will he be persuasive, or would he undermine our efforts?"

"How do you get inside the mind of an infidel, Salman? They do not think like us. I will meet with him a few more times. Hopefully I will have a better understanding of how valuable our Captain Orne can be to us."

Chapter 7
Rabat: September 1784

The crew of the *Betsey* had been held captive, first in Agadir, then in Rabat, for over three months without a word of encouragement from America. Captain Orne and his crew had tried to remain optimistic, but without a word from home, they weren't even certain that their letters had been received in America. For all they knew, the letters had not left Morocco, though that seemed unlikely in view of what they'd been told of how the Moroccans would benefit as much as they would by their letters reaching U.S. officials.

All of the crew members had lost weight. It was a combination of abusively hard work 12 or more hours a day and a sparse, unappealing subsistence diet. Over time, the tiny portions of stale bread and chickpeas had become sightly more varied, but hardly more appetizing. On occasion they would be give a small amount of chicken in a watery broth. On other occasions they received a small piece of roasted lamb. This was deemed the most edible by the members of the crew, though in most cases it was so charred that half of it could not be eaten. Once in a while they would be given a small amount of fruit. This was the highlight of those rare days when they received such a treat.

As the days went on certain crewmen emerged as leaders. Some tried to do their part to buoy the morale of the crew. One such man was James Fitzhugh, who turned out to be the comic of the American crew. He entertained them with endless jokes and witty, barbed comments about their captors. While most of the crew tried to maintain a hopeful, positive outlook, it became more and more difficult with the passing of each day. It didn't help that some of their guards now taunted them with threats of death. It was not uncommon for a guard to say, "If your government does not send money, the sultan will have you all killed. What good are you to the sultan if you do not fetch money?"

Summer temperatures in Rabat were usually quite pleasant—not nearly as high as in some places in North Africa, but occasionally they could rise to 100 degrees Fahrenheit or more. One particular day in early September was one of those exceptionally hot days. On this day the Moroccan guards or handlers—Will Proctor was not sure what to call them—led about 12 prisoners to a work site in the local cemetery. Two or three of the prisoners had dug graves here before, but today, 12 were needed because ten locals had been executed for various crimes.

As the prisoners were herded over to the nearby graveyard, Proctor learned from one of the guards that the crimes ranged from theft to murder. As a Muslim country you could be given the death penalty for adultery, apostasy, homosexual behavior, atheism, fornication, sodomy, idolatry and more. Proctor also learned that, while most of the executed 'criminals' had been killed by hanging, one had been beheaded and one woman had been stoned to death.

After digging for more than two hours in the oppressive heat, the men were bone weary and in need of water. One man yelled for water. A guard said, "Be quiet. You will have water later. Dig, or you will get no water today."

"We need water now," said the prisoner with a dry, raspy voice. "We cannot continue without water." The guard took three steps toward the complaining prisoner and shoved him into the open grave.

On seeing this another prisoner exploded. "You miserable son-of-a-bitch!" As he said this he landed a great blow to the jaw of the abusive guard, sending him into the grave next to the first prisoner. A roar of protests arose from the other prisoners, and they began to attack the other guards.

Crack! A gunshot was heard and the prisoners became quieter.

"Who did that?" demanded the leader of the guards, holding a smoking gun. Because of the tumult it was unclear who had struck the guard.

"Speak up or you'll all feel the wrath of Allah."

Will couldn't believe what he saw next. It looked as if a prisoner on the periphery of the skirmish was pointing to crewman James Fitzhugh and speaking furtively to a guard. That guard then quickly approached the trembling Fitzhugh. He spoke animatedly in Arabic. The group suddenly fell silent.

Crack! A second gunshot. The guard had fired his pistol at Fitzhugh, sending a ball into his chest, and then, without hesitation, kicking his body into the open grave. He jammed his pistol into his waistband and smiled.

"You evil scoundrel," roared Proctor. "You've killed a good man. For what? Because he came to the aid of a man asking for water? Something he and all of us need if we are to continue doing your evil work. Do you not value human life?"

Showing no remorse the guard snapped, "An infidel's life is worth very little. Especially if he cannot perform acceptable work. Now get back to your task, all of you, or you will join him in the grave."

Chapter 8
Annapolis, Maryland: 1784

Thomas Mifflin stared out the window at the town of Annapolis. He had been president of the Continental Congress now for ten months. He'd been pleased when his fellow delegates elected him to succeed Elias Boudinot. It was a great honor to be elected by his fellow delegates, many of whom he had the greatest respect for. He knew the job would be challenging. He'd seen what Boudinot and the congress had to face during the preceding year. He expected no less during his own term. The problem was things had only gotten worse. Much worse.

The inability to raise sufficient revenues to carry out the business of the government had been onerous. The individual states simply were not as forthcoming with what Mifflin considered a reasonable contribution to the national government. Many of the states were reluctant to yield much power to a central government for fear of losing control of their own affairs. Dealing with the debt to veterans had been heartbreaking too. The struggle to gain the respect of the European powers had been frustrating at best, as nobody wanted to lend money to a new, untried country that had astonishingly denied itself the right and the authority to raise the funds it needed to function. On top of that was the matter of the merchant ship *Betsey*. That, in fact, was the matter he needed to talk to Jefferson about now.

He heard a knock on the doorsill. It was Jefferson, looking perfectly groomed and dashing as always.

"Come in, come in, Thomas. Tea, or coffee?"

"No, I'm fine."

"Then let's get down to business. I need your help on this *Betsey* matter. The more I talk to members of Congress, the more I find it nearly impossible to come to a resolution. Meanwhile, as we deliberate *ad nauseam*, those poor crewmen are rotting in a Moroccan prison. As you know, the debate is between paying ransom or tribute in order to get the men and ship back or standing firm and refusing to pay anything for fear that by paying we only encourage further attacks on our ships. You can see why we are deadlocked? I've always respected your thinking, your ability to cut to the heart of a matter, Thomas. I'm hoping you can help me now."

Jefferson steepled his fingers and thought for a moment, then spoke, "There's another way, you know. It would mean that those men would have to suffer there a while longer, but it might eliminate this problem once and for all."

"You mean send ships to the Med as a show of strength?"

"We couldn't do that now because we don't have enough ships. Our navy is no threat to anyone. It would be a show of weakness—not strength."

"Then I fear I don't know what you have in mind?" said Mifflin.

"We need to build a respectable navy. We need to put the fear of God into these criminal corsairs who violate the very laws of civilized society. We can't do it now, but if we build a respectable navy, we can. In my judgement we could build enough ships to make a forceful presence in fewer than two years."

"The cost would be prohibitive. We'd never get the member states to commit that kind of money. Their financial resources are already stretched thin. I'm afraid, Thomas, that we simply can't afford to have a respectable navy."

"I believe we cannot afford *not* to have a good navy. The alternative is to lose countless more ships and crews to these Barbary Pirates. Not to mention the cargoes. The cost to our economy could be catastrophic. Already, after the loss of the *Betsey* I understand that insurers have raised their rates for merchant cargoes. To make matters worse it's been reported that Britain encouraged the Moroccans to attack our ships because they want us to fear the very act of sailing in the Mediterranean. If our merchants are afraid to sail to the Med, it eliminates competition for British merchants, and we have no commerce in the Mediterranean. Our fledgling nation depends on overseas trade. While admittedly investing in a navy will be costly, I believe failing to do so will be far more costly to America."

Jefferson had always preferred negotiation to war, so this

recommendation for an expanded navy was not easy for him.

"I will take this to the Congress, Thomas, but I fear that it will be rejected. The mood at this time supports negotiation or even a reasonable tribute—not the expense of building a navy.

Chapter 9
Rabat Jail: September 1784

The prisoners were herded back to jail at the end of the gruesome, nightmarish day. The Rabat jail was remarkably similar to the grim, damp filthy jail in Agadir. Even the layout with cells on the periphery of a large room were almost identical. Obviously, thought Proctor, the Moroccan had little imagination when it came to jails. Will couldn't help but think that the Moroccans had little imagination when it came to architecture.

The guards, showing no mercy or sympathy for the executed prisoner, seemed, if possible, more abusive of their charges than ever. No doubt it was because they had seen that the American prisoners were not as compliant as slaves they had guarded in the past. As far as they were concerned, the fact that one of the prisoners had struck one of the guards only lent fuel to their belief that infidels were not worthy of mercy.

After their guards had secured them in their cells they left the immediate confines of the jail room. Will Proctor knew that some of the guards, at least, were standing just outside the room, but hopefully far enough away that they could not hear conversation between their prisoners—at least not when the crewmen kept their voices down so as not to be overheard. There was probably little risk of being overheard, anyway, as it was doubtful that any of the guards understood English. Still, best not to take the chance. One never knew.

When all of the men were locked up, Captain Orne, who had been with the sultan and not with his men, asked to be brought up-to-date on the day's grave-digging labors.

Will quickly filled him in on what had happened. Other crewmen added details from their own observations. When the terrible events of the day had been absorbed fully, Orne said, "Several of you claim that Peter Lisle identified James Fitzhugh as the one who struck the guard, knocking him into the grave." Orne then raised his voice slightly and asked, "Is that true, Lisle?"

"It is true," yelled Lisle loudly from his cell across the room. "I thought it better that the guards punish one of us than take it out on all of us. You may not agree with my thinking, but it worked out as I predicted. I'm sorry about Fitzhugh, but better one than all of us." Lisle seemed unconcerned about his voice reaching the guards outside the jail room. "I have come to understand our Moroccan brethren, and since they dislike Christians anyway, I believed it better that they not be given an excuse to kill the entire crew."

One of the men sharing Lisle's cell turned on him. "You miserable lowlife," he roared as he lunged toward Lisle. The other prisoner in the cell forced himself between the two men, saying, "No, leave him be—for now. We can't afford to give these Moroccan animals any excuse to come in here and execute someone." He then turned his attention to Lisle and said, "Don't think this means you go free. It's clear to all of us that you identified Fitzhugh in order to ingratiate yourself with these Moroccan savages. You'll get what's owed to you at the right time."

A red-faced Lisle shook off the hands of the first prisoner and said, "That's not true. I was just trying to protect the rest of the crew. Lord knows I didn't enjoy it, but better to sacrifice one than all."

"You don't know what they would have done, you sick son-of-a-bitch. It's most unlikely they would have killed us all. We're too valuable to them. What you *did* know was that once you pointed your finger at James, they would kill *him*."

"Let it be, John," interrupted Captain Orne from across the room in his cell. "Let it be. We'll deal with the Judas at the right time. In the meantime I suggest you and your cellmate alternate your sleeping. Obviously, you can't trust the turncoat Peter Lisle."

The next day a guard came and removed Lisle from his cell. Without a word of explanation the guard took the man from the jail room, leaving the rest of the prisoners to wonder what the traitor's fate was.

Chapter 10
Sultan's Palace 1784

The guard, with his American prisoner one step in front of him, was stopped at the entrance to the throne room by one of the two footmen who controlled access to the sultan. After a brief discussion the guard was allowed to approach the sultan with his prisoner.

Anyone granted an audience with the sultan was expected to remain silent until spoken to by the monarch.

"What brings you forth?" demanded the sultan in Arabic.

"This American wishes to convert from the infidel Christian belief to our glorious Islamic faith, Your Majesty."

The sultan frowned and remained silent for a moment before saying, "What evidence do we have that he is sincere and not just seeking preferential treatment?"

"I think he is sincere, Your Majesty. When one of the infidel prisoners attacked another guard, this man identified the attacker so that we could punish the man for his act."

"And did you punish him?"

"We executed him on the spot as an example to the other prisoners. I think it was very effective, Your Majesty. I would expect the infidels to be easier to deal with in the future."

The sultan turned his attention to the prisoner now. "What is your name?" he asked in an accented, but surprisingly good English.

"Peter Lisle, Your Majesty."

"If we permit you to convert to the one true religion of Allah, you understand that you will have to take a Muslim name for yourself?"

"I understand that, Your Majesty. I am willing and eager to do that."

"You will have to live like a Muslim. You cannot go back to your decadent infidel ways. Can you accept that?"

"Yes, Your Majesty. That is my desire."

"I see. Why did you choose this moment to convert to Islam? You must understand that it is very suspicious that you would choose to become a Muslim at this time when it would give you freedom from your incarceration."

Lisle was in awe of the sultan's command of English.

Unfortunately, it meant that it was going to be harder to convince the monarch that he was in earnest about his desire to convert. Clearly the sultan was capable of understanding every nuance of their conversation. It was ironic, he thought, that the sultan doubted his sincerity, since he was every bit as committed to becoming a Muslim as he had said he was. He snapped out of his thoughts as he saw that the sultan was waiting for his reply.

"I beg you to give me the chance to prove my sincerity, not only by word, but by deed. I know these prisoners, and I can give you information about them and the thinking of other American seamen as well. When your men take possession of other ships in the future I can act as intermediary to insure that the infidel sailors understand what will be expected of them when in captivity. I will be helpful in maintaining control of them and for getting the most out of them in their work details. I will also be helpful in determining what they are thinking, which as you know is not always what they are saying.

"I know you don't need me, Your Majesty, but I think I can be of help to your maritime warriors. I can make their seizure of enemy merchant ships more successful. I can help make the exploits of your corsairs more successful and more profitable for Morocco."

The sultan forced an insincere smile. "How do I know that what you say is true and not what you are thinking? You seem to understand deception and guile. Perhaps it is an art which you are practicing now."

"As I said, Your Majesty, I only ask that you give me a chance to prove my value and to prove my commitment to you, Morocco and to Islam."

"That all sounds very good, but I still don't understand why you have chosen this moment to convert to the only true faith?"

"I have never felt comfortable with the religion that was thrust upon me at birth. I have always sensed that there was a better way. In recent years I have read about the Muslim religion. I have learned about its holy plan to become a world-wide religion. I believe in its willingness to punish those who do not adhere to its teachings. I—"

"I hear what you are saying. There is no need to say more. We shall see, Peter Lisle, we shall see. I am going to put you in the hands of Ahmad. He will determine if you are truly sincere in what you say. You will need to learn a great deal if you are to become a Muslim. He will help you if he believes you to be sincere. At some point we shall see how successful your conversion has been."

Chapter 11
Rabat Jail 1784

Several days passed before the prisoners learned what had happened to Lisle. No one knew whether the benighted crewman had been executed or given favorable status because of his betrayal of a fellow prisoner.

In the meantime, the *Betsey* had been brought from Agadir to continue the conversion from merchant ship to warship. Rabat had larger cannons than were available in Agadir. One day Proctor, who was laboring on the *Betsey* conversion, overheard two talkative guards mention the name Lisle. Proctor had picked up some Arabic and was able to make out that Lisle was in the process of converting to Islam. The guards beamed at this, proud that one of the prisoners had seen the wisdom of becoming a Muslim. Proctor seethed at this. Lisle had proven to be more than just a turncoat who caused the death of a fine crewman—clearly to curry favor with his captors. Now the worm of a human being had joined the very people who had forced them all into captivity.

More weeks went by before the men heard anything more about Lisle. Then one day Captain Orne returned from meeting with the sultan to say that Lisle had now become a favorite of the the sultan. The mood of the prisoners grew sullen.

As the weeks went by things only got worse. Orne sensed that the crew had started to resent his relationship with the sultan. From their perspective another member of the crew had found favor with the Moroccan leader. This time it was their captain. More and more talk among the prisoners focused on expressing this resentment. While they wanted to see Orne's command performances with the sultan as different from Lisle's willfully going over to the other side, they couldn't help but lump the two situations together and found themselves resenting both men. Proctor agonized over this because he had respected the captain for his fairness and leadership skills. He even saw him as a friend. He tried to accept that the captain's time spent with the sultan was a command performance. Logic told him that this must be so. Still, he couldn't help but resent the fact that Orne was having an easy time of it compared to the grinding labors imposed on the other prisoners. While the members of the crew were toiling away in the Moroccan sun for over twelve hours a day, the captain was having stimulating conversations with the monarch in the comfort of the throne room.

Orne sensed the resentment of the crew. One night he brought the matter to a head.

"I know that each of you must wonder if I'm currying favor with the sultan in order to secure preferable treatment for myself. I hope you know me better than that. Believe me, that is not the case. The sultan finds me useful and a source of information about the outside world. He has little communication with Europe and certainly not America. Despite his power he is cut off from the outside world. I don't have to tell you that Morocco is an insular land not connected to the civilized world. Most Moroccans we've come in contact with have little or no interest in the outside world or in expanding their knowledge about much of anything. Most of them haven't traveled more than a few miles from where they were born. The sultan is the exception. He received a university education in Cairo and misses his contacts with that great metropolis. He knows that there are even greater centers of learning and culture in Europe. He's seized this opportunity to probe an outsider for information and ideas that he's unable to get to here in Morocco.

"Why am I helping him with this? Why am I telling him things he didn't know before? Believe me, it's not to give myself favorable treatment. It's to persuade him that all of us are or could be more useful to him than we are as mindless slaves doing physical labor that any of his Moroccan subjects could do. I'm trying to convince him that I am not the only one from our ship who knows about the world."

One of the prisoners yelled out from his cell. "All well and good, Captain, but how does that help us? You're the one who eats fine meals and natters away in comfort with His Majesty."

"The sultan says that he'd like some of his men to learn English. Some of them can speak a bastardize Spanish. Some, a little French, but not many of 'em know much English. I'm trying to talk him into having some of you boys teach English to some of these mercenaries. I know, your sense is to do as little as possible to help these vermin, but if we teach them English, in the process they'll get to know us better and maybe find it harder to kill us. Certainly it's better than most of the work you've been forced to do. And if it takes some of the unpleasantness out of being enslaved prisoners while we wait for the U.S. to come through with a ransom payment, I think it makes sense."

"Is it definite?" asked another prisoner.

"No, the sultan is considering it. He doesn't make hasty decisions. Do I think he will do it? Yes, I think there's a good chance he'll want to do it."

The same prisoner then asked, "You said he might want some of us to teach English. Where would that leave the rest of us?"

"The sultan has a very active mind. He's thinking that others of you might teach his men other things. Things like geography and mathematics and navigation."

"I thought mathematics was born in the Arab countries?" commented Proctor. "What could we teach these people that they don't already know?"

"That was during the Golden Age of Islam. The 9th and 10 centuries. Since then, the Islamic countries have been sliding into cultural decline. The sultan says most of his men know only the simplest arithmetic. A bit of addition maybe, but most can't do simple subtraction."

"Are you saying, Captain, that if we do this the sultan would treat us civilly and not as slaves?"

"Certainly better than now. Not as equals, though. Don't forget, as infidels we are considered inferior to any Muslim and therefore not entitled to the same treatment as a Muslim. So I would say things would be better than now, but it wouldn't take much for them to punish us for the least infraction."

Chapter 12
The Sultan's Throne Room: Late 1785

After more than a year of massaging Sultan Abdullah's ego while keeping him company in their daily sessions, Orne wondered how much longer he would have to do this. Had his country abandoned them? Had it forgotten them?

He was tired of struggling to maintain a balance between showing more deference to the sultan than he would have liked and retaining a semblance of self respect. The sessions were always stressful, for he knew that Abdullah had a volatile temperament and could turn on anyone who said the wrong thing. Adding to the tension was the fact that it was not always clear to Orne what the wrong thing was.

As if always being on edge in the presence of the sultan weren't enough to deal with, Orne was always conscious of the underlying resentment of his crew. He had done his best to convince them that he was not seeing the sultan to feather his own nest, and most of them had assured him that they understood. Still, he knew that many of them couldn't completely let it go.

As he entered the throne room now, he forced himself to put those thoughts aside. He couldn't afford to let his mind wander in the presence of the mercurial monarch.

"You seem distressed today, Captain. I do not like it when your mood darkens, for it darkens mine. Come, come. Entertain me."

"Entertain you, Your Majesty? I am not an entertainer," said Orne sourly. "I am a ship captain." As soon as the words had left his lips he regretted saying them.

The sultan frowned. "You have entertained me many times with your curious stories and novel comments on things. I do not summon you to dishearten me. Come now, tell me something interesting."

Orne was tired of being treated like a trained monkey. Would it never end? Where in God's name was the ransom payment they had begged for so many months ago? Had their country abandoned them? He had to control himself now. The sultan was clearly impatient. As much as the man exasperated him, Orne knew that his and his men's lives depended on his keeping the sultan "entertained."

"Did you know, Your Majesty, that in Boston, where I come from, most men can read and write? More so even than in England."

"I do not believe it."

"It is true, Your Majesty." Orne knew that this was a shock to the sultan because Moroccan literacy was limited to a very few. There were not many schools and those were available to the very few families that could afford them. In general, though, Orne sensed that because most Moroccans were unaware of the outside world, they didn't realize what education could do for them. In short, they didn't realize how ignorant they were. They were not unintelligent. They were simply unaware that they knew so little. Orne continued, "Our country was settled by some of the most literate people in Britain. When they got to America they continued stressing the importance of education in each successive generation.

"As I have told you when I first entered into your service, my men can teach your people mathematics and science and other things that they are not aware of now. You did not accept my offer at the time. You did not seem interested. My men can still do this if you wish their service."

"Can they teach them to read?"

"In English—not Arabic. My men know very little Arabic."

"All very interesting, captain, but the education of my people is of little interest to me. It would only make them demand more from me. As it is now, I am not challenged by my subjects because they do not know what they do not have."

"But I had the impression from our previous discussions that you had some interest in our teaching your people certain things."

"Yes, it seemed a good thing, but, as I have just said, in the long run it would lead to further demands. I cannot afford to take the chance."

"You do not feel the need for having educated people as your support staff?"

The sultan smiled, a smile that was not reflected in his eyes. "You, my good captain, are enough."

"I am flattered, Your Majesty, but when you receive the ransom payments from my country, I will no longer be at your service."

"I wouldn't count on that, captain. I wouldn't count on that. It's interesting that you should mention ransom, as there is something I haven't told you. Yesterday, near the close of day, I received word that your country was, after much delay, sending their ransom payments. However—"

"That is excellent news, Your Majesty. Very good news." Orne was so excited that he interrupted the sultan. Something he never would have dared doing. He couldn't stop himself from smiling. At last they were going home.

The sultan frowned. He was not used to being cut off in mid-sentence. "I was not finished, captain. I was not finished. Before you interrupted me I was about to explain to you that you would not be returning to America with your crewmen."

Orne fought to catch his breath. His elation of only a moment ago had turned to despair. "What do you mean, Your Majesty? If the ransom is being paid, I should return to my home."

"I have decided that it would be better for you to remain here. I've found you to be good company and most valuable because you are an educated man of the world. More than that, you make my days more interesting. Your mistake, captain, was being too valuable to me." He allowed that to sink in; then he said, "There is another reason that I am asking you to stay. By retaining you here I hope to extract another payment from your country. I expect when they see that you have not returned, they will see the value in offering Morocco a monetary tribute in return for safe passage on our seas for their merchant ships. It is what Britain and Spain already do. Others will soon pay tribute, too."

"By retaining me here you are contradicting your agreement to return the *Betsey* and the *Betsey's* crew for the ransom you will receive. Does that not bother you, Your Majesty?"

"Not in the least, Captain. My duty to Morocco and to Allah is to extract as much as I can from the infidel states. You may not like it, but I'm sure you understand."

Orne looked crestfallen. He was deflated.

"Have no fear, captain. You will be treated well here. You will be comfortable and even have your own personal slave to help you with everyday conveniences."

Three weeks later local fishermen saw two American ships anchored at the mouth of Rabat harbor. The sultan sent a longboat out to invite the ships into the harbor. Captain Beveridge of the lead American ship refused the request and sent word back that he would turn over

JIHAD AT SEA

the ransom when the Moroccans sent out the American crewmen being held prisoner. After some exchange of messages it was agreed that the ransom would be paid at the same time the last prisoner was turned over to the American ships. The two American ships were well armed with 24 cannons each, but Captain Beveridge was hoping he and his accompanying ship would not have to use them. However, as he looked around, the possibility of conflict seemed very real. Several armed Moroccan xebecs and other smaller boats had encircled the two American ships and looked ominously threatening. Xebecs were Mediterranean type vessels of medium and smaller size, often with square sails.

At this point Beveridge had no idea that the exchange almost didn't come off, as Captain Orne's crew had refused to be repatriated when they learned that Orne was being retained by the sultan. Three days earlier Will Proctor, speaking on behalf of his fellow crew members, spoke to Orne. "Sir, the crew and I will not leave you here alone. If you can't leave, then we shall not leave."

Orne had been adamant in his refusal. "Damn it, Will, you tell the men that they must go now that they have the chance. And that goes for you, too. I'll not hear another word about this."

"But, sir, this is not fair."

"Things are not always fair, son. This is the best deal we can get. I want you and the men to leave while they still can. By staying here you aren't going to free me. Then we all suffer. Besides, when you return home you can plead my case. Maybe if the government agrees to pay something, American ships will get safe passage through Moroccan waters and maybe I'll even get to go home."

"It's still not right."

"Look," said Orne heatedly, "if you and the men refuse to leave, the sultan won't get his ransom money, and he'll take it out on the men. I appreciate the loyalty, Will, but if you and the others stay, things'll only be worse for all of us. These vermin will only be more abusive than they are now. Worse than that, the sultan might auction us all off or have us killed since we will no longer be of any value to him. No one will win."

A crestfallen Will Proctor said, "All right sir. I'll tell this to the men, but they won't like it."

"You tell them they owe it to their loved ones back home to come back safely, and not in a box."

Even after this fervent plea of Orne's, many of the men were reluctant to leave without their captain, but Proctor finally convinced them that this, of two very bad choices, was what they should do.

43

Chapter 13
The Mediterranean: One day later

The two American gunships escorted the *Betsey* out of Rabat Harbor and 20 miles into open water. At this point the freed prisoners set an eastern course past Tangier and into Gibraltar where the goal was to take on water and supplies as well as any cargo that would help defray the loss suffered when the *Betsey* was captured two years earlier. Captain Orne had delegated Will Proctor to be captain of the ship in his absence. The rest of the crew welcomed this, despite Proctor's youth. At 21, he was now one of the youngest ship captains out of Boston. Nevertheless, he had proven to his crew on the voyage over that he was more than capable of taking charge of the ship.

Upon leaving the Rabat harbor the crew burst into a loud cheer in celebration of their liberty. "Thank God we are finally out of that hellhole," said more than one crew member as they slapped each other on the back in sheer joy. They weren't completely comfortable entering Gibraltar, as it was only three years ago that the American colonies and Britain were still at war. How they would be received in that British outpost was uncertain, but Captain Proctor and his crew felt certain it would be an improvement over Morocco. As it turned out their reception was mixed. Some in the port city greeted them icily, but others were accommodating, apparently willing to view the American rebellion as a thing of the past. Besides, during the war, many Britons had sided with the Americans.

While the crew of the *Betsey* was eager to return home, Proctor persuaded them that the trip would be more profitable for all of them if they made a stop in Malaga before returning to the U.S. Hopefully they'd be able to take on cargo that would be well received by merchants back in Boston. It would mean sailing eastward about 60 miles, but Proctor said it would probably only add a week to ten days to their trip and be far more profitable than returning home with an empty hull. Proctor had nothing to trade, but fortunately he still had the money he'd stashed aboard ship when they'd left Boston. The owner of the ship, Robert Carlisle, had a policy of stashing cash on board his vessels in the event his captains came across desirable merchandise that foreign merchants wouldn't trade for. Proctor had secured the money in a double-bottomed slop bucket.

In the meantime, while they were in Gibraltar he encouraged them to enjoy themselves, but cautioned them against getting into trouble. The Brits wouldn't need much of an excuse to lock up American sailors.

Proctor knew that many of the crew would be looking for one-night liaisons with local women in this international port town. He couldn't blame them either, as it had been a long time since he'd been with a woman. He missed two women in particular. One was his mother. His father, who'd been Will's hero and role model, had lost an arm fighting in the War of Independence. He'd become a successful cod fisherman, despite his handicap. His fellow fishermen were in awe of his ability to keep up with them on a boat. He'd died five years ago, leaving his mother to raise six of the children still living at home. Proctor wondered how she'd been getting along these last few years. She'd be worried. That's for certain, especially if she'd received his letters about their imprisonment in the Moroccan jails. Before the Moroccan confinement, he'd contributed to the household finances as much as he could.

He also missed Elizabeth. The girl of his dreams. He smiled. By now, he supposed, she'd be a woman. He and Liz had grown close. They'd even talked about marriage after he returned from the Med.

His thoughts were interrupted by Billings, who wanted to know whether all of the crew could leave the ship at the same time. Proctor said he wanted four men aboard ship at all times. The crew could decide who.

Meanwhile, the two American gunships, after taking on water and food in Gibraltar, sailed into the Mediterranean to take on cargo themselves in the port of Algiers before returning to America.

The *Betsey* was now on it's own, but Proctor felt comfortably safe from marauding pirates, knowing that he had a document on board signed by the sultan of Morocco himself stating that they were not to be boarded or captured by any Moroccan corsairs they might encounter.

On the first day out of Gibraltar the sailing was smooth, and the sky was clear and welcoming. The crew was finally able to relax. Yes, it would be two or three months before they reached Boston, but at least now they knew it was just a matter of time. Their good spirits were saddened by the loss of two of their own to the pirates, not to mention the fact that Captain Orne was not allowed to leave with them. Still, they realized that it could have been even worse.

The second day out Proctor noticed more clouds in the sky, but thought little of it because the sea was calm. Past midday, though, the sky turned ominously gray. The gray gradually turned to black as the gentle breeze they had been enjoying quieted down to a deadly calm. Definite signs of an oncoming storm. Captain Proctor turned to Josiah Billings, his newly appointed first mate, and said "We best head toward land, and hope we find a port that can handle us."

"Aye, Captain, I think yer right. This could get nasty."

They set a northward bearing toward the nearest Spanish coast and prayed they would find safe harbor before the storm broke. There was no way they could reach Malaga, as it was more than 80 miles to the northeast.

Proctor stared ahead at the darkening sky and said, "Have the men batten down the hatches, Josiah. I think we're in for rough seas."

No sooner had he said this than the wind picked up noticeably, and the calm sea suddenly became disturbingly choppy.

"Lower the sails," yelled Proctor in order to be heard over the worsening conditions. He knew that in winds of high velocity, a sudden, powerful gust could topple even a stable ship if all the sails were unfurled.

"Aye, sir," said the first mate as he ran to pass along the order to the other seamen. Within minutes Billings was back at the captain's side.

"They're comin' down, sir. Good thing, too. Looks like we're in for it."

"I fear you're right, Josiah. I fear you're right. Best you get most of the men below. And do it quickly. Whoever needs to stay on deck, be sure they're lashed to something firm. A man from Salem was washed off the deck in a bad storm on a brand new cargo brig a few years ago."

A half hour later it was clear that they were not going to make it to shore before the storm hit. Already the sea was roiling mightily; the rough chop had become six-to-eight foot waves. A light rain had started up. Off in the distance lightning flashed through the clouds on its journey to the surface of the water. Seconds later they heard thunderous, ear-splitting cracks, followed by rolling booms reminding everyone of nature's devastating power.

Soon the waves were at least fifteen feet, tossing the ship around as if it were a toy boat. Sea water cascaded over the deck, and spray descended on Proctor and Billings as if they were under a waterfall.

As they desperately held on, they both realized that the main part of the storm had not even hit them yet. Minutes later all hell broke loose. The wind whipped into them so fiercely that they feared they would be blown off the deck despite being lashed to the brass wheel stanchion. Suddenly the rain that had pelted down on them became an angry deluge. Then, as if things weren't desperate enough, they heard a loud snap.

"Foremast down, Captain," yelled Billings as he tried to be heard above the deafening noise of the storm.

Proctor uttered an "Aye," that was almost swallowed up by a clap of thunder. He saw that the foremast had cracked just below the second spar. It was now tilted precariously to the port side. Proctor cursed. Could things get any worse? They would have to deal with the mast when they reached some port on the coast of Spain. That is, if they reached the coast. At this point in their trip they were slightly closer to the coast of Algeria, but there was no way they would attempt to dock there. Proctor had enough of the North African coast for a lifetime.

He was worried about the men in the hold of the ship, but dared not check on them. There was no way he or Billings could untie themselves from the stanchion and make it to a hatch without being blown overboard.

"It's only going to get worse," cried Proctor, thinking that his first command of a ship might be his last. "If you're a God-fearing man, Josiah, now would be good time to pray."

Chapter 14
Fraunces Tavern: New York City 1785

Richard Henry Lee, the new president of the Continental Congress, had asked some of his key delegates to Fraunce's Tavern in New York to discuss the latest matter of concern. The U.S. capital had been moved here in January of 1785 from Trenton, New Jersey. Prior to that the capital had moved from Annapolis to Trenton in late '84, where it remained for only two months. Rather than create a fixed national capital the delegates had chosen to move the capital to various state capitals so as not to show preference to one state over another.

Fraunces Tavern in New York City had been selected as the temporary seat of government because Samuel Fraunces, back in 1776, had foiled an assassination attempt on General Washington. He'd also served as a spy for the Americans, exposing Benedict Arnold as a traitor. The war left him insolvent, and the new government, as a show of appreciation for what he'd done, rewarded him by leasing his tavern for two years as a government center.

Lee nodded as William Blount of North Carolina breathlessly took a seat on the other side of the long wooden table.

Blount caught his breath and said, "Got lost for awhile. Need to get familiar with New York. Sorry I'm late."

"I understand," said Lee, who was from Virginia. "Took me a few days before I felt comfortable. Still get lost sometimes."

Lee scanned the five delegates sitting around the table and said, "We should get started. We have a difficult matter to consider." Lee was a popular leader and famous as the man who, in the Continental Congress, had moved that the colonies separate from Britain. His oratorical skills were legendary. When he had their attention, he continued, "We're all familiar with the attack on the *Betsey*, the merchant ship out of Boston, and the subsequent enslavement of its crew." The five delegates at the table nodded somberly.

Lee continued, "You're also aware that the United States

recently paid the Sultan of Morocco $80,000 ransom for the release of those men and the ship. We have not yet had confirmation of their release. Let us pray that we hear good news soon." His fellow delegates nodded their agreement enthusiastically.

"I assume we shall hear something within the month?" said Blount.

"Yes, that would be my expectation. Until then I will hold my breath. However, that is not the main reason I asked you all here. Unfortunately, I have just been told that two more American merchant vessels have been boarded. They've been taken into the port of Algiers. And we should not forget that just a few months ago we received a report that an American ship had been captured by the Tunisians. As if these losses were not enough for us to consider, there is no guarantee that the Moroccans will not seize more of our ships in the future."

"We cannot afford to pay ransom for every one of these seizures," said Zephaniah Platt of New York. "It's a terrible problem. As I calculate it, if we paid $80,000 to these scoundrels six times it would come to nearly 20 percent of our annual revenue. You think we have problems now with our nation's mounting debt. Imagine if we gave away 20 percent of our revenue on top of what we already owe. And as appalling as that prospect is, each time we capitulate and pay ransom we encourage more seizures. It would be the end of our noble experiment as a nation."

Lee could see that the others agreed with him. "It is a terrible dilemma that we face. We have already paid for the release of the crew of the *Betsey*. Thank God they will be coming home soon, though we know that at least two of the seamen were murdered by these pirates. Fortunately the others should now be free and on their way home. However, I think we agree that we will not relax until they are back on American soil.

"But back to our dilemma. None of us wants to sacrifice American crews and ships to these Barbary pirates. If we do not rescue them, it will mean that we have abandoned American citizens. Furthermore, it will mean that we are unable to safely engage in commerce in the Mediterranean. Unthinkable, but if the seizure of our ships continues, I see no other outcome. Already I'm told that the insurance on cargoes to the Mediterranean has tripled. Soon it will mean that it will be unprofitable to send merchandise to that region of the world, even if it is not seized."

Blount spoke. "Then what do we do? We cannot afford ransom. Good God, even if we could it would mean that we'd be rewarding these wretched Moors for their vicious conduct."

"I think we must try diplomacy," interjected Stephen Hopkins of Rhode Island. "Surely there must be a way that we could reach common ground with these people."

"You mean negotiate?" said Platt. "Other countries have negotiated with the Barbary States and ended up paying them large monetary tributes so that their ships might pass safely through Moroccan waters. The mighty British Empire now pays such a tribute. Even they could not negotiate a better arrangement than that. How could we expect to do better?"

"Don't forget," said Lee, "we already negotiated such a tribute with Morocco back in '77 or '78. It failed because we forgot to thank the sultan for being so generous as to grant free passage to the ships of a new nation. It seems quite unreasonable to us that we would need to pay homage to him in this way, but such things apparently are important in the Barbary states. Perhaps if we try again, paying sufficient deference to the sultan, we will have a better result. I think we should at least make the effort."

Blount leaned forward and said, "I, for one, am uncomfortable paying a monetary tribute to a foreign state for the right to sail in international waters. We fought a lengthy war to free ourselves from just that sort of oppression and abuse."

"All well and good, William," said Hopkins, "but we are not capable of demanding our freedom from Morocco and the other Barbary states. We have considerable debt, an army that still demands back payment for its service during the war for our independence, and virtually no navy. If we wish to do commerce in the Mediterranean, I fear that we must come to some understanding with Morocco and the other North African states—even if it means the payment of a tribute. It's repugnant to me, but I see no other realistic course of action. We are in no position to make demands."

Chapter 15

The Mediterranean: Off the coast of Malaga, Spain 1785

At dawn the next morning the sun rose in the east, casting an orange-red glow over the surface of a tranquil sea. During the early part of the night the storm had maintained its violent fury, but as midnight approached, it slowly abated. As Captain Proctor surveyed the ship he took comfort from seeing that they'd suffered no serious damage except for the foremast. Proctor and the crew thanked God that they had lost nothing more than a mast. Yes, it was a major inconvenience because it meant that they would have to limp into the nearest port at a much slower speed than under full sail. It also meant that they would have to spend a week or two in port having the mast replaced. The actual time would depend on the availability of a mast of the proper height and when the workers in that port could start on the job.

Despite this inconvenience and expense, many of the crewmen welcomed the chance to explore a friendly port and enjoy decent food and any other enticements that might appeal to them. Fortunately, Proctor had sufficient funds to pay for work and the layover. The two gunships that had delivered the ransom had provided them with enough money to purchase modest cargoes and to sustain themselves until they returned to Boston. It was understood that Robert Carlisle, the owner of the company that sailed the *Betsey*, would repay the funds at a later date.

They eventually made their way to Malaga, which had been their destination in the first place. Malaga, as they were to discover, was a very old city, having been settled by the Phoenicians in 1000 BC. Around 200 BC it was brought under the aegis of the Roman Empire. As luck would have it, none of the local ship workers had the right mast available. One of them said they could fashion one, but it would take some time. Proctor gave the go ahead, but pleaded with the tradesman to do it as quickly as possible.

In the meantime, Proctor and the rest of the crew explored the old city and slowly got their health and strength back.

Not surprisingly, the replacement of the mast took much longer than promised. After almost four weeks, the remains of the old mast were removed and a new one installed. While in port Proctor shopped for goods that could be sold back in Boston. Fortunately there was an ample array of such goods, including cheeses, olive oil, wine, vinegar, olives and cork. When the hold was sufficiently filled with this new cargo, it became unnecessary to stop off in Tenerife, where they originally planned to stop on their way home. The crew was delighted at this turn of events, since everyone was eager to get back to America.

Finally they were ready to set sail. As they eased out of the Port of Malaga, the Med was calm and the skies were clear. Proctor turned to his first mate and said, "Josh, I think we can finally relax. Looks like our new mast is holding up nicely. We'll stop for water in Gibraltar, and then our next port is Boston."

The next day they calculated that they had made excellent time and would be in Gibraltar sooner than they had expected. As the day went on they encountered several ships, and Billings commented on it. "It's a busy day on the Mediterranean today, sir. Apparently nobody's worried about pirates."

"Aye, Josiah. Maybe we were just unlucky. Maybe it's not as common a thing as we feared."

"Well, sir, we have the sultan's signature so we don't have to concern ourselves with the Moroccans, and we're too far west to worry about the Algerians or the Tunisians."

"Aye. Should be good sailing from now on."

Chapter 16
The Mediterranean:
Between Spain and Morocco 1785

Murad Rais was now captain of his own vessel out of Tripoli. The Tripolitan pirate vessel under his command was heading westward toward the Strait of Gibraltar. Rais couldn't believe his luck. His own command and he'd only been in Tripoli for a few months. Miraculously, in that one year, he'd become a favorite of the pasha.

Two years ago he'd been a lowly seaman on the American ship *Betsey* out of Boston. At that time becoming a Muslim and a citizen of Tripoli were the farthest things from his mind. Two years ago he just wanted to win the favor of Captain Orne and earn a promotion. Back then he was still known as Peter Lisle from Scotland and more recently of East Boston. Unfortunately, Captain Orne acted as if Peter Lisle didn't exist. He got virtually no recognition for his skills as a seaman or his leadership ability. To the contrary, within a week of sailing from New England he had made several enemies and was despised by most of his shipmates.

He'd always felt he was better than the average sailor. In fact he'd always felt he was better than most people. Back when he received his schooling he'd done well in the classroom. He wasn't well liked, but he did well. Until recently he assumed that was why people disliked him. They were envious. It never occurred to him that he had the kind of bearing that made him hard to like.

Later, when he and his fellow crewmen were taken prisoner and forced into labor on a work crew, another crewman, James Fitzhugh, pushed one of the guards. All of the guards were furious and threatening to take out their resentment on the crewmen. At that moment, he made the decision that changed his life. He pointed to the guilty crewman and said, "He did it." His thinking at the time was better one prisoner be punished than all of them. Unfortunately, one of the guards shot the man on the spot, mortally wounding him.

After that he, Peter Lisle, was reviled by his fellow crewmen. It was an injustice. He'd made the right decision but instead of being thanked, he'd been condemned for it. He should have been praised for it. Try as he might, he was unable to convince the others that his intentions were good. He had stressed that he had no idea they would kill Fitzhugh.

Feeling abandoned by his fellow crewmen, he decided to use his brain. The first chance that he got to talk alone to a guard he told him that he wanted to convert to Islam. The guard sneered and said you only say that to avoid prison. Eventually he'd persuaded the guard to take him seriously, and he'd been seen by one of the sultan's advisors. He smiled. The advisor had been easier to convince than the guard. Eventually he'd convinced the sultan. After a period of testing, the sultan had allowed him to convert, made him change his name and accepted him as an advisor on American and European thinking. He'd proudly taken the name of an earlier pirate, Murad Rais.

Within a month, as Rais, he'd been sent as a courier to the pasha of Tripoli. As he thought about this he was pleased with himself at how easily he'd manipulated both a sultan and a pasha into granting him extensive privileges and even a degree of power. He'd become such a favorite of the pasha, that the leader had persuaded him to remain in Tripoli as his advisor. Having no allegiance to Morocco, he, Murad Rais, became one of the pasha's chief advisors. His job was to help the monarch negotiate with foreign governments for tributes and ransoms. The pasha felt that Rais would understand the way of thinking of European and American negotiators, thus giving the monarch the edge in such negotiations. Rais was thrilled. In a matter of months he'd gone from imprisonment and enforced slavery to privilege and considerable comfort.

Then something unbelievable happened. The pasha summoned him and said, "As you know, we have recently acquired a Portuguese merchant vessel called the *da Gama*. We've fitted it out with 16 cannons. I had hoped for more, but my captains have assured me that 16 is more than enough to confront undefended merchant ships."

"That is true, Your Excellency, but why are you telling me this?'

"I thought you might like to be its captain."

Chapter 17

The Mediterranean:
Between Spain and Morocco 1785

"There's a swift moving brigantine coming up on our port side, sir," said Billings. "Can't see her flag yet. Still too far."

"Let's keep an eye on her," said Proctor. "Shouldn't be a problem since we're in Spanish waters." Even though Morocco was just to their south, that no longer worried him. Knowing that he had the sultan's signature on a document granting free passage helped to put his mind at ease. Nevertheless, he still wouldn't feel completely secure until they were a hundred miles out into the Atlantic. If they were sailing along America's Atlantic coast or even in the Caribbean, they wouldn't have been concerned about unknown ships. However, this was the Mediterranean, and after what they'd gone through with Moroccan pirates, Proctor could not help being a bit skittish.

"She's gaining rapidly on us, Captain. I think I can make out her flag. Appears to be Portuguese."

"Fine, if we can trust it. We'll hail her as she passes us." Proctor scanned the sky ahead of them. Clear, sunny and welcoming. What a day to be sailing. Hopefully there'd be many more such days on their voyage home.

Billings interrupted his thoughts. "Looks as if she has guns, sir. Probably eight or nine pounders. Can't tell how many yet."

Proctor frowned. "A Portuguese gunship here. Doesn't make sense. Best watch her closely. Hail her as she goes by."

"She's headin' our way, sir. Not passing. Obviously wants to make contact."

Proctor could think of no legitimate reason such a vessel would want to make close-up contact unless it was in distress. From how swiftly it was moving, that didn't seem likely. He pursed his lips grimly. He didn't like what he saw. Still, no need to panic. He considered the situation for a full minute before saying, "It's not a xebec or lateen, so it's probably not a corsair vessel. Most likely nothing to worry about, but alert the men to arm themselves with whatever they have at hand. Only to defend themselves, though. We don't attack because, if they're pirates, you can be sure they'll be better armed than us. Best to be prepared and not assume anything until they're in our wake. More than likely they're just curious or friendly, but you never know."

Ten minutes later the friendly sky they had enjoyed so recently turned ominous. A sudden storm was brewing. A rumble of rolling thunder off in the distance sounded menacing. Proctor couldn't help but think that the onset of a sudden storm seemed to be connected in some way with the sudden appearance of the Portuguese ship. He wasn't particularly superstitious, but it seemed portentous that the two things should be happening at the same time. The other vessel was now within a hundred yards of their stern and gaining fast. Proctor could see men at the bow of the fast-moving ship. They were not in naval uniforms. He turned to his first mate, concern now showing on his face.

"Now I think we should worry." As he said this the sea became turbulent and a nearby clap of thunder startled them.

"Aye, sir. Probably not Portuguese seamen. More likely pirates under a flag they acquired from a Portuguese merchant ship they boarded and took possession of."

"Yes, Josiah, very likely. Cannons probably added by the Muslim criminals." Ironic, thought Proctor, the cannons added to the *Betsey* by the sultan had been removed when he granted the crew their release. The sultan was not going to provide valuable fire power on a ship now under the command of his freed infidel prisoners. They could easily be turned against his own corsairs.

"If we're right, sir, we can only pray that they're Moroccans and not from some other lawless state. Do you think our document would protect us from Algerians or Tunisian pirates?"

"I doubt it, but it's worth a try. We're fairly far west for Algerians or Tunisians. If they're pirates, I'd wager they're Moroccan, which should not present a problem "

Billings let out a sigh of relief.

Chapter 18

The Mediterranean:
Between Spain and Morocco 1785

Captain Rais at the helm of the *da Gama* turned to his Tripolitan first mate and said in Arabic, "The American ship should be easy. They are usually unarmed and naive about sailing in the Mediterranean—even after losing several of their ships to our brethren."

His first mate seemed less confident. "Yes, captain, but these seas will make it quite dangerous to board the vessel. If we get a bad wave at the wrong time we could damage her so badly that she would take on water and sink. We would not be able to sail the ship into port. Even worse, the *da Gama* might be seriously damaged, too."

Rais was not going to pass up this opportunity. It would be his first capture. It would prove to the pasha that his faith in Rais had been justified. To sail on without taking possession of a ship and its cargo would signify failure. The pasha didn't tolerate excuses; he liked proven performance. It wouldn't matter that the weather conditions made the seizure somewhat risky. Rais ignored his first mate's warning and said, "Lower the Portuguese colors and raise ours."

The first mate shook his head in disbelief, but dared not protest further. To do so could be fatal. One didn't challenge men in authority on the Barbary Coast. Even if they were western men who'd converted to Islam. While Murad Rais had been in Tripoli for less than a year, he already had the reputation of being inflexible and ruthless, qualities the pasha admired.

Rais then said, "Pull in along her port side. Be prepared for boarding."

"Yes, captain," said the first mate grimly.

As the gap between the two vessels narrowed, the turbulence of the sea intensified. It became hard to maintain one's balance on the deck.

As he tried to keep his footing, Rais squinted. There was something about the other ship that was familiar. It seemed remarkably similar to the *Betsey*. As they got closer he realized that it was the *Betsey*. How it was free of Moroccan control was a mystery. Unless it *was* under Moroccan control. In which case he probably should leave it alone. He looked carefully now. The crew didn't look like Moroccans. More like Europeans or Americans.... Somehow the Betsey had become free of Moroccan control. His heart raced with excitement now. Undeterred by the perilous weather, Rais ordered his first mate to announce to the *Betsey* that they should be prepared to be boarded. He then added, "Tell them that if they resist, they will be killed."

Chapter 19

The Mediterranean:
Between Spain and Morocco 1785

"They're closing in, Captain. Obviously want to make contact."

"Looks like they plan to board us." Proctor was sick at the very prospect. After roughly two years in Moroccan jails, the thought of further confinement under slave conditions was more than a little unsettling.

"Let's assume the best and be prepared for the worst. Let me handle the talking." As he said this lightning hit the surface of the water within a few yards of the ship's stern. The thunder clap that followed shook the ship and everyone on board. At the same time a huge swell washed over the ship's deck.

"They're not going to be able to board us if this keeps up, sir."

"Might call it a mixed blessing, Josiah. Hold on, our Portuguese friends are still coming at us. In these seas, no telling what will happen if they make contact." Normally when ships drew abreast of each other to converse or exchange cargoes, they would do it gingerly so as not to damage either vessel. With the roiling of the sea in storm conditions like these, it was more than likely that any contact could result in damage to one or both of the ships.

"They don't seem to be deterred by the conditions, Captain. They're still closing in on us."

As the gap narrowed to ten feet, a collision seemed imminent.

"Tell the crew to be prepared for hard contact," yelled Proctor. "What in God's name is wrong with them? They'll get us all killed."

"Wait! That's not the Portuguese flag!"

"Order the men to let up on the mainsail," barked Captain Rais. "Allow some space between the two ships. Conditions are not safe for boarding now." He gave the command as if avoiding a collision was his idea—not his first mate's. He then added, "We'll stay with her until the storm lets up. Then we'll board her."

The first mate shook his head in amazement as he carried out the captain's orders.

Chapter 20
The Mediterranean:
Between Spain and Morocco 1786

The bow of the *Betsey* dipped precipitously, going well below the surface of the angry sea. Seawater flooded the front third of the deck nearly washing two crewmen into the sea. After what seemed forever, the bow came up, righting the ship, at least for the moment. Billings and Proctor breathed a sigh of relief, though they both knew things weren't going to be getting better soon.

Proctor saw that the pirate vessel had allowed the gap to widen. Apparently they'd seen the wisdom of avoiding contact.

"Looks as if they've changed their minds," said Billings.

"Not as crazy as we thought," said the young captain. "Good, maybe they'll leave us alone. Now all we have to do is weather the storm. The sea is enough to contend with without being rammed by those damned pirates."

"Aye, sir, they do seem to be pulling away. Good riddance to 'em."

"If I know anything about these bloody devils, they'll just lie in wait till the storm subsides. Unfortunately, we can't outrun them. First things first, though. We need to ride out this storm."

As they held on to keep from being blown away or washed off the helm, they saw that several of the pirates on the other ship seemed to be making faces at them. Apparently they were so confident of their ultimate victory that they were taunting their victims before they'd even made contact. Since boarding seemed inevitable, barring a miracle, Proctor prayed that they were Moroccan pirates—not corsairs from some other Barbary state.

A half hour later, the storm began to abate. It was still raining hard, but the wind was letting up and the sea was growing calmer. Proctor had mixed feelings. They were now out of danger from the storm, but the threat from the nearby pirate ship loomed large and imminent.

Already the other ship was heading their way, this time with no storm to interfere with her plunderous intentions. As the pirate vessel drew near, someone from the deck yelled in broken English that they intended to board the *Betsey* and that resistance would be met by death.

Minutes later the pirate ship pulled alongside the *Betsey*, bumping the side of the ship gently. The name on the ship said *da Gama*. The spokesman for the pirate vessel said, "My captain would speak with your captain."

Moments later Captain Proctor was standing midship at the port gunwale facing the side of the pirate ship. "I'm the captain. Where is your captain?"

As he said this a man came from behind the mainmast and walked slowly to the side of the ship facing Proctor. Proctor couldn't believe his eyes.

"You're . . . you're. . ."

"Yes, Proctor, I'm a former crew member of yours. Used to be Peter Lisle, though I surprised that you even remember me. You never acknowledged me then. You can call me Captain Rais, my new name I chose when I became a Muslim." Can you imagine my surprise when I saw that we were approaching the *Betsey*. Of all the ships at sea, it would be the very ship I served on that we came upon. Talk about irony. I'm flattered that you remember me since I served in relative obscurity on your ship. You never even acknowledged me on our voyage across the Atlantic."

"Oh I remember you all right. I remember you. You certainly made your presence known when you turned against one of your own and got him killed. I'll never forget your duplicity. I'll never forget that you're a traitor to your crew and to your country."

"My fellow crew members and my country turned against me long before I chose the side of Allah. My Muslim brothers in Morocco and in Tripoli have treated me far better than anyone treated me in America or on that sorry ship you command. As you see, I am now in command of my own ship, a ship of dedicated seamen who are taking possession of the *Betsey* and putting you and your crew in chains. Ironic, isn't it. I had no chance of becoming a captain on an American ship; yet in my new country my ability is recognized and rewarded within months. But enough of my new success. I see that somehow you managed to escape the grasp of the sultan. How you managed this I look forward to learning. However, as Allah would have it, your escape came to naught. This time you will not escape. Pardon me for enjoying this, Proctor."

Chapter 21
Fraunces Tavern: New York City - October 1786

The new president of the Continental Congress, Nathaniel Gorham of Massachusetts, called the informal meeting to order. Gorham had replaced John Hancock, who'd recently been elected president for the second time. The first was back in 1775. Hancock did not actually serve his second term, as he remained home in Massachusetts, too ill to carry out the duties of president.

Gorham, a direct descendant of a *Mayflower* Pilgrim, was a self-made man, having become a hugely successful import-export merchant in Charlestown, Massachusetts. In addition to his business activities, he served in various political roles including being elected to the the Massachusetts General Court and delegate to the Continental Congress.

Gorham turned to James Monroe, of Virginia. "We've wrestled with the Barbary pirate matter for years. As most of you know, months ago, after much deliberation, we finally decided to pay a ransom for the *Betsey* and its crew members. They still have not yet returned to Boston. Apparently the Moroccans have not honored their end of the agreement.

"Shortly after the *Betsey* was taken the Algerians took the *Maria* and the *Dauphin*. Our negotiations with Algeria have borne no fruit so far. Both ships and their crews remain in Algeria. In the meantime, in good faith, we've negotiated a treaty with the sultan of Morocco that gives our ships free passage in Moroccan waters. We've paid a tribute to insure that free passage. We can only hope that this time the sultan will honor the agreement."

"Yes," said Monroe. "We can only hope. If he does not, what options do we have?"

Edward Carrington of Virginia said, "I think we will be forced to take action."

"What sort of action do you have in mind, Edward," asked Gorham. "We've taken action by the very act of negotiating this treaty with the sultan. Surely you can't mean military or naval action?"

"That's exactly what I mean. These barbaric North Africans only understand force."

Gorham interjected, "Think of what you're saying, Edward. If we had a navy up to the task, which we don't, in addition to Morocco, we'd have to take on Algeria, Tunisia, and Tripoli. There's no way that we could send our tiny navy half-way around the world to take on four Barbary states. These are states that have kept at bay far larger, more powerful nations than our little country."

"Then what do you propose?" demanded Carrington heatedly.

"That's why we're here," said Gorham. "We need a plan that we are capable of carrying out in case we find that negotiation has failed us in Morocco and Algeria. I still have hopes for the treaty, but the Muslims or Mussulmans of the Barbary Coast, have proved unreliable and unpredictable. We know from Adams and Jefferson that these North African Muslims think Allah gives them the right to attack and even kill non-Muslims. I have a letter from Jefferson that makes the point quite clearly. He and Ambassador Adams met with Sidi Haji Abdul Rahman Adja, the resident Tripolitan ambassador to Britain, and asked him why his government was so hostile to the new American Republic. Let me read from the letter what it says about Tripoli:

> "...that it was founded on the Laws of the Prophet, that it was written in their Koran, that all nations who should not have acknowledged their authority were sinners, that it was their right and duty to make war upon them wherever they could be found and to make slaves of all they could take as prisoners, and that every Mussulman who should be slain in battle was sure to go to Paradise..."

The others in the room seemed stunned by the reading of this excerpt. James Monroe broke the silence. "If the leaders of these Barbary states all think this way it will be close to impossible to negotiate favorable agreements with them. How do you negotiate with people who think they are superior to yourself? How do you negotiate with people who think that their god has obligated them to kill anyone who does not believe in that god. If they think that way, they can justify anything they do, regardless of how shocking or unreasonable it is."

Edward Carrington suggested, "Perhaps we should negotiate with Britain to put us under their wing as they did when we were their colonies? Surely they would rather see us . . ."

Monroe interrupted abruptly. "I wouldn't get my hopes up,

Edward. As soon as we were free of them the British cast us to the winds. I have it on good authority that they are gloating among themselves as they witness our troubles in the Barbary region. There is no way that they would help us now, as it would be giving aid to their competition in commerce. As it is now they are enjoying our suffering as it is beneficial to their economy."

"As you know," said Gorham, " the Spanish helped us with our negotiations for the return of the *Betsey* and her crew. It is certainly not their fault that the results have not been what we hoped for. They have also advised us to pay tribute to these rogue states because, in their opinion, it is the only way to carry on commerce in the Mediterranean. They pay tribute, the British pay tribute and several other European states do the same. Since all of these countries are far more powerful than we are, it would seem that that is our only option. Even if these Muslim states feel justified in treating Christian states badly, it is in their best interest to treat us more fairly if they are being paid to do so."

Carrington said, "I hate to pay tribute for something that should be free to all nations. It is wrong, unfair, downright evil."

"We all agree with you, Edward," said Gorham, "but I think all of us in this room have lived long enough to learn that it is an unjust world. If we are going to survive in it, we shall have to learn to cope with the inequities. Right now, as a new nation, our first priority must be to survive. Someday when we are more powerful, perhaps we shall have more bargaining power."

"In the meantime," said Carrington somberly, "our citizens are left to rot in Barbary jails, forsaken by their own government."

"We have not forsaken them, Edward," said Gorham. "You know as well as any of us that we're doing all we can short of declaring war on Morocco and Algeria. And I think you know that such a declaration would be reckless on our part."

"Then what do we do?" demanded Carrington in frustration. "Just forget about them?"

Chapter 22
The Mediterranean: Approaching Tripoli – 1786

"How many are you?" demanded Rais. I know when we left Boston there were 22 including your esteemed Captain Orne. By the way, why is he not here?"

"He was detained by the sultan. The sultan saw value in him."

"You mean the sultan kept him as someone to be used for bargaining sometime in the future."

"No, I don't think so."

"Doesn't matter. He's not here. When I was chosen by the sultan there were two dead. Did you lose any more men?"

"No, sorry to disappoint you."

"I would advise, you, Proctor, to show a little more respect or that number will grow. All right, here's what we are going to do. We're going to divide your crew between the two ships. Some of my men will board your ship to insure that you sail it into Tripoli without attempting something rash. I, too, will board the *Betsey*, so you and I will be on the same ship." Then he added with a sneer, "We can catch up on old times."

The two ships were well into their fifth day heading east toward Tripoli. The weather had been good. Captain Rais came jauntily up to Proctor and said, "Just another beautiful day on the Mediterranean, Proctor. Soon you will begin to enjoy Tripolitan hospitality." He smiled coldly. "I'm afraid our jails are not always as comfortable as the ones in Morocco. We Tripolitans don't believe in pampering our prisoners. Then again, maybe you won't be confined that long. The pasha likes to auction off his prisoners as slaves. Far more lucrative than feeding ungrateful prisoners."

Proctor struggled to control himself. He wanted to strike the man in the face. Better yet, kill him. He knew this would be suicide and certainly no help to his crew. Even by controlling himself he understood that this time they might not be as fortunate as they were in Morocco. At the very least it could take a half year or more for negotiations to release them. Then again, maybe his government would refuse to continue paying ransom on the assumption that such payments only encourage further attacks. Worse than the endless months of moldering in filthy, rat infested jails was the thought that, if he and his men were sold off as slaves to various slave owners, any attempt at ransom would be impossible. How could an American negotiator reach each and every slave holder without himself being taken captive?

As he considered their grim options, Proctor found himself thinking about the possibility of launching a mutiny. The odds against success of such a mutiny were not good, especially since they would have to make the attempt on two ships. How could he even communicate a plan to his men on the pirate ship without alerting the pirates on their ship?

Proctor considered his odds. There were nine of his men on the pirate ship. There were nine more including himself on the *Betsey*. There were eight pirates including Captain Rais on the *Betsey*. He assumed that there were somewhere between seven and nine pirates on the other ship, since it would make sense to have close to an equal number on each vessel.

The fact that the Americans outnumbered the pirates was a slight plus. Even more of a plus was the fact that the Americans were not shackled, since there were no shackles on the ship. At least not on the *Betsey*. He was surprised that Rais and his band of pirates didn't find a way to bind the crew, but they didn't even try. No doubt, thought Proctor, it was because the pirates had found through experience that non-combative merchant seamen tended to be intimidated by pirates and by their barbaric reputation. Besides, the pirates had made sure to disarm the few armed seaman on the ship.

That the pirates were armed was a factor against the Americans. Proctor had done a quick assessment of the situation and concluded that the eight pirates on the *Betsey* had a total of six cutlasses and five pistols. By comparison, before being boarded the American crew had six pistols and seven or eight knives. However, since the Americans were now prisoners, their knives, their guns and their powder had been confiscated, so the odds against them were much worse. Still, while the chances of success were not good, a mutiny was worth a try—especially if you weighed it against the certain prospect of being prisoners or slaves possibly for the rest of your life.

It was risky, extremely risky, but not to try would mean certain enslavement. To Proctor it was a risk worth taking.

First, though, he had to convey his plan to the other crew members, and he had to do it without being seen or overheard by Rais or his fellow pirates. That his fellow crew members might not want to stage a revolt never occurred to Proctor. He knew his men, and he just assumed they'd prefer the risk of a mutiny attempt over certain imprisonment. They'd all had enough of pirate jails. However, if he was going to communicate with his crew members, he had to do it soon as they only had a day or two before they reached Tripoli.

His strategy was to quickly get his plan across to two or three of his men and urge them to pass it on to the others. To do this his message had to be brief, as any attempt to explain the plan in detail would take too long and call attention to their conversations. The shortened message would go something like this:

"We attack tonight at midnight. Pretend you are asleep to get their guard down. When you hear me say, 'Now,' take down the man nearest you. Pass this on to the others."

After five days at sea, the pirates had relaxed somewhat their surveillance of their prisoners. They'd even attempted, with their limited English, casual conversation with some of the Americans, since the *Betsey* crew had not caused any disruption or shown any sign of causing trouble. Because of this loosening of their guard, the Americans were allowed to have brief verbal exchanges with each other. However, if these exchanges lasted too long, the pirate guards would bark, "That's enough, you two. Move on." Consequently, it wasn't difficult for Proctor to get his plan across to two men, and it was just as easy for those two to pass the word along to the others.

Now Proctor had to get his plan to the crew members on the pirate ship. This was not going to be easy. He considered his possibilities. He could not yell across to the other ship as it would obviously reveal the plan to the captors. The pirate ship was now abut 100 feet off the starboard side of the *Betsey,* and the wind seemed to be pushing it closer. Suddenly an idea occurred to him.

Chapter 23

The Mediterranean: Approaching Tripoli – 1786

Proctor approached the cast-iron brazier at mid-deck. The crew's cook used a charcoal fire to roast fresh meats when they were available. Fresh meat was a delicacy, so the brazier was rarely used. The only time they had fresh meat of any kind was shortly after they left a port. Most of the time the meat served was dried and salted. Now the ashes in the brazier were cold. Proctor's eyes lit up when he saw a number of pieces of charcoal in the bottom of the brazier pan. He looked around to see if he was being watched. He wasn't, so he reached in and grabbed a sizable chunk of the spent fuel. He pocketed it in one quick motion.

In the next few minutes he waited for his next opportunity. He needed to go to the gunwale facing the pirate ship and lean over the side as far as possible. Easy to do, but not without calling attention to himself. Still, he had to do it. It was the only chance of alerting his crew members on the other ship to the planned mutiny. After several minutes he realized that he was not going to get enough time to do what he intended to do without being seen. There had to be a way, though.

Then it hit him. He would actually call attention to himself. All along he'd been trying to do just the opposite, but that wasn't going to work. He wasn't sure this idea would work, either, but at least it had a chance. He looked out toward the pirate ship. It was easing closer now. *No time like the present.* He put his hand to his throat and made a gagging sound loud enough for anyone on his part of the deck to hear him. He gagged again, only this time louder. As he did this he stumbled toward the side of the ship.

"What's wrong?" yelled a guard coming forward from the stern. Proctor could barely understand him, the man's English pronunciation was so bad.

"I'm sick!"

He now leaned over the gunwale, making a retching noise. As he did this he took his piece of charcoal from his pocket and wrote on the side of the ship in huge letters, AT MIDNIGHT MUTINY! It wasn't easy writing upside down, but he managed.

As he pulled up from the gunwale a couple of his men came over and asked if he was all right. Proctor winked at them and said fairly loudly that he was fine now.

Chapter 24
The Mediterranean: Approaching Tripoli – 1786

As his men trimmed the sails to adjust for increasing winds, Murad Rais was at ease with himself. Things could not have gone better. He let his mind wander to what lay ahead. He imagined with satisfaction the reception he would get when they returned to Tripoli. He and his ship had been out less than two weeks, and they were already returning to port with a major prize—a captured merchant ship, its cargo and its crew.

Not just any ship, but an American ship. And not just any American ship, but the very ship he'd come over on from Boston just two years ago. By capturing an American merchant vessel he would erase any doubt that he could serve the pasha faithfully and effectively. He smiled inwardly. Certainly there wasn't any doubt now. There probably wasn't any doubt before, he thought confidently. Obviously the pasha thought well of him, or he wouldn't have made him the captain of the Tripolitan corsair flagship.

Rais's thoughts went back a few days to the moment when he and his men had boarded the *Betsey*. Oh how he'd enjoyed the look on the face of Proctor. A few years ago the man had barely spoken to him when they were shipmates. Now Proctor was speechless, but for a very different reason.

How much greater it would have been to see the expression on the face of Henry Orne. Unfortunately, according to Proctor, Orne now enjoyed a favorable relationship with the Sultan of Morocco, so it was unlikely they would meet again.

Rais looked out at the clear blue sky and sighed. It would be nice to celebrate his success with a pint when he returned to port. But of course that wouldn't happen. As a Muslim he had sworn not to partake of spirits. Too bad. He did like his beer. Oh well, a small sacrifice to make for the privileges he enjoyed now as a Tripolitan ship captain and advisor to the pasha.

Chapter 25
The Mediterranean: Nearing Tripoli – 1786

It was a cloudless night. A million stars dotted the ebon sky overhead. The only sound was the rippling water as the ship's bow cut steadily through the calm Mediterranean. Far in the distance the lights on the shore of Tripoli flickered silently.

Proctor estimated that they were within five or six miles of the coast. His silver-cased pocket watch had been confiscated by the Moroccan pirates two years ago, so he could only guess at the time. Still, from the position of the moon and the star alignments he could make an accurate guess. He was fairly certain that it was midnight—or very close to it.

He had been given a berth in the hold, but the last two days he'd said he preferred sleeping on deck. From his position midship, only two pirates appeared to be awake on deck. Obviously they'd been assigned guard duty. Two other pirates were asleep on the hard plank surface. The rest of the pirates were below. Proctor knew from when he'd slept below that two men would be on guard down there and two would be asleep.

He swallowed hard and took a deep breath. They had to move now. The element of surprise was the only advantage they had over the armed pirates. They would never have a better chance than right now when some of their captors were asleep. Besides, to delay further would put them too close to Tripoli where their insurrection was more likely to be noticed. He prayed to God that his men on the pirate ship had noticed his message.

Of course it was possible that the pirates also noticed his message. He was counting on one thing, though. From his observation of their captors, he saw no evidence that they understood much English. Even the few pirates who attempted some verbal English were able to say only a few phrases and seemed to understand even less. True, Rais could read English, but he was on the *Betsey* so he would not be in a position to see the message.

Okay, now or never. He watched as one of the guards slowly approached midship. It had been the man's routine for the last few hours. As the guard passed by within a few feet, Proctor lunged at him from behind, grabbing the man's dagger from his belt and plunging it into the man's chest just below the ribcage. The dagger pierced the pirate's heart killing him instantly. He made only a barely audible gasp as he fell to the deck.

Proctor could no longer keep silent. It was important that his crew members knew now was the time to strike. "Now!" he yelled, hoping against hope that his men would be successful without sustaining too many losses. They all knew that losses were inevitable, but they also knew that everyone would be lost if they didn't at least try to gain their freedom.

Seconds later Proctor heard a scuffle from the bow of the ship. There was one American and two pirates in the bow section. One of them was sleeping. The scuffle was followed by a thumping sound as someone fell to the deck. Was it the standing pirate guard, or was it Proctor's man?

Chapter 26
The Mediterranean: Nearing Tripoli – 1786

Before Proctor could check the bow, the sleeping pirate near him began to rise from the deck. Proctor fell upon him and sent his already bloody knife deep into the man's chest. At the very same moment the American seaman in the bow rushed to the other awakening pirate and dispatched him quickly with a knife he had taken from the first pirate. The seaman had felled the first pirate with a loose section of anchor chain he'd found on the deck.

With the threat on the deck ended, Proctor went to the hatch and listened. Unlike on the main deck, a full-blown battle was underway down below. Proctor heard screams of men being hacked or skewered by cutlasses. He grimaced at the sound of swords clashing against swords and the occasional thud as men fell fatally to the lower deck. Had his men survived or been defeated? He feared the worst. He shuddered at the very thought of what he might learn. He thought, I must go down there to help.

Suddenly it went silent below deck. Whatever had happened in the hold, it was over. The silence seemed to go on forever, confirming in Proctor's mind the worst possible outcome.

"Captain." A faint voice came from the open hatch. Proctor stared in horror as one of his men slowly emerged drenched in blood.

"Daniel," cried Proctor at the sight of his blood-soaked crewman. "Are you all right?" *Stupid question. Of course he wasn't.*

"I'll survive, sir, but some of the men won't."

"You're bleeding."

"Just a few cuts, sir. They'll heal. Mostly the other fellow's blood. But we lost two good men."

"What about the Tripolitans?"

"Two of them are dead. I think there's still two alive. One of them is Lisle or Rais, but they're both in bad shape."

"Then we're in control of the ship. I'm going down there to see what I can do for our men."

As he said this he heard a scream from the pirate ship. He then he said, "Come up here, Daniel, and help me listen."

"The other ship, sir?"

"Yes. If the Tripolitans are still in control over there, our losses here could be for nothing. Listen."

The savage, feral sounds coming from the pirate ship made him wince. If anything, the fighting sounded even more savage than it was on the *Betsey*. He wondered if his decision to take on armed men who made it their life's work to fight and kill might have been the wrong one. As far as he knew, only a few of his men had ever killed anyone. Three or four had fought in the War of Independence, but most of them had not, as they were too young. Certainly he had not. And that made him sick at the very thought of what he'd just done. God help them all, he thought.

What do you think, Daniel?"

"Sounds like all hell's broke loose over there. Sounds bad, but it's impossible to tell who's winning."

"I know. We can only wait and pray. In the meantime let me look below and see what help we can give to our men here. You stay above and keep me informed as to what's happening over there."

"Aye, sir."

JIHAD AT SEA

Chapter 27
The Mediterranean – 1786

Proctor slowly went down the ladder into the charnel stench of the darkness below. As his eyes adjusted to the lack of light, he slowly made out human forms lying silently in ghastly repose. Four of them appeared dead: two Tripolitans and two Americans.

One of the surviving Tripolitans was bleeding into the ship's muddy bilge, adding still more crimson to the foul standing water—a dark red reminder of the the carnage that had just ended.

Proctor did a quick count. Five of his men appeared to have survived, though most of them had sustained injuries of one kind or another. The other surviving pirate was Rais, who glared malevolently at Proctor.

"I hope it was worth it to you, Proctor. You lost two men here, and I'm guessing more up above and on my ship, too. My best men are on the *da Gama*, so I'll wager we came out ahead."

"We're just going to have to wait a while, aren't we, Lisle. They're still fighting over there. You may think your men are better than mine because they're trained killers. And that they are, but my men are trained seamen. Easily as fit as your sadistic devils. Don't bet on winning."

One of the surviving crew members interrupted. "Want us to get these bodies out of here, captain?"

"Aye, give 'em a watery grave. And if this traitor opens his mouth again, toss him over, too."

When Proctor came back up to the main deck, he could tell that the fighting had moderated somewhat on the *da Gama*. There was nothing he could do but listen. Soon the pirate ship went ominously silent. After what seemed an eternity a voice was heard from the deck of the pirate ship. "It's over cap'n. We're pulling in closer so you can come aboard and see for yourself." Proctor was afraid to ask how bad it was. Apparently his men had prevailed, but at what cost.

A half hour later, after dressing the wounds of his men on the *Betsey*, Proctor boarded the *da Gama*. One of the men, apparently the one who'd called across to the *Betsey*, met him on deck and explained excitedly. "We took 'em by surprise, cap'n, but they rallied quickly and put up a hell of a fight. I'm proud of our boys." Then he lowered his head and spoke more slowly. "Unfortunately, we didn't all make it."

"How many?" asked Proctor somberly.

"Three brave men, Cap'n. Three of the best mates a feller could have."

"Injuries?"

"Mostly bad cuts, but one of the boys may lose his arm. Looks bad to me, sir."

"And the Tripolitans? What are their losses?"

"Three dead and five injured. Thank God we outnumbered them."

"That's it? There were just eight of them?" asked Proctor. He was surprised that a pirate ship would go to sea with only a total of 16 men.

"Yessir. What do we do with 'em now, sir?"

"Send the dead ones to Davy Jones' locker, and shackle the others securely in the hold."

"What'll we use to shackle 'em, sir?"

"Find something. Let's not make the mistake they made with us."

"Maybe we should let them join Davy Jones, too, sir. Best we get rid of 'em."

"No, sailor, we're better than that. We'll drop 'em off in Gibraltar with the local constabulary."

The sailor shrugged his shoulders skeptically and said, "If you say so, sir."

"I do."

JIHAD AT SEA

Two days later Proctor spoke to his first mate.

"So far, so good, Josiah. Three more days and we should be in Gibraltar. We can rid ourselves of these Tripolitan scum, stock up on food and water, and be on our way home." He looked across an expanse of water at the *da Gama*, now under the control of some of the *Betsey* crew members. "We'll have our own prize, too. The *da Gama* should make a nice merchant ship for Mr. Carlisle."

"If we don't run into more pirates before that," said Billings pessimistically.

"Let's hope we have some good luck for a change." He knew as well as Billings that they would be sailing in treacherous waters until they were past Gibraltar and well into the Atlantic. The only thing in their favor now was that by acquiring the guns, cutlasses and knives of the pirates, they were better prepared to ward off any new attack.

Being attacked twice had shown Proctor how naive all of them had been when setting out from Boston several years ago. In his opinion now, all merchant ships that entered the Med should be armed and prepared to defend themselves. He knew, too, that such preparedness would change the shipping business dramatically. For one thing, it would make the cost of shipping and importing goods much more expensive. Insurance would go up, adding to the cost of each cargo shipment. Every ship would have to be armed, and the sailors would have to be trained in defensive methods. Just as critical, though, would be the difficulty in recruiting men willing to fight. Most seamen, while tough and used to hardship at sea, were not fighting men and wanted nothing of it.

His hope was that the U.S. government would work out agreements with the Barbary states granting free passage to American vessels. He knew that they had tried—that a treaty with Morocco had been signed. He also knew that the Moroccans had ignored the agreement. Barring effective treaties, Proctor was convinced the only long-term solution was to go to war with the Barbary states and defeat them. Until that happened shipping to and from the Mediterranean would only become more perilous.

While relieved that they were out of the pirates' hands, Proctor took little pleasure from their hard-won freedom. Since leaving Boston the *Betsey* had lost a total of nine men from their original crew of 22. Seven were dead. Orne was still in Morocco and Lisle, the traitor, was in chains in the hold of the ship.

Proctor was not happy leaving Orne in Morocco at the mercy of the mercurial sultan, but could do nothing about it. There was no way that one unarmed ship, a crew of 13 and one pirate ship could take on the nation of Morocco. He fully intended to remind the authorities in Boston about the status of Orne, and hope that they would convey the plight of their former captain to the U.S. government. He wasn't optimistic, though, having seen how long it took the federal government to pay ransom for the crew when they were imprisoned in Morocco.

Chapter 28
Gibraltar – 1786

Immediately upon tying up in the port of Gibraltar, Proctor sent First Mate Billings into the port town to the local constabulary to announce that the *Betsey* had seven Tripolitan pirates secured in its hold. Since Gibraltar was a British military garrison, the policing was the province of the military, so Billings had to find the garrison headquarters.

A tall sergeant at the front desk greeted Billings curtly and asked what his problem was. The sergeant was fitted out imposingly in his red military uniform. He looked dubiously at the man before him. The weatherbeaten soul with his tattered, dirty rags made a stark contrast to the crisp military bearing of the sergeant.

"I'm Josiah Billings, first mate on the American merchant ship *Betsey*. A few days ago we were attacked by a Tripolitan pirate ship." Billings proceeded to explain how the pirates had attacked and overpowered them, how they were being brought into Tripoli as prisoners where they were to be put into prison or slavery. He went on to explain how in desperation they had, with a surprise uprising, overcome their captors and won their freedom. He added that in the process they had lost five men. However, he said, they had captured seven of the pirates.

The sergeant smiled indulgently and said, "That's a very interesting story Mr. Billings. Very interesting. I'm happy for you that you and your crew members are free, but why are you telling me this? What business is it of mine?"

Thinking it obvious, Billings was taken back by the sergeant's question.

"My captain thinks they should be locked up in your jail. He thought you should prosecute them. We're bringing you seven men who won't be able to continue their piratical ways, if you put them away in prison."

The sergeant forced a tolerant smile that he reserved for the naive or the uninformed.

"Apparently you don't realize that we have treaties with these

Barbary states that grant us free passage in the Mediterranean waters. If we arrest these men, we violate our treaty with Tripoli."

"But they attacked our ship and took us prisoner. They intended to make us slaves in Tripoli. They took possession of our cargo and our ship."

The officer grinned indulgently. "You Americans think you can have free passage everywhere you go at no cost to yourselves. I don't blame you and your crew for believing such nonsense, but I hope you understand that your little country has let you down. They've exposed you to imprisonment and enslavement because they refuse to pay tribute to these Barbary states. We in Europe learned long ago that we could do business in the Med if we went to the trouble of negotiating treaties with these Barbary states, something your pitiful country has not learned to do." He thought for a minute, then said, "I'm sorry, but you can't expect the sort of help from us that you enjoyed before you separated yourselves from Britain. By fighting your so-called war of independence, you forfeited any protection you enjoyed as British citizens. Now your commercial enterprise is direct competition to British commerce. You must see that. Even if you don't, I'm surprised that your captain did not. You Americans have a lot to learn. Maybe your experience with these Tripoli corsairs will make you smarter in the future."

Billings frowned in frustration. He felt his neck redden. He was humiliated and totally at a loss as to how to proceed next. He dreaded breaking the news to Proctor, though he doubted the captain would blame him for the failure. He sighed. There was nothing to be gained by remaining in the garrison headquarters any longer, so he said, "What do you recommend we do with these seven lowlifes?"

The sergeant snorted disdainfully. "There's only two things you can do. Either you can take them back to America with you, or you can let them off here where they can enjoy our Gibraltar hospitality." Then he added, "If you do decide to leave them here make sure a representative from this constabulary is present at the dock to insure that none of these rascals has a weapon or a disease."

Back on the *Betsey*, Proctor and Billings considered the two alternatives.

"It's a bad couple of choices, Josiah. Either way it makes me sick in the stomach just to think about. If we take these rogues back to Boston, we risk a mutiny by them on our Atlantic crossing. It's almost certain they'll try something. At the very least it means we get very little sleep, as most of us will have to stand guard 24 hours a day. I wouldn't underestimate what lengths these men would go to when facing imprisonment. Remember the risk we took against them." He closed his eyes as he frowned, struggling with the terrible choices that he had to deal with. Finally, he said, "I blame myself for this. I should have known that the Brits wouldn't take these fellows into custody. If I'm honest with myself, I really did know, but was so caught up in our own situation it never occurred to me that these people in Gibraltar no longer considered us British."

"May I make a suggestion, Captain?"

"Yes, yes. By all means. What have you got?"

"Considering the disadvantages of taking seven vicious killers home with us, why don't we leave six of 'em here, and. . ."

"And take Lisle or Rais, whatever his name is, back to Boston to face trial for treason."

Chapter 29
Gibraltar – 1786

Captain Proctor slowly descended the wooden ladder into the dark, dank hold of the *da Gama*. As he stepped onto the slippery deck of the hold, he approached the seven prisoners confined to the bow section of the ship. While there were no shackles as such on board, the American crew had managed to find enough unused rope in the hold to tether the hands and feet of the seven pirates. Proctor had given strict orders to his own crew not to release any of the buccaneers under any conditions. Even if they needed to relieve themselves, they were to remain secured. They were given two buckets and were told to use them when needed. It was far from dignified, but under the circumstances, necessary. Besides, the Americans were not concerned with protecting the dignity of their former captors. Proctor knew that the granting of the least bit of freedom opened his crew up to great risk.

"I have news for you, Lisle."

Rais glowered at Proctor. "The name is Rais, Murad Rais."

"You're Lisle as far as I'm concerned."

Rais considered a response, then decided there was no point in pursuing a losing cause, "I assume it's bad news."

"As a matter of fact I have some good news and some bad news."

"You're enjoying this aren't you, Proctor?"

"It so happens, I'm not." Then he allowed himself a slight smirk. "Well, maybe a little."

"Get on with it then. What is it?"

"The good news for you is that your crew will be set free here in Gibraltar."

"They will not be arrested?"

"No, the Gibraltar authorities don't want them. However. . ."

"They want me. Is that it?"

"No, they don't want you either. We want you. You're going

home to Boston with the rest of us where you'll go on trial for treason, piracy and whatever else the authorities want to throw at you. Aren't you glad you're going home? You must be homesick by now."

"Just let me off in Gibraltar with my crew. You can be rid of me. That should make you happy."

"No, Lisle, that won't make me happy. Bringing you home to face charges of treason and confiscation of an American vessel will make me happy."

Chapter 30
Gibraltar – 1786

Two days later, when the *Betsey* was fully loaded with supplies, water, and newly acquired cargo—mostly wine, dried fruit, furniture and tools—Proctor sent Billings to the police station at the Gibraltar garrison headquarters.

As Billings went up to the front desk he saw that the desk sergeant was the same man he'd talked to on his first visit two days ago.

"Ah, my American friend from the *Betsey*. What brings you here today?" the sergeant inquired patiently.

"We're about to depart for America. You said we needed to have someone from this constabulary present as we released our prisoners. We intend to leave today."

"Yes we do. Give me a minute, and I'll have someone go with you to the docks." He disappeared into a hallway behind the desk. After what seemed like a half hour, but was probably no more than ten minutes, the sergeant reappeared followed by a slightly older, stockier man.

"This is Leftenant Woodley-Smith. My superior officer. He'll be accompanying you to the docks. I'm sorry, I don't remember your name?

"Billings, sir, Josiah Billings." Billings offered his hand to the leftenant, who ignored it as if it were beneath him to greet a common seaman the way two gentlemen would greet each other.

Woodley-Smith seemed annoyed that he had to make a trip to the docks for an American ship. "Come, come. Let's get this over with."

The headquarters building was less than a half mile from the waterfront, yet the leftenant called for a cabriolet to carry them to the docks. The small, two-wheeled carriage was brought around from the rear of the building by a civilian driver in the employ of the military. Within minutes they were at the wharf where the *da Gama* was tied up.

JIHAD AT SEA

Woodley-Smith stood for a minute peering at the pirate ship. Then he spoke to Billings.

"This ship is not the *Betsey*! What is this?"

"It's the pirate ship, sir. The one that seized the *Betsey*. We then overcame the bloody wretches, took our ship back and took possession of their ship, too. It's called the *da Gama*. The pirates took it from the Portuguese. If you'll look out there in the harbor you'll see the *Betsey*. She's at anchor. The *da Gama* is a wee bit more maneuverable, so we brought her in here to the wharf." Larger ships were usually anchored in the harbor rather than tied up at docks and wharves because they were less maneuverable by sail. If they remained at anchor out in the harbor there was usually more wind to help them get underway.

Woodley-Smith shook his head. This was supposed to be a simple transfer of Tripolitan corsairs to Gibraltar soil. How involved should he get in the ownership of the two vessels? Should he take possession of the *da Gama* and return it to the Portuguese? No. He wasn't paid to get involved in international affairs such as this. Besides, he wasn't sure how to handle the situation anyway. Better to keep it simple and just do a cursory check of the prisoners and be done with it.

"All right, take me to your captain."

"Follow me, sir."

As they approached the ship, Billings yelled out to a seaman on deck. "Tell the captain he's needed up top."

Billings introduced Captain Proctor to Woodley-Smith, explaining that the leftenant wanted to supervise the debarkation of the Tripolitan prisoners.

Proctor was not happy with this, but understood why the British controllers of Gibraltar would want to see for themselves what sort of men were being dropped on their wharf.

After Proctor and Woodley-Smith discussed procedure for a few minutes, Proctor said, "I'll have them brought up now so you can see what you're getting."

Woodley-Smith nodded his assent.

Soon the sounds of scuffling and muttering could be heard from the hold. Then, a man emerged through the mid-ship hatch, blinking at the brightness of the Gibraltar sunlight. Proctor told him to stand along the gunwale on the opposite side of the ship. As the other pirates came up they lined up alongside the first man.

As the sixth man took his place on the deck, Proctor said, "That's it. These are the men who will be set free here. As far as I'm concerned they may debark now, if you have no objection."

"I'm afraid I do have an objection," snapped Woodley-Smith curtly. "I was told you were holding seven men. Where is the seventh man?"

"He's their captain, an American traitor. Name's Peter Lisle, though he now calls himself Murad Rais. We're taking him back to Boston with us. He'll face charges in our courts. There is no need for you to see him."

A normally suspicious sort, Woodley-Smith had the feeling that the Americans were attempting to put something over on him.

"I'm afraid I'm going to be the judge of that, captain. Bring him up here."

"But..."

"No buts. Bring him up so I can see him, or you'll be taking all seven of these good-for-nothings home to America with you."

Proctor gave a resigned shrug. He turned to Billings and said, "Bring him up."

When Lisle came up from the hold he was smiling. "So I'll be getting off, too. I'll bet you'll miss me, Proctor."

Woodley-Smith took a step toward the prisoners now lined up against the gunwale. So you're the pirate captain. Is this your ship?"

"Yes sir. the *da Gama*." He looked at the uniform and said. "I mean, Leftenant." He was still grinning at his apparent good luck.

"Why are the Americans retaining you, yet letting your crewmen go?"

"I'm not sure, sir, er, Leftenant. I think it's something about my being born in America and now working for the Tripolitan pasha. Strictly a matter of seizing the best opportunity available for a mariner of my experience."

"If this were simply a matter of employment, I could understand the point you're trying to make. However, it appears that your choice of employment requires you to plunder other ships. This violates international law. However..."

"We do not plunder British ships, sir, as you British have a treaty with Tripoli. The Americans have no such treaty, so they are fair game for people like me who fight to defend Tripoli from states that are unwilling to pay tribute for the right to pass through our waters. We only attack to defend our rights."

Woodley-Smith smiled at the clumsy deceit. He had no illusions as to the intent of the Barbary pirates. He was torn between his allegiance to Britain and his sense of what was proper. He naturally took satisfaction in knowing that his country enjoyed the rights of passage through Tripolitan waters. Still, he had to admit that this was only because Britain found paying a monetary tribute less costly than fighting to defend their rights to the sea. Because the British Empire was rich, paying for passage was much easier and much less costly than going to war.

He knew, too, that smaller countries, countries like the United States could barely keep the wolf away from the door, so monetary tributes were not an easy choice. In a way, he felt for the Americans. But only so much. His first loyalty was to the Crown, not America. His patriotic sense told him that America deserved this problem because of their disloyalty to Britain. They had rejected the benevolence of the Crown, and now they were paying the price for such childish, impulsive behavior.

He understood how the Americans resented the traitorous behavior of Captain Lisle, but he considered the irony of that resentment. By fighting a revolution against Britain, the Americans had engaged in traitorous behavior against their own mother country.

If he were dealing with a crew from a ship of another country, he would allow the captain of that country's ship to keep his traitorous prisoner. Today, though, he would free Lisle. It was his little revenge against the Americans.

Part 2

Chapter 31
Salem, Massachusetts, Early April 1801

Pickerings had lived in the same house on Salem's Broad Street for 150 years. The large house was set back from the street and shaded by tall elms and maples. The current occupants were Timothy and Rebecca Pickering. The last few years, Timothy had spent more time at the U.S. capital in Philadelphia than he had at home, as he had served as secretary of state under both Washington and Adams until May 1800.

Several days ago 36-year-old sea captain, Will Proctor, had sent a letter to Pickering asking him if he might be granted an opportunity to meet with the former secretary. Proctor said that it was a matter of great importance. In the letter Proctor explained that he'd been referred to Pickering by Jonathan Mason, U.S. senator from Massachusetts and a personal acquaintance of Proctor's in Boston. Proctor had mentioned to Mason that he wished to be part of the new naval squadron President Jefferson intended to send to the Mediterranean to blockade the port of Tripoli. Mason had told him that he should seek a commission in the navy. He thought Pickering could help him get that commission. Mason believed that with his experience in the Mediterranean region, the navy would very likely take him and include him in the mission, especially with a recommendation from Pickering. It had taken a bit of encouragement by Mason. Proctor had serious doubts as to whether a man of such importance would see him. He had no doubt that he could lead men, if he got a commission, but gaining access to Pickering was another thing.

Mason reminded him that he, Will Proctor, was also somewhat famous, not only in Massachusetts, but in the rest of America. His exploits 15 years ago were well known and highly thought of throughout the country. Mason was confident that Pickering would see him.

Pickering, who'd been ousted from his position as secretary of state by President Adams, was now home in Salem considering what he would do next with his life. He was intrigued by this request from Proctor, a man he vaguely remembered reading about 15 years ago. While he never met Proctor, he recalled that the man was part of the crew on a merchant ship called the *Betsey*. The ship had been attacked by Moroccan pirates. He remembered reading in the newspapers that the crew, including this man Proctor, had been imprisoned in Morocco and eventually released a few years later after the U.S. had paid a ransom to the sultan. He recalled that the original captain of the Betsey had never been released. As far as Pickering knew, the unfortunate fellow was still being held prisoner in Morocco. That is, if the Moroccans had not killed him.

Proctor rapped on the door with an ornate brass knocker. He heard footsteps within. Seconds later the door was opened by a stately middle-aged woman. Proctor was taken by her finely chiseled cheek bones and her gray, intelligent eyes. She must have been ten or fifteen years older than Proctor, but she carried those years well.

"You must be Mr. Proctor."

"Yes, ma'am. Are you Mrs. Pickering?"

"Yes. Come in, come in. Let me take you into the library. I'll let Mr. Pickering know you're here."

Proctor was browsing the extensive bookshelves when Pickering entered the room. Pickering was the type of man who took over a room. Tall, thin with an angular face dominated by a slightly aquiline nose, he had a bearing that somehow commanded respect.

"Mr. Proctor. Are you any relation to the Salem Proctors?"

"Yes, as a matter of fact I am sir. My aunt and uncle."

Pickering smiled. "An old Salem family. Both of our families go back a long time."

"Yes, I suppose they do, sir."

"Please sit down. Coffee? Tea?"

"Coffee will be fine, sir."

When they were both sitting Pickering got down to business. "I was intrigued by your letter. Tell me what brings you to Salem and to my house in particular?"

"Before you were secretary of state, I was first mate on a merchant vessel out of Boston heading for the Mediterranean."

"Yes, the *Betsey*, if I'm not mistaken."

"Yes. That was it. You may also recall that the ship was attacked by Moroccan pirates, who seized the ship and its cargo and imprisoned the entire crew."

"Good God, man, what you must have gone through." Pickering

seemed sincerely appreciative of what Proctor and the crew had endured. "As I recall, you were eventually released when we paid a ransom to the Sultan of Morocco."

"Yes, after a couple of years working as slaves for the sultan."

Pickering appeared pensive. "If I'm not mistaken, your captain was not released. What ever happened to him?"

"That's one of the reasons I'm here, sir. He's still being held by the sultan. Last I knew the sultan was using him as some sort of advisor on how to deal with European and American negotiators. I think the sultan felt that knowing how westerners think would give him an advantage when negotiating ransoms and tributes."

"Did your captain do this willingly?"

"He did it because he had no choice. He was afraid if he balked, the sultan would take it out on the rest of us. Besides, he—his name is Orne, Henry Orne—he hoped that by being close to the sultan, the man might find it harder to abuse the rest of his crew."

"How do you feel about all of this, Mr. Proctor?"

"I feel deeply for the captain. All of the men do. He was a good, fair-minded man. Treated the men well. He's been away from Boston and his family for over 17 years now. I know his family, and they're distraught about this. They don't want to give up hope, but they're discouraged, since no effort has been made to bring him back."

"As well as I can remember," said Pickering, "we did send some negotiators to Morocco, but unfortunately nothing came of it."

"If I may be blunt, sir, these Muslim pirate states only negotiate when it's in their favor. You can't appeal to their sense of decency because they justify their actions by saying their religion makes it proper to do these things. If you're an infidel, they say they're obligated to kill you or convert you to their religion. They don't think like we do, sir."

"Then what are you saying—that we should go to war with these blackguards?"

"I'm saying that we will never be able to do commerce in the Mediterranean safely until we teach these people a lesson. They must know that they can't attack our ships without paying a price. We've paid an enormous price over the last 17 years. As you know, the *Betsey* is not the only ship to be seized by these North Africans. We've lost far too many. Worse than the loss of ships is the loss of hundreds of men. Even though my crew and I came back eventually, we lost seven good men to these killers." He went on to explain that the seizure of the *Betsey* by Moroccan pirates was not the only seizure he and his crew endured. He pointed out that they had been captured by Tripolitan pirates soon after being freed by Morocco. He added that to add insult to injury, the captain of the Tripolitan pirate ship had been an American traitor.

Pickering got up and walked to the mullioned window looking out on the woods to the rear of the house. He stood there for a minute or more, then said, "I sympathize with you, and your desire to bring your captain back. You do realize that I'm no longer active in the government, so I have very little to say about this, despite my sympathies."

Proctor was impressed by Pickering's grasp of the situation. He was a man who seemed comfortable in the presence of anyone he came in contact with. He clearly was able to see directly to the heart of a complex matter. Proctor could see why the man had occupied such important positions under both the Washington and Adams administrations.

"Yes, but . . ."

Pickering raised a hand and said, "But even if I were still active, I would advise you that the United States is a small country that doesn't have the sort of army or navy that could put the fear of God into these Barbary states. It's unfortunate, but a fact that we must face. I'd advise my fellow officials in Philadelphia that we should not go to war. I do know from my Philadelphia contacts that Jefferson is considering sending a squadron of ships to blockade the Port of Tripoli. I think there is considerable risk in such an action, but I suppose it is better than going to war."

"But, sir, as I understand it, he's doing that because the Tripoli pirates continue to harass our merchant trade in the Mediterranean. It gets worse every month. Anyway, I'm not asking you to persuade the government to go to war, sir. What I am asking is for you to help me get a commission in the navy so that I may help with the blockade and possibly even free Captain Orne."

"Then you already know about Jefferson's squadron?"

"Yes, sir. Senator Mason told me about it."

"I don't know if you realize that I didn't leave my employment with the government under the best of circumstances. Adams and I had a little disagreement, and he found the best way to deal with me was to remove me from my post. Even if I did want to help you, I'm not sure I carry as much weight in Philadelphia as I did in the past."

"But Mr. Adams is no longer the president. Perhaps President Jefferson or his associates will be more amenable to your request—assuming you are willing to make such a request. I know how these

Barbary buggers think, sir. I believe I can be of help to whoever it is that commands the squadron."

Pickering thought for a few seconds, then said, "I like you Proctor, and I like your kin here in Salem. More to the point, though, I'm impressed by how you, as a very young man, conducted yourself when your captain was no longer available. I'll do what I can. I know Secretary of State Madison quite well, though we seldom see eye to eye. He gets on quite well with Secretary of the Navy, Smith, though. I would think he'd want someone with your background and experience. I'll send Madison a letter, and we shall see."

JIHAD AT SEA

Chapter 32
Nearing Tripoli, Late July 1801

The squadron of seven ships left America in late June. While Jefferson had authorized the squadron on May 15, it had taken almost a month to fit out the ships and prepare them for what lay ahead. The squadron was led by Commodore Richard Dale, who simultaneously served as captain of the *USS President*, the flagship of the small fleet of warships.

Dale had a checkered and somewhat hair-raising career leading up to this command. In 1776 he left the merchant service and signed on as a lieutenant in the navy of the Virginia Colony. Soon after, he was taken prisoner by a British ship. He knew many of the British crew from his days as a merchant seaman, and soon those friends on the British ship talked him into signing up with the British navy. He served under Lord Dunmore, the royal governor of Virginia. Under his command, Dale was wounded in a clash with American armed boats. While recovering in Norfolk, he decided to return to the patriot cause when the opportunity presented itself. En route from Norfolk to Jamaica, the British warship on which Dale was serving was captured by the *USS Lexington*. Always a persuasive talker, Dale somehow convinced the captain of the Lexington that he was truly a loyal patriot, despite his time with the British navy. He immediately volunteered to serve on the *Lexington* and astoundingly was granted the rank of midshipman. Soon, Dale was promoted to Master's Mate.

Once again, Dale found himself on a ship that was captured. This time it was by the British ship *HMS Pearl*. Dale and other officers from the Lexington were taken aboard the *Pearl* as prisoners. Dale was released in a prisoner exchange in January 1777. He returned to the *Lexington* under still another captain, Henry Johnston.

For the fourth time Dale was taken prisoner by enemy forces when the *Lexington* was captured off the coast of Ireland and imprisoned in the Mill Prison in Plymouth, England. After more than a year in Mill Prison, Dale managed to escape by walking out of the prison wearing the uniform of a British officer. (He never explained how he came into possession of the uniform). He immediately took himself to London where he obtained papers allowing him to leave England and escape to France. While in France Dale signed on as a Master's Mate under John Paul Jones on the *USS Bonhomme Richard*. He was soon promoted to First Lieutenant. As the war progressed, so did Dale's navy career. Recently he'd been promoted to commodore. The name Dale became legendary in the U.S. Navy.

The squadron now heading toward Tripoli was not large, but it carried considerable fighting power. The *President*, for example, was one of the largest fighting ships in the world. The other ships in the small fleet were the frigates *USS Boston*, the *USS Essex*, the *USS Philadelphia*, and the *USS Trenton*. In addition there was the sloop the *USS George Washington* and the schooner the *USS Enterprise*.

To his surprise and utter delight, Will Proctor had been made captain of the *Trenton*. He'd been shocked at how readily he'd been accepted by the navy and by the famous Commodore Dale. He was shocked even more when he was awarded command of one of the largest frigates in the navy.

Chapter 33
Five miles outside Tripoli Harbor,
Late July 1801

Commodore Dale signaled to his squadron ships to come to rest three miles outside of the city of Tripoli. Shortly after dropping anchor he summoned the captains of the other six ships to the *President* to discuss their next move.

When they were all assembled in the commodore's quarters, Dale dispensed with social conventions and launched directly into what was on his mind. "Gentlemen, I'm sure you've all taken notice of the three frigates just outside the harbor. A midshipman from the Swedish frigate *Thetis* was just sent here by his commander, a Rudolf Cederström. He told me that the *Thetis* and two other Swedish ships were attempting to blockade the Port of Tripoli. The other two are the *Fröja* and *Camilla*. All three are 40-gun frigates.

"The midshipman gave me a message from his commander explaining their attempt to blockade the port so that Swedish merchant ships might have safe passage in the region. The message stated that, unfortunately, they were having rather poor results despite their best efforts, primarily because they have only the three ships. Clearly, three ships can't blockade such a large port, and according to the Swedish commander, Tripolitan vessels are able to enter and leave the harbor with little difficulty. The message also said that, because their three ships are large frigates, they are unable to maneuver in close to the port, so smaller pirate vessels have no trouble doing their nasty business. Their captain closes by welcoming a joint effort, saying that our combined forces should be able to accomplish far more than they could alone."

Dale looked up from the wrinkled paper he was holding and met the eyes of his officers. "I'm inclined to accept his offer. Do any of you see any problem with such a proposition?"

One of the captains spoke up. "Do you know if we share their objectives? Our orders are to blockade the harbor so that the

Tripolitans cannot conduct seaborne commerce and so that their pirate ships cannot prey on unarmed American merchant ships. We were to provide safe passage to our merchant vessels whenever possible. However, we are not supposed to initiate military action against the Tripolitans, and can only respond with fire if attacked or if we witness a Tripolitan attack on one of our merchant vessels." The reason for this nonaggressive approach was that the American government was in the midst of ongoing negotiations with the Tripolitans.

The ship captain continued. "Do we know if the Swedes are under similar order?"

"The note was brief, but it seemed to imply that they were here under similar orders."

At this, Will Proctor could no longer remain silent. He had endured too much at the hands of Barbary pirates to accept a pacifist approach now. "It will be frustrating to sit back and maintain a blockade when we could defeat these bastards once and for all. With the aid of the Swedes, we have more than enough fire power to do the job."

Dale could see by the vigorous nodding of heads that the other captains were in agreement with Proctor. He was tempted to do as they quite obviously wanted. A major victory toward the end of his career was no small consideration. In the end though, his sense of duty forced him to adhere to the orders he had been given.

"We shall proceed as ordered. I will notify the Swedes that we welcome their assistance."

Proctor was disappointed with Dale's reluctance to stretch the limits of his mandate. To his knowledge the U.S. had never been in a more advantageous position with regard to the Barbary pirates. To strike now would send a message to all Barbary states that America was not to be trifled with. It would mean the end of costly tributes to buy protection for American merchant ships. He knew that Dale was just following orders, but he felt certain that Jefferson would understand if the squadron took advantage of this unanticipated opportunity to end the seizures for all time.

What Proctor did not know was that Jefferson, in authorizing the squadron, had overcome his strongly held belief that the U.S. should reduce its small navy, not strengthen it. The mounting cost of losing countless merchant vessels to the Barbary pirates finally convinced him that the country could justify the expense of a small fleet for the purpose of a blockade of Tripoli. But in so doing he had made it clear that he was against engaging in a war with these rogue states.

Commodore Dale was well aware of Jefferson's aversion to war and even to a large navy, but Proctor and most of the squadron's captains and crews were not.

None of them was aware that shortly before Jefferson authorized the blockade, the pasha of Tripoli had declared war on the United States. Word had not reached America when the squadron set sail, so Dale and his squadron were unprepared for what lay ahead.

Chapter 34
The pasha's palace, Tripoli, Late July 1801

Pasha Yusuf Karamanli leaned back on his royal couch and motioned Captain Rais to sit down in front of him. Karamanli was the latest pasha in the long line of Tripolitan rulers in a Karamanli dynasty going back nearly 100 years.

Karamanli, in his mid-thirties, exuded a controlled, latent energy that bespoke of the power of his sovereign authority, not to mention his personal physical power. In many ways he appeared primitive and crude to Rais. Not what he'd expected in a monarch, but his looks were somewhat deceiving. That the leader had competency in at least four languages, English being one of them, was known throughout the realm. In addition to English, he was fluent in Arabic and the local Berber language, Tamasheq. He also had a passing knowledge of Turkish, as he was descended from a noble line of Turks. Rais had long felt that Karamanli was far more worldly than his fellow Tripolitan subjects or anyone he had met in Morocco, for that matter. In his opinion, the pasha was one of the few Tripolitans he'd come in contact with that could exist comfortably in European or American society.

"You summoned me, Your Excellency?"

"Yes, Murad. We must discuss how we shall deal with the arrival of the American warships. First the Swedes, now the Americans. We must consider them a threat to our security."

"They have never posed a threat in the past, Your Excellency."

"They have never confronted us with anything more than pitiful offers of peace and harmony. Now they come with guns. Many guns. We cannot dismiss them so easily now as we have in the past. You know these people, Murad. Do you honestly think we have nothing to fear?" It was not a simple question, but more of a challenge to Murad Rais's judgement.

"No, I suppose not. I don't know the Swedes, but the Americans have a history of fighting for what they believe in. As you know, they defeated the great British Empire, much to the surprise of the rest of the world."

"Yes, I agree. We cannot underestimate them as a threat. The Swedes alone made a feeble attempt to blockade our harbor, but with only three ships, they were unable to interfere with our commerce or our warships. Now, with the added threat of seven American gunships, the chessboard has tilted in their direction. I summoned you, Murad, because I have decided on our course of action."

"And what is that, Your Excellency?"

"I want you to lead our fleet of gunships against these infidel invaders and teach them a lesson that they cannot threaten the territory of Tripoli without paying the consequences."

Rais tried to hide the smile of satisfaction upon hearing these words. The pasha was known for his tendency to misinterpret facial expressions. He measured his response carefully. "I am honored that you have so much confidence in me, Your Excellency, but are the Americans not still in negotiations with you about proper tributes? Perhaps you can rid Tripoli of these infidel warships by persuading them to pay a generous tribute. This way you would not have to risk a single Tripolitan vessel, and you would still reap a handsome revenue."

"As you know, Murad, we have already declared war against these Americans. If I agree to any monetary settlement without teaching them a lesson, they will continue to harass us. They will see it as a sign of weakness, but if we defeat them, the tributes will come, and they will be handsome indeed."

Murad realized that it would be foolish to protest further. "Of course, Your Excellency. What you have concluded makes much sense. When do you want us to begin our attack on these infidels?"

"Quickly. Every day we do nothing we encourage them to think that we are cowering in fear. Soon they will attack us and put the kingdom in jeopardy."

"It will take some time to organize the attack, Your Excellency. To do this right I will need a month."

The pasha knitted his brows and peered menacingly at Rais. "That is too long. By then the infidels will have attacked us. I will give you two weeks."

"Yes, Your Excellency. If you give me complete authority over both the navy and the corsairs and their ships, I can do it in two weeks."

The pasha smiled condescendingly. "I was confident that you could. As a show of my confidence in you I have decided to elevate you to the rank of *amiral* or admiral as you say in English. Do not let me down, admiral."

Chapter 35
Tripoli, Late July 1801

After he left the palace, Murad Rais couldn't believe his good fortune. Originally Peter Lisle from Scotland and then from East Boston, the first years of his life had been cheerless and discouraging. His father, a merchant seaman, had rarely been home, and his mother was cold and distant, uninterested in her one child. She definitely wasn't the motherly type. When he was 17 he left Scotland for America, thirsting for a better life. It hadn't been much better. Fifteen years ago he was a mere deckhand on the American merchant ship *Betsey*. Ignored by the officers on the ship, he was treated like a common lackey, given virtually no respect and treated by all as if he didn't exist—except when they wanted him to do something menial. He'd been treated especially poorly by the other deckhands on the ship. For some reason, they didn't take to him. It never occurred to Lisle that he had an off-putting manner that kept people at their distance. Lisle had been nothing in his native Scotland and, despite what he'd been told about America, things were no better in Boston.

He'd been told by more than one person that he had a bad attitude, but these critics tended to be people who never appreciated him for what he was. They never liked his ideas about how things should be done. They were naive, trusting people who accepted unfair treatment without comment and blithely took whatever abuse was thrown at them. He, Rais, had never been one to ignore abuses. He'd always spoken out, regardless of when or where the abuses occurred. He had never taken any rubbish from anyone, even the most minor offense. People didn't like his direct, often insulting approach, but he didn't care. He had the courage to speak his mind.

Now, he had the opportunity he'd dreamed about all his life. He was an admiral and had the opportunity to send a message to the the ungrateful Americans. He liked the sound of the word admiral. When he was done people might not like him, but they'd respect him, and more important, they'd fear him.

He forced himself to think about what his next steps would be. Now that he had the job of a lifetime, he dare not fail. Having never organized anything in his life, it dawned on him that the next two weeks were a test that he had to pass. It wouldn't be easy, either. He would have to command the respect of a great number of hardened Tripolitan men—both regular navy seamen and calloused, violent corsairs. To them he was still an outsider. Once again he would be unappreciated for his abilities. Somehow, though, he had to get them to obey his commands. Hopefully they would be persuaded by his leadership skills. If not, they would have to be forced to obey. Not an easy alternative, since he was a lonely Westerner in an Arab-Berber world, a world that was and always had been mistrusting of foreigners, especially infidels. Berbers and Arabs often lived side by side in the same communities. Berbers looked more like Europeans than Arabs and often spoke their own language. Arabs tended to be shorter and slightly darker. Still, despite their differences, when it came to Westerners, they were united in their mistrust. Rais felt like a pariah in the company of both groups. True, he had converted to Islam, but did most of the men under his command believe he was truly Muslim, or did they think he'd converted out of convenience in order save his own neck?

Then it came to him. He would model his behavior after Captain Habib, the Moroccan pirate captain who'd kept the American crew in line by killing the first man who got out of line. Kill that first agitator and the others will obey. Naturally he would try persuasion first, but he knew himself. He lacked the skills of persuasion that Captain Orne possessed. Rais did not consider this a failing, though, for he considered Orne far too tolerant and permissive. Admiral Rais would issue commands, and if anyone failed to obey, he would teach them a lesson. Rais couldn't afford to waste time catering to the personal feelings of hardened, violent men. Unlike Orne, he didn't need his subordinates to like him. They just had to fear him.

Immediately after meeting with the pasha, Rais went into seclusion in his personal quarters. He needed time to think—time to decide what his next steps should be. After an hour of this seclusion he grew more and more agitated as he thought about the great burden he had accepted from the pasha. Prior to this, one of his biggest commands had been the *da Gama* back in '86. Things had started out well with the capture of the *Betsey* and its American crew. Then, his own crew had begun to show him a little grudging respect.

Within days, though, his hard-earned victory had been reversed by the mutiny of the American crew. He and the few survivors of that violent mutiny had been captured and set free ignominiously in Gibraltar. Because his men had been lax and reckless while watching their captives, the Americans had won their freedom. True, they'd suffered losses, but they still were free. The men under Rais's command defended their captain, despite their dislike for him. Failure to do so would have meant that Rais would take it out on them in the future. It wasn't a chance most of them were willing to take. Tripolitan men, no matter how tough, were conditioned by their culture to accept authority.

The pasha had cautiously given Rais more rope to test him. At first he'd given him lesser commands of various smaller ships. Gradually, though, the pasha had put him in charge of some of the largest ships in the Tripolitan navy. Rais had risen to the occasion every time. The pasha now fully respected him and demonstrated that respect by making him admiral of the Tripolitan navy.

Now Rais faced the greatest test of his life. True, it was the opportunity of a lifetime, but he was aware that success was far from guaranteed. The fact that seven American and three Swedish warships were at anchor just outside the harbor, could not be easily dismissed. Facts were facts. Eight of the ships lying in wait in the outer harbor were large well-armed frigates. By contrast, the Tripolitan navy had just two frigates, a number of medium-sized sloops, several medium-sized dhows, smaller lateen-rigged dromans and feluccas. All but the two frigates had light armaments, putting them at considerable disadvantage against the American and Swedish frigates, most of which were armed with 40 eight or nine-pound cannons. He knew, of course, that his smaller ships could out-maneuver the large frigates, but he also knew that the frigates could inflict far greater damage when they hit their targets.

The longer Rais thought about the enormous responsibility he'd just accepted, the more his initial euphoria waned, gradually being replaced by diminishing self-confidence. Rais was a lot of things, but he was not stupid. The more he thought about the task he'd been assigned, the more it became clear that success was far from certain. Between marshaling his men and formulating an attack strategy, the challenge he faced was formidable. Unlike an admiral in the

American or a European navy, he had no advisors. It suddenly occurred to him that his voluntary isolation from most of the Tripolitan populace meant he had no friends or colleagues to turn to for advice or support. He had no civilian friends, and he had always kept other naval officers at a distance. He trusted no one. His self-imposed isolation meant that he was unwilling to share his personal views with anyone, so no one shared their views with him, no matter how useful they might have been.

For a moment he considered telling the pasha that he could not accept the honor of commanding the Tripolitan armada against the Americans and the Swedes. But only for a moment, for such an act would almost certainly result in his execution. The pasha would consider his refusal a personal insult. There was only one way the pasha dealt with insults.

Rais took a deep breath and plunged into the initial planning stages of the navy's assault on the infidel ships. He was smarter than most people, so his plans would succeed because he would outsmart the Americans and Swedes. A part of him actually believed this.

Chapter 36
Tripoli, Early August 1801

Commodore Dale had brought his captains together for their daily meeting on the *President*. For this meeting he'd also invited the Swedish commander, Rudolf Cederstrom. The squadron had been hovering at the outer edge of Tripoli Harbor for eight days now. Thus far no contact had been made by the Tripolitans. A few curious small boats had cautiously approached the blockade, but before they came too close they retreated and returned to the inner harbor. Perhaps they were just curiosity seekers. More likely they were doing reconnaissance in preparation for an attack.

"Gentlemen," said Dale. "I think we would all agree that, to date, our combined efforts to restrain the Tripolitan pirate activities have been successful. Not only that, their limited legitimate commerce has all but come to a halt—at least in this, their largest port. We don't know about Derne or some of the smaller ports in the kingdom. We're fairly sure, though, that the majority of their commerce and piratical activities is based here in Tripoli City.

"Two things must concern us, though. The first is that inevitably these rascals must lash out at us. They cannot sustain this for much longer or their criminal economy will wither away and die. My second concern is that, while we have done a competent job of blockading Tripoli, we are also running low on supplies. Soon we will need to send one or two ships to Malta for food, water and other necessities. In doing so we become more vulnerable to attacks by these barbarians."

Captain Proctor spoke up. "Fortunately, the Swedes make us less vulnerable. We should probably be able to withstand any offensive by the Tripolitans."

"Yes, I agree, captain, but I would like to see this end peacefully. No doubt we will prevail if they attack, but we will still suffer losses. Do you think we should negotiate with these people?" Before Proctor could respond, Dale scanned the other captains and added, "What do the rest of you think about negotiation? Or do you have some other idea as to how we might end this without an engagement?"

One of the other captains said, "We might send an emissary to the pasha and see if he will voluntarily end his attacks on American merchant vessels. If he agreed to this we could say that we will have a treaty drawn up to certify the agreement." He smiled self-consciously, then added, "I know, that sounds naive, but he might be persuaded, knowing that ten warships are ready and able to lay waste to the city."

Proctor said, "He will want more than our assurances that we will not attack. He will want a monetary tribute or he will want to hold some of our men to insure that we stick to the agreement. I know these people. They don't think like us. They believe they are morally justified in attacking us because we are infidels. Their holy book tells them that it is their obligation to destroy infidels."

"But," said the other captain, "we have more and greater weapons. They have no chance against us. Surely even religious fanatics will see that. Besides, we have tried tributes in the past and they have not honored them."

"It is true that they only honor tribute payments for a year or so. Then they get greedy and want more. As for our having more fire power, that will not discourage them. Because they are religious fanatics they will resist us even though they know that we outgun them," explained Proctor. "They are willing to accept the loss of a few hundred men if they believe in their cause. Besides, the *Koran* tells them that if they die fighting a *jihad* against infidels, they will go to paradise. They are not afraid to die."

Dale cleared his throat and said, "That may very well be true, Proctor, but I think it is our obligation to give negotiation a try anyway."

Before Will Proctor could respond to the commodore, the other captain said, "How do you know all this, Proctor?"

"I was held captive by the Moroccans for nearly two years. You learn a lot when you have to listen to those devils every day. They tell you more than they should because they are so full of their Muslim righteousness. Not once do they ever question their maniacal views. They know they are right because the Koran tells them they are."

Commodore Dale waited a few seconds, then turning once again to Proctor, said, "As I said, I think we must try diplomacy, hopefully we can deter them from attack."

This was not what Proctor wanted to hear. Since they had arrived at Tripoli, he had gotten the distinct impression that Commodore Dale wanted to avoid confrontation at all cost. No doubt this was his last command. It seemed to Proctor that Dale wanted to complete his assignment with as little risk as possible so that he could go home and retire comfortably at his Virginia homestead. This was a far cry from the bold naval officer who served bravely as First Lieutenant under John Paul Jones during the battle of Flamborough Head, England, in 1779. It was also a far cry from the man who became one of the original six commodores in the newly founded U. S. Navy.

Proctor tried to understand. After all, the man had served his country well and was now at a point in his life when a man might want to retire from military service. All this was understandable, but Proctor considered it unfortunate that his commander should be pulling back when his skills and courage were so sorely needed. In Proctor's opinion, now was the time to defeat the Tripolitan corsairs—not the time to back off and let them off the hook. There would never be a better time to strike. The United States could not afford to keep a squadron of ships on the outskirts of Tripoli Harbor indefinitely.

Chapter 37
Tripoli, Early August 1801

Commodore Dale wasted no time moving ahead with his plan to negotiate. "I need a volunteer to take our offer to the pasha. Who would be willing to go into Tripoli and meet with the pasha or his officials to discuss our desire for peace?"

Proctor spoke up. "While I don't have much confidence that the pasha will agree to any proposal we make to him, I suppose it makes sense that I be the negotiator. I know how these people think, and I even know some of their language."

"I appreciate your willingness to do this, Captain Proctor," said Dale earnestly. "However, I'm reluctant for two reasons. One, you have already suffered at the hands of Barbary criminals twice. I don't think it's fair to put you at risk a third time." He looked at each of his other officers and added, "I would rather no one had to take the risk, but I fear we must try. That is why I'm asking for a volunteer. Frankly, I don't think there is great risk in a single negotiator being taken hostage. The Tripolitans would then have no means of communicating with us. The risk would be greater if we sent two or three negotiators. They could then take one as hostage and send the others back to us with their demands."

Proctor took note that the commodore had not volunteered himself as negotiator. Then, as he thought about it, he realized that the pasha might actually hold Dale as hostage, since an American commodore would be a far bigger prize than a ship captain. In such a situation, the pasha would probably expect another American to meet with him to negotiate for Dale, thus giving the Tripolitans a major advantage in the horse trading.

Dale met the eyes of everyone in the room to see if anyone appeared to disagree with his logic. He then said, "Secondly, I don't think you, Captain Proctor, have your heart in the mission. I sense that you believe any effort at negotiation will be a waste of time."

"As for putting myself at risk, sir, it is far less risky than it would be for one of the other officers here to negotiate. My experience with these pirates gives me a slight advantage. I know what to say and what not to say. Besides, I agree with you that one negotiator is less at risk than two. As for having my heart in the mission, you are right. I am not optimistic, but it's also true that I hope I'm wrong. If we can arrive at a peaceful solution, everyone will benefit. I believe it's worth a try."

"Very well then, you shall go. Are you sure you can gain access to this pasha?"

"Probably not right away. The local authorities will almost certainly stop me to see why I am there. They may even put me in the local jail, since I represent the American squadron blockading their harbor."

"Then how will you be able to negotiate with them if you are incarcerated?"

"I can assure you, sir, that the pasha will learn of my presence and want to see me in person in order to learn what our intentions are. What better way to find out your enemy's intentions than to interrogate one of their officers. Once I'm granted an audience, I'm sure he'll want to make some demands of us, and he'll need me to convey these demands to you. Hopefully, instead of demands, he'll want me to convey his agreement to a peaceful accord or treaty—whatever he wants to call it."

An hour later, after conferring with Dale and the other captain on terms to be negotiated with the pasha, Proctor set off toward Tripoli in a small dinghy equipped with a single sail. A faint breeze teased the sparkling surface of the outer harbor to a light chop—perfect conditions for sailing the dinghy into the unwelcoming harbor. Less than an hour later Proctor eased into the crowded port, made even more crowded than usual because nearly all its vessels were tied up to quays or at anchor in the inner harbor.

As he neared the closest quay Proctor felt curious eyes watching him from every direction. He was not one of them, which made him a very unusual visitor. No one made a move to help him as he tied up at the nearest quay. Whether they feared him or despised him, Proctor was not sure. No doubt it was a little of both. What he did know was that the local people found him to be fascinating, but at the same time, someone to avoid.

Centuries of living as a piratical state had conditioned the subjects of the Tripolitan pasha to view outsiders as at best unwanted and, at worst, inferior types to be preyed upon. Almost all outsiders in Tripoli were either in prison or held as slaves by the pasha and some of his relatives and friends.

Wealth and power in Tripoli were concentrated at the top. The pasha, his relatives and close friends owned and controlled anything of value in the benighted kingdom. The vast majority of the pasha's subjects lived in abject poverty with virtually no options to improve their status in life. If they were born poor, they stayed poor. They were so conditioned to their powerless existence, that they expected nothing more.

However, when pirate ships brought in merchant ships and their crews from other nations, the local Tripolitans took pleasure in taunting and abusing these foreigners. The foreigners were infidels and, as such, deserving of mistreatment and abuse. It was times like this when powerless, wretched indigents no longer felt like inadequate serfs. In these instances it was the infidels who were inferior and deserving of abuse and malice. In these situations the common man of Tripoli gained a modicum of power.

It was no surprise, then, to Proctor that no one offered help. What *was* surprising was that no one made threats. As he stepped onto the quay from the dinghy, he did a quick scan of his surroundings, looking for someone who might be inclined to help him reach the pasha's palace. He didn't expect friendliness, but was hoping for neutrality or at the very least, a lack of hatred in someone's eyes. As he walked along the quay toward shore he felt eyes boring into him from both his left and his right. He expected at any minute to be rushed by men hoping to gain favor with the local officials for their vigilance and willingness to attack an unwanted stranger. Whether he'd survive such an attack was questionable.

He stepped onto solid land without incident. Up ahead a man bent over from age and, no doubt, decades of carrying heavy loads on his back, approached him cautiously. As Proctor came within a few feet of the man he realized the man was not offering help or guidance, but was expecting a handout.

He gave the man a coin, not knowing if American money would be accepted or even recognized in Tripoli, but that was all he had. The man nodded vigorously, obviously appreciative of the money.

Will smiled and tried some of the limited Arabic he'd learned while in captivity. *"Ayn hu alqusr? (Where is the palace?)"* The old man pointed. The palace was obviously in the direction he pointed, but not visible from the harbor side. Proctor needed more than just a general direction. He was reaching the limits of his Arabic, but ventured one more time. *"Hal tastatie 'an triny? (Can you show me?)"* The man nodded and held out his hand. Proctor reached into his pocket for another coin.

As he followed the hunched-over old man through the narrow winding streets busy with hawking street merchants and carts being pulled by donkeys and even goats, he couldn't help but compare what he was witnessing in Tripoli to everyday life back in Boston. It was as if here in Tripoli he were back in Biblical times. At the same time he felt like a spectacle in a circus with all eyes taking him in as if he were some kind of freak

Ten minutes later the man came to a halt and pointed to what must have been the largest building in Tripoli. The two-story white stucco building was topped by a golden dome. The palace appeared even more opulent than the sultan's palace in Morocco. The economies in these North African countries, being almost totally dependent on piracy, were generally weak and incapable of providing for the general populace. The pasha and other leaders clearly didn't care, since the pirates brought in enough money and goods to make them extremely wealthy.

The entrance to the palace was flanked by two burly guards. Proctor had no choice but to approach the entrance and hope for the best.

Chapter **38**
Royal Palace, Tripoli, Early August 1801

As Proctor reached for the massive bronze door handle, two guards closed ranks in front of him, demanding where he thought he was going.

Proctor wasn't sure what they said exactly, but got the general drift. It was time once again to dip into his limited Arabic vocabulary.

"*llaqad jit min alkumudur al'amriki* I Come from the American Commodore."

One of the guards rattled off something quickly and entered the palace. The remaining guard stood in place holding Proctor's bicep in a firm grip.

Two minutes later the first guard emerged from the palace and said something else. It was spoken too fast for Proctor to understand, but he figured he'd know soon enough as the two guards were now ushering him into the palace. Normally he would have enjoyed the cool interior of the building, but he was too nervous to get pleasure from anything right now. It was dark inside the building, and he found that it took a minute or two for his eyes to adapt to the limited light after coming in from the blazingly bright sunlight outside.

The first guard ushered him toward the rear of the large entrance hall. Proctor could now make out a closed doorway just ahead. The guard knocked sharply. Seconds later the door opened and a gray-bearded older man garbed in a deep-crimson silken robe invited him in with a slight wave of his right hand. Hunched over, the man then slowly retired to what appeared to be a padded lounging chair. He motioned Proctor to approach, but did not invite him to sit.

The older man studied Proctor for what seemed an eternity, but was probably only a minute or two. He then spoke softly in Arabic. "*ant rajul shijae (You are a brave man.)*"

Proctor thought the man had said something about courage or bravery, but was not sure.

He was running out of Arabic phrases, but he tried one more. "*hal tatahaddath al'iinjlizia (Do you speak English?)*"

The man furrowed his brow. "I have some knowledge of your

language. What do you want to say? Why you come to pasha's palace when you must know he wishes Allah's wrath fall upon you Americans? You must know, too, that you might not leave here alive." He paused, then said, "You're either very brave or very foolish."

Proctor felt his stomach turn over and his heart beat faster. He took a deep breath and said, "I come to talk peace with the pasha."

At this, the old man smiled, the smile of someone who feels superior. Someone who knows more than the one to whom he is speaking.

"You do know that Tripoli is at war with the United States?"

Proctor was caught completely off guard by this. When they departed from America that had not been the case. As far as Proctor knew, nobody in the squadron was aware that war had been declared. He was sure that Commodore Dale did not know. The declaration must have been made when they were at sea. Under the circumstances, would Commodore Dale want the negotiations to proceed as planned? Unfortunately he could not return to the *U.S.S. President* to confer with Dale. This was almost too much for Proctor to consider without consultation, but he had no choice. Now, more than before, he had to negotiate for peace.

Proctor was aware that the U.S. had been negotiating with the Tripolitans for some time even before the squadron left for Tripoli. The only thing he knew about those proceedings was what had been rumored among his fellow naval officers—that the Tripolitans apparently were asking for an outrageously large tribute. If the professional diplomats could not come to terms with the pasha, how could he be expected to do any better? Obviously, if Tripoli had declared war, the negotiations had failed.

Apparently either the United States had been unwilling to pay a tribute, or if it was, the amount was not enough to satisfy Tripoli. Was the negotiating about price or was it about whether a tribute was justified in the first place? Should Proctor try to move the discussion in another direction? If so, what direction, and why could he even hope that the pasha would accept anything but a monetary tribute?

In other words, should he, Proctor, negotiate on principle or be pragmatic?

The Barbary states had been sponsoring and benefiting from piracy for centuries. It was part of their culture—their way of life. To them, it was not only acceptable, it was admirable. It was a major part of their economy, especially the pasha's economy. It was justified by their religion. If the pasha argued on principle, no doubt he'd not be willing to give ground on tributes. Proctor feared that, disappointingly, the U.S. had apparently been willing to argue on the pasha's terms—the only disagreement being the amount of tribute. Proctor knew why, too. The pasha was negotiating from strength. If the U.S. wanted to engage in commerce in the Mediterranean anywhere near Tripoli, it would have to pay a tribute. Tripoli had armed pirate ships to enforce their demands.

Until now. It was true that Tripoli had more armed vessels than the U.S., but it was also true that the American and Swedish navy vessels lying in wait on the periphery of Tripoli Harbor, were bigger and more powerful than all of the Tripolitan vessels combined. Surely the pasha must know this.

The slow-moving elder official was staring at him impatiently, wondering why this strange, foreign specimen did not talk. Proctor was not sure what role the man played in the pasha's court, but he was obviously important—some sort of gatekeeper. Unless you were known by the pasha, you didn't get by this shaky, but clearly alert man. Proctor also knew that he'd better say something now.

"I did not know that Tripoli was at war with the United States. When we left the United States, we believed we were engaging in peaceful negotiations with your country."

"Apparently word did not reach your country before you departed. We have declared war against the United States because it has refused our demands for just tribute to His Excellency, Yusuf Karamanli."

"Then I take it that negotiations have ended?"

"There is no need for further talk. Our ships now are free to strike your ships whenever they wish. Obviously the United States is not interested in coming to an agreement. Return now to your commanding officer and tell him to return to the United States."

"But that doesn't make sense. Surely the pasha must know that the American and Swedish ships at anchor near your harbor could destroy your fighting ships and much of the city of Tripoli."

"If that were possible, the pasha believes they would have already done it."

Proctor shook his head from side to side in disbelief. "They have held back, hoping that the pasha would prefer to talk. Now it is clear that he does not want to talk. Do not underestimate the naval force you and your navy would face."

The old man smiled condescendingly in his belief that Europeans and Americans were not fighters. "I urge you to return to your ship before the pasha decides to make an example out of you."

Proctor was sure that the pasha might do exactly that, but he had to try one more time before returning to the fleet. It was a risk, but he was representing his country. He could not slink away without one more effort.

"I would like to talk to the pasha. I think when he hears what I have to say, he may decide that talking will be more profitable than war."

"Tell me what it is that you wish to say to the pasha. Then I will decide if it is something he will be interested in."

"My instructions are to say it directly to him."

The old man considered this for a minute. Finally, he said, "Very well. Remain here. I will see if the pasha is interested." With that he left the room through a large, massive door overladen with elaborate bronze filigree. Proctor paced the floor tensely, knowing his fate was in the pasha's hands. Was the man reasonable, logical, practical? Or was he deranged, rigid, fanatical? Based on his experience in the Barbary states, Proctor feared it was the latter. He knew that within minutes his fate would be decided. Not to mention the fate of relations between the United States and Tripoli. Right now Proctor was worried about his own fate. He pictured flogging, beheading, burial in sand up to his neck or things he couldn't even imagine. At the very least he could find himself locked up once again in a North African prison.

Ten long minutes later the huge door opened and the wizened old man reappeared. Closing the door behind him he stood grim-faced and said, "The pasha will see you. Follow me."

The throne room was not as large as the entry hall, but still impressive. The room was lined with flickering torches. As Proctor and his guide entered the room, Proctor's eyes were drawn to the figure at the far side of the room. Sitting erect in a gold-encrusted throne, that looked rich, but terribly uncomfortable to Proctor, Pasha Yusuf Karamanli eyed his guest warily.

"You may approach," said the old guide. "Say nothing until spoken to."

As he approached the throne, Proctor was taken aback by the pasha's appearance. He was a large, unkempt beast of a man. Not at all fitting Proctor's image of royalty. He seemed more like a hulking backwoodsman who'd never been exposed to civilized society. Surprisingly, the pasha seemed younger than Proctor had imagined. Definitely younger than mid-life. Perhaps several years under 40. The Tripolitan monarch appeared to be a man of fearsome, feral vigor. A man wielding untamed power.

Proctor came to a halt 15 or so feet in front of the fearsome monarch. He waited for the pasha to speak. Off to the side, the old advisor remained silent, but attentive to every word.

Karamanli leaned forward on his throne and said in a surprisingly deep voice, "Sharif here tells me you are an American ship captain, and you have something to say to me."

Proctor was surprised at how good the pasha's English was. "You speak excellent English, Your Excellency."

"My corsairs have kindly brought me educated Englishmen who have taught me your language. I have also learned French and Spanish this way. These languages are important if I am to deal with foreign states. But I am sure this is not what you wish to speak to me about."

"No, Your Excellency, it is not. What I . . ."

"I am impressed by your courage. I have declared war on your new country, and you now have many warships threatening my harbor and my city; yet you risk your security by coming to see me. Do you think I will treat you kindly when you represent our enemy?"

Chapter 39
Royal Palace, Tripoli, Early August 1801

"Since I come in peace, I had hoped that you would be willing to hear me out," said Proctor more confidently than he felt. "Hopefully we can come to an agreement that will satisfy both countries. The United States wants you to be satisfied at the end of any discussions we have."

The pasha snorted. "We have had ongoing discussions with your country in the past, but your Mr. Adams and Mr. Jefferson would not agree to our terms."

This was true. When Jefferson and Adams met with Tripoli's ambassador to Great Britain in 1786, they asked the diplomat, 'By what right does your nation attack American ships and enslave their crew members. The ambassador replied that Islam

> *"was founded on the Laws of the Prophet Muhammad, that it was written in the Koran that all nations who did not acknowledge their authority were sinners, that it was their right and duty to make war upon these sinners wherever they could be found, and to make slaves of all they could take as prisoners, and that every Musselman (Muslim) who should be slain in battle was sure to go to Paradise."*

Proctor understood that when the pasha stated that Jefferson and Adams refused to agree to Tripoli's terms, it meant that Tripoli intended to set the terms. Tripoli did not intend to negotiate in the normally accepted sense of the word. There would be no give-and-take in such a discussion. No compromises.

How Proctor responded to the pasha was critical. He took a deep breath and said, "As I understand it, you and the United States have been negotiating more recently."

"We have discontinued those discussions. Now that your Jefferson is president he is still unwilling to accept our terms. Your country continues to show disrespect for Tripoli and for Islam. That is why we declared war on your country. Now they insult us further by sending you, a mere ship's captain to do their negotiating. Are you Americans not so intelligent, or do you think we are not so intelligent? I do not understand you people."

Proctor was amazed at how articulate the pasha was, especially in a language that was not his native tongue. Looks were deceiving. The pasha definitely was not stupid. Proctor would never get used to how different the thinking was in this part of the world. It was difficult to agree on the most basic idea of what was right and wrong. Things were not going well. It was not going to be easy to persuade the pasha to compromise. Nevertheless, he had to make the effort.

"I don't think you or my leaders are lacking in intelligence, Your Excellency. Far from it. What I do think is that it would be unwise for our countries to remain at war now that a powerful fleet of warships lies only a few miles outside of your harbor. I know that they have no desire to strike Tripoli, but if a state of war continues, the fleet will remain in position in order to protect the merchant ships of the United States and the Kingdom of Sweden. Such a condition can only continue to limit your country's seagoing commerce." By implication he meant piratical activities as well as their few legitimate shipping activities.

The pasha spoke. "By maintaining the presence of ships intended for warfare you reveal your true intentions." Proctor noticed that off to the side of the room Sharif nodded his approval of this. Will was beginning to think that the tired-looking old man was not as tired as he looked—that he wielded greater influence on the pasha than he first thought. He was not just a doorkeeper. The pasha continued. "How can your country expect us to think that you want peace, when you bring a warlike show of force to my very doorstep?"

Sharif looked pleased with the way the conversation was going.

Proctor continued. He could not back down now. "Respectfully, Your Excellency, you must understand that the United States believes that Tripoli has not acted in a friendly way toward U.S. shipping. You have allowed your corsairs to lay siege to our ships and enslave our citizens. You have allowed them to confiscate our cargoes and turn our ships into hostile vessels of aggression. These are not the acts of a nation that wants peace."

Sharif appeared to be shocked that an infidel would have the audacity to speak to the pasha so brazenly. The pasha frowned as he considered the American's insolence. After a moment, he responded.

"Clearly, Captain, you and your isolated little country do not understand how things work in the rest of the world." The Tripolitan ruler seemed to be enjoying the clash of minds. He was not used to others disagreeing with him. To him, the debate was a stimulating cerebral exercise, not a means of getting to the truth. He enjoyed the mental fencing, but he had no intention of being influenced by what this bold infidel had to say. He already knew the truth. From the moment he had learned to speak he had been indoctrinated with the great truths by his imams, his teachers, his father and his mother. Pasha Karamanli was enjoying this, while his advisor, Sharif was becoming furious at the disrespectful behavior of the American.

Finally, the pasha replied. "It is not the obligation of Tripoli, or any Islamic state, to make friends with infidel states. To the contrary, it is our duty to make war against these sinner nations whenever we have the opportunity." Sharif nodded vigorously in relief. The pasha was not becoming soft.

"Does that mean that you prefer war to peace?" asked Proctor incredulously.

"Whenever we believe that such a war can end in victory, yes."

"Then I assume that you would find peace acceptable if your chances of victory were not favorable?"

"You mean when faced with ten warships in our outer harbor?"

"Yes. Certainly you must see that you could not win against such a show of force."

For the first time the pasha hesitated. He glanced quickly at Sharif, as if for guidance. Sharif nodded his encouragement, and the pasha continued.

"I think you underestimate the power of Allah and his people. Tripoli does not tremble at the sight of a few American warships. *Allahu Akbar (God is great).*"

Sharif had far too much influence on the Pasha, thought Proctor. "I am sure Tripolitans are brave people. They do not live in fear. Still, there are times when even brave soldiers must know that they cannot win."

"There are no such times in Tripoli. We cannot lose because Allah is on our side. Now go back to your infidel commander and tell him he would be wise to sail his ships back to America, for he and his sailors will die if they remain in the waters of Tripoli." Off to the side of the room Sharif beamed with pride at how well the pasha had conducted himself.

Chapter 40
Royal Palace, Tripoli, Early August 1801

After Proctor left, Karamanli and Sharif retired to the pasha's inner quarters to discuss the recent meeting with the American ship captain.

Sharif opened the conversation. "You did well, Your Excellency. Allah and your honorable ancestors must be proud of you. Not once did you hesitate or show the slightest sign of weakness in the presence of the American captain."

"Thank you, Sharif, but do not mistake the American captain. He is not a weak man. He did not hesitate in my presence. Most men show weakness in my presence. He did not."

"It is all show, Your Excellency. Inside he is weak like all the Europeans. Americans are very much like Europeans. When you make demands of them they talk boldly, but eventually they capitulate. They do not want to fight because in their hearts they know they must submit to our greater authority. Look at the mighty British Empire. They have many more naval ships than Tripoli or any of our brethren Barbary States. Yet they do not use that strength against us because they are afraid of us. Instead, the mighty British Empire pays you tribute. If *they* won't fight, do you think the tiny American state will fight?"

"The ships they have massed in our outer harbor, plus the three Swedish ships, could hurt us badly," said the monarch. "I don't think we should challenge them. Perhaps we should at least come to an arrangement that will leave our navy and our city unharmed?"

Sharif smiled condescendingly. The pasha was his sovereign ruler, but he was inexperienced. He needed guidance. "You have not been pasha very long, Your Excellency. I am old, and I have seen these European types for many years. They are always the same. They threaten and bluster, but they do not attack. Maybe it is because it is easier to just pay what we demand. Maybe they are simply too afraid to go to war against a state protected by the might of Allah. Either way, past history shows that they will not attack.

"Note, Your Excellency, that even when we tell them that we have declared war against their little country, they still wish to talk of peace. If they had declared war on us, we would immediately strike against them with the wrath of Muhammad. You see, Your Excellency, that is the difference. You have nothing to fear from these blustering Americans."

"What would you have us do, Sharif? We cannot go on like this. Our commerce is but a fraction of what it was before these ships blocked our harbor. Our noble corsairs can only operate out of Derne. They are farther to the east, and therefore have less contact with merchant ships in the western part of the Mediterranean. If a merchant ship makes it past Tripoli, there are far fewer corsairs to contend with. By being blocked from using Tripoli Harbor, our corsairs have become much less effective."

"We should strike these American ships now. I gave Rais two weeks to be ready to strike so we should be ready. It is the perfect time. They will never believe we would strike. In their minds I am sure they think that if we were going to strike, we would have done so in the first few days of the blockade. Now they will believe that we lack the courage or the firepower. Now is the time to strike—when their guard is down and their will is lacking. It is your decision, Your Excellency, but that is my advice."

Yusuf Karamanli, the all-powerful, but inexperienced leader of the ancient Kingdom of Tripoli, considered what his ancient advisor was telling him. The man had served three generations of Karamanlis. His advice could not be ignored.

Chapter 41
The *U.S.S President* Outside Tripoli Harbor,
Early August 1801

Commodore Dale frowned as he and the other ship captains listened to Will Proctor's report on his conversation with the Tripolitan pasha. Dale was shocked to learn that Tripoli had declared war on the U.S. Proctor sensed from looking at his superior officer that the man found the pasha's behavior incomprehensible. The commodore scanned the faces of his senior officers, then looked out to sea and said, "Can these people not see that they are outgunned? Can they not see with their own eyes what they face if they attack us?" He turned to Proctor and said, "You say this man seems intelligent. Do his decisions sound like the decisions of an intelligent man?"

"No, sir. Not in our world, but these people live in a different world."

"Obviously. Still, are not facts, facts—even in their world?" asked Dale incredulously.

"I'm not so sure they are, sir."

"Come now, Captain. I'm afraid you're going to have to clarify that."

"I'm reminded of what Hamlet said about prisons. Something like *'tis neither good or bad, but thinking makes it so.*'" The people in this part of the world base all of their decision-making on their holy book, the *Koran*. They believe they live by facts, the facts preached by Muhammad in the *Koran*. These are often not facts to our way of thinking, but to them they are the word of their god, Allah."

"Yes, yes, I know. These people are very religious. Or at least they use religion to justify their criminal activity."

Proctor was finding it almost as difficult to reason with Dale as he had with the pasha. Dale's assessment of the thinking of the pasha and other North Africans was going to make it almost impossible for the commodore to understand the mind of their enemy. Proctor had to choose his words carefully.

"I don't believe the pasha is cynical about his religion. From what I have seen of these North Africans, most of them truly believe in their Muslim faith. Their lives are guided by it to a much greater extent then our lives are guided by Christianity. Religion is central to their lives. Everything they do is dictated by their religion. They live it every minute of the day. They pray five times a day. The first prayer is at 3:30 in the morning."

"You sound like they've converted you," snapped the commodore.

"I'm sorry, sir. I must have given the wrong impression. I am simply describing what I've observed. It is not the kind of life I could ever subscribe to. They use the words of their *Koran* to justify all of the evil they perpetrate against the rest of the world, but I don't think they do it in a cynical fashion. They don't see it as evil. I think they really believe that it is their duty to attack nonbelievers. To them we are the nonbelievers."

"Then we must be prepared to show them that attacking us will be a big mistake."

"Yessir. I think you're wise to be prepared for an attack."

"I still find it hard to believe that they would be foolish enough to attack us."

"They really have no alternative, if you think about it, sir. They suffer more each day because of our blockade," explained Proctor as deferentially as he could.

The commodore said, "If they want the blockade to end, all they have to do is make peace with us. Why is that so unreasonable?"

"If they make peace with us, they know they will no longer be able to demand payments of monetary tribute. These tributes are the cornerstone of their corrupt economy. They have no sense of how to go about honest trade between nations. It is not part of their history. Everything they do is at the expense of infidels in Europe and now America."

"Nevertheless, they must see that attacking us would be suicide?"

"I'm sure they don't see it that way at all. First of all, the pasha and his close advisor, Sharif, believe we are afraid to fight, despite our superior fire power. They have seen this reluctance to fight in the British. They have seen it in the Spanish. They believe people in Europe and America lack the backbone to take on Muslim warriors. They think if we had the courage to attack them them we would have already done it. When we negotiate they view it as a sign of weakness. Every time we or the European states have negotiated, we have ended up making concessions to the Barbary states."

Dale closed his eyes and looked downward as he considered everything Proctor had said. When he opened his eyes he said, "Then we should prepare ourselves for an attack, though I am still not convinced." He scanned his officers, stopping briefly at each person. Finally, he asked, "Do you all agree that such an attack is likely?"

Each of the officers nodded his assent or agreed with a cautiously spoken yes. They would not show enthusiasm as they weren't comfortable challenging their commodore. He was not known to encourage opinions contrary to his own.

"Then let's put the officers on alert. It may not be necessary, but we should not underestimate this enemy either. Some of the most vicious wars have been fought by religiously motivated foes."

The captain of the *USS Essex* spoke up. "Before we run low on water and fresh food, sir, shouldn't we send another ship to Malta or some other friendly port to refresh these supplies in case we're in for a long battle?"

Dale was quick to respond. "Sterett on the *Enterprise* made a run up there, as you all know. Wasn't an easy trip, I'm sure you'll agree," he said with a flicker of a smile. "Still, a successful one." He was referring to an engagement between the *Enterprise* and the Tripolitan warship, the *Tocra*. The result was a resounding victory for the Americans: 30 enemy sailors killed and 30 more wounded. The battle lasted several hours en route to Malta. After the battle ended, the *Enterprise* went on to Malta, got the supplies, and returned safely to the squadron.

"I'm sure we'll be fine with the supplies that we have, thanks to them," said Dale. "I want you all to be prepared, and make no mistake, if they attack, they will regret it."

Chapter 42
Royal Palace, Tripoli, Early August 1801

Murad Rais was summoned to the palace. He had not spoken with the pasha in days. His ongoing responsibility had been to keep what there was of the Tripolitan navy stocked with ammunition and functioning guns, ready for when they would attack the Americans. He was prepared for the eventual encounter, but he had mixed feelings about it. Yes, it would be his big opportunity to show his ability as a commander, but he couldn't ignore the awesome strength of the squadron out in the outer harbor. It wouldn't be easy.

Today he sensed a change as he entered the palace and was given a perfunctory nod by Sharif as he entered the pasha's chambers.

The pasha dispensed with civilities and said, "Sit down, Murad, we have much to talk about."

"I'm aware, Your Excellency, that an emissary from the American fleet met with you yesterday. I assume that is why you have called me here?"

"You assume correctly, Murad. Recently I made you admiral of the Tripolitan navy. It is now time for you to prove to me that you deserve it. You should be ready. I want you to ready the navy and our corsair forces for an attack on these infidel ships, both the Americans and the Swedes."

Rais had dreaded this day. While he was honored to have been made admiral in charge of the Tripolitan navy, he knew bad odds when he saw them. Far better to revel in the honor bestowed upon him by the exalted leader than to have to actually execute against clearly superior forces. Though he had converted to Islam in order to gain favor in the Muslim nation, he did not believe everything many dedicated Muslims believed. For one thing, he did not believe that Allah would protect him and his navy in all instances. He doubted that the Muslim God was any more powerful than the Christian God. For another thing, he was fairly certain that if he fought the good fight and died in the process, there would be no virgins in Paradise for his personal pleasure to reward him. Of course he could not share this thinking with his fellow Tripolitans.

While he had gained a certain degree of respect and prominence in Tripoli, he had to admit that much of that respect came from the pasha. Not bad, of course. If you were looking for respect, you couldn't ask for more than the respect of the most powerful man in the country. Yet he was uncomfortably aware that, outside of the palace, the pasha's approval of him was a disadvantage in everyday living. Most Tripolitans resented the fact that their leader had elevated a former infidel over many deserving home-grown naval officers. They couldn't understand this and took it out on Rais. Except for his official standing in the navy, Rais was reviled in Tripoli almost as much as he had been in Boston and Scotland before that.

In light of this, Rais had known since the day the pasha had ordered him to prepare to attack the Americans that he would have to find some way to inspire his sailors to rise to the naval confrontation ahead of them. It hadn't been easy, but despite their obvious dislike of Rais, he had given them reason to be excited about the prospect of attacking the Americans. What a glorious way to please their pasha and their god Allah. Since he was admiral of the navy they had to fight for him. Worse yet had been the necessity of inspiring the many pirates that would be needed to co-exist with his navy against the Americans and Swedes. Again, the prospect of pleasing the Pasha and doing Allah's work had overcome any hesitation they might have had to comply with Rais's commands. It was an uneasy alliance, but it seemed to be holding. Rais prayed to Allah that it would continue.

"Do you think this is wise, Your Excellency?" As soon as the words left his lips, Rais knew that he had chosen those words carelessly.

"Do you believe, Murad, that I would utter an unwise statement?"

"No, your excellency. I misspoke. What I meant was. . ."

"I know what you meant. I am not asking for your opinion on this matter. I have called you here to give you your orders. Do you understand that?"

Rais swallowed hard. "Yes, Your Excellency."

"Good. Now listen to what I have to say. A Captain Proctor from the American fleet came to see me. He expected us to cower in fear of the warships at anchor in the outer harbor."

Rais was put off balance by this. His voice quavered as he asked, "Did you say Proctor, Your Excellency?"

"Yes, Captain Will Proctor."

Rais couldn't believe his ears. Could this be the same Proctor he'd escaped from back in '86? It must be. How many Will Proctors could there be in the U.S. Navy? Rais was flustered. He had to say something now. The pasha's eyes were boring into him in expectation of a comment or response.

Rais dared not mention the *da Gama-Betsey* encounters back in 1786—long before Karamanli was pasha of Tripoli. If the pasha were to know of Rais's ignominious defeat at the hands of a civilian ship captain, the monarch would remove him from command of the navy and no doubt demote him. He'd be lucky to survive the disclosure with his life. Thank God or Allah that the pasha did not recognize the name Proctor. Nevertheless, the pasha was expecting a comment.

"I knew a Proctor when I was a seaman on an American merchant vessel back in the eighties. I thought for a moment it might be the same Proctor."

"Perhaps it is, Murad. Perhaps it is. Describe this Proctor for me."

Did he dare give an accurate description? Since it was unlikely that the pasha would see Proctor again, he proceeded to give his recollection of what Proctor looked like 15 years ago.

"That sounds like the man I met with. This might be an old friend of yours. Will you hesitate to kill him if you have to?"

This was an easy one. "No, Your Excellency. He was not a friend, and he certainly is not of the Muslim faith. No, I would not hesitate to kill him."

"Good. Then prepare your men for an attack within the week. I suspect that the Americans will find it necessary to attack us soon, as their crew members will not want to remain aboard their ships much longer. Sickness will set in, food will be in short supply. They will have to attack or depart from Tripoli. I know they don't want to fight, but they will not want to return to America and say they have accomplished nothing. They will be compelled by circumstances to stage an assault. Better that we attack first. One week or less, Murad. Can you do that?"

Rais swallowed hard. "Yes, Your Excellency. We will attack within the week."

Chapter 43
The *U.S.S. President*, Outside Tripoli Harbor, Late August 1801

Commodore Dale dipped his head a fraction of an inch in the direction of Proctor. It was the daily officers meeting, and Proctor actually had something new to discuss.

Proctor explained what was going to affect all of them, and soon. "Our scout reports a build-up in the Tripolitan navy."

Dale had sent a scout into the inner harbor in a one-masted dory. It was an extremely dangerous mission as there was enormous risk in entering the enemy's harbor. To minimize the risk, the scout had entered the port at night. While there was less risk of being seen at night, it was still risky. His orders were to seek a remote part of the inner harbor and cautiously get a sense of a military build-up for an offensive. He was to spend half the night there and then make a stealthy retreat back to the squadron. The scout wasn't satisfied with what he learned that night. He couldn't see well enough, and there wasn't much activity at night anyway. Because of this he took the initiative and remained in the harbor into the following morning. Technically, he was disobeying orders, but he felt he could justify it by bringing back more useful intelligence, which he did. Amazingly, he managed to elude detection and returned to the *President* to report directly to Proctor.

Proctor continued, "Thanks to the brave efforts of seaman Barnes, we know that it's almost certain that the pasha's forces are getting ready to attack. It's no longer speculation. We must be prepared for an attack any time now. We out-gun them, but don't let that mislead you into a false sense of security.

JIHAD AT SEA

"These people will fight to the death. They do not fear death. They welcome it. I know, this is strange, but it's a religious thing. They've been brought up believing that dying for Allah means they will go to paradise and be greeted by a vast number of virgins for their enjoyment in the afterlife." At this, several of the officers snickered.

"I know it seems funny, but they are deadly serious about this. Someone who welcomes death is a lethal opponent."

"Shouldn't we launch a preemptive attack then?" asked one of the ship captains. "Hit them before they can mobilize their forces."

"Our orders are to blockade the port, not attack it," snapped Commodore Dale.

The ship captain, somewhat taken aback by the commodore's answer, said, "But sir, if we know they're going to attack, can't we justify hitting them first?"

Dale was near the end of his career and was undecided as to whether to retire upon returning to America or perhaps take on the challenge of one just more command. He had no desire to launch a full-fledged assault on the Tripolitans. In his opinion, the risk of attacking the Tripolitans was far greater than fending off an attack by the Tripolitans. This view was not shared by his officers, but he was the one in command. Generally Dale was admired by his officers. He was considered a man of great integrity and courage. This was the first time since leaving the United States that they found it hard to adhere to his orders. Being duty-bound naval officers, they would follow his orders—as much as it went against their better judgment.

Rais was about to launch an offensive against American forces on behalf of the pasha of Tripoli. There could be no greater honor. Especially for someone not born in Tripoli. Tripoli had already declared war on the U.S., and now he, Murad Rais, had the pleasure of leading a major offensive—an offensive that would convincingly defeat the U.S. forces and allow Tripoli to control the waterways for years to come. He would become a national hero.

As he considered the prominence this would bring to him he savored the opportunity to take revenge on his old nemesis, Will

Proctor. He would enjoy this sweet revenge even more than the satisfaction he'd get from defeating the American squadron. Rais had never forgotten how Proctor and his crew had gotten free after being captured by Rais and his corsairs. Total humiliation! It was an embarrassment that he had lived with for years. Rais was all too aware that many in the Tripolitan inner circle still laughed behind his back. Somehow, miraculously, the pasha continued to have faith in him. A resounding revenge would put the embarrassment behind him once and for all.

As Rais reveled in contemplation of what lay ahead, a grim curtain began to descend on his spirits. It was a cloud of gloom that was all too familiar. He'd been plagued by this feeling of depression off and on most of his adult life. Every time he dreamed of some wonderful event or some great accomplishment, the cloud descended and forced him to face the truth. This was one of those times.

In an instant his feeling of euphoria was overwhelmed by dark, negative thoughts about the responsibility he was burdened with. For one thing, he had never led the Tripolitan or any other navy to battle against anyone. He had no idea how his navy would perform. Secondly, even if it performed heroically, it was still unlikely the poorly trained and poorly equipped Tripolitan navy would be able to defeat the combined American and Swedish forces. Their opponents just had too much weaponry and their navies were far better trained than the men fighting for him. The feeling of well-being of just a moment ago was replaced by an overwhelming melancholy.

Rais was now overtaken by a sense of fear for his very life. He knew it was not an exaggerated fear, either, because failure in Tripoli was not looked upon favorably. He had been fortunate 15 years ago following the disaster of the *da Gama* incident. Somehow the previous pasha had seen the release of Rais in Gibraltar as a sign that Rais had outmaneuvered the Americans, despite their clever mutiny. Amazingly he had been a favorite of that pasha. Back then, Rais could do no wrong. Not so with Karamanli. He, too, had confidence in the abilities of Rais, but unlike the old pasha, he was ruthless if someone failed to perform for him. Certainly losing a naval battle against the Americans would bring down Karamanli's wrath.

But the pasha might not get the chance to punish him. It was highly possible that he would be killed in battle. There was no alternative, though. He could not avoid leading an assault. His only chance was that he and his men would catch the Americans by surprise. Not likely, but something to hope for.

He knew that Tripolitans could be fierce warriors. It was just hard to control them. They had no patience for the details of a military assault. Rais prayed that this Tripolitan ferocity combined with the element of surprised could save Tripoli . . . *and, more importantly, his own life.* Anything less would mean his neck. Literally.

Chapter 44

The *U.S.S. President*, Outside Tripoli Harbor, two days later

The sun was just peeking above the Mediterranean's eastern horizon. The brilliant orange half sphere had now become a low-hanging rubescent ball painting a bright yellow-orange streak on the surface of the sea all the way from the horizon to the side of the ship. The water was calm. It was never noisy in the outer harbor, but this time of day was particularly quiet.

Dale felt something on his shoulder. The hand shook him several times as a voice said, "Sir, please wake up." The commodore moved, and after one more shake on the shoulder, opened his eyes.

"Yes, what the bloody hell is it? It's barely dawn."

"They're coming, sir. Ships from Tripoli Harbor. Straight at us."

Dale was now fully awake. He cleared his throat before speaking. He wanted his voice to be clear and commanding. "Signal the alert to the other ships, and wake our crew. Don't waste a minute. Get to it, lad."

As the commodore peered into his telescope toward the inner harbor at the slowly advancing flotilla of Tripolitan warships, it was clear that the upcoming engagement was not going to be easy. Yes, the Americans and Swedes should win, but Dale had not expected to be facing so many small boats in addition to larger warships. There appeared to be five larger ships: two brigs, two frigates and one xebec. What he hadn't expected was the array of smaller boats. There must have been eight or nine of them. Maybe more. There were fustas, lateen-rigged dhows and boats he had never seen before. What made the imminent battle so dicey was this unexpected group of smaller boats and their ability to maneuver agilely and quickly around larger ships like flies around honey. He should've anticipated this, but he hadn't. He'd based his judgement on his experience with pirate ships at sea. They were almost always sizable ships with heavy armament.

He had to act quickly. He ordered his first mate to signal for Captain Proctor to come over to the *President* by dory immediately. Fifteen minutes later a breathless Proctor made his way to the bridge. He saluted Dale and said, "Yessir. You wanted to see me?"

"Yes. I'll get right to the point. We need a strategy for these pesky smaller boats that will be annoying us in less than an hour. They could do a lot of damage if we concentrate our fire on the larger ships coming at us from the harbor. These smaller boats will move too fast to make for easy cannon targets. Our cannons are stationary, so it will be almost impossible to aim accurately. Obviously, small arms will not be enough. Any ideas?"

Proctor needed only a minute. "Both the *President* and the *Trenton* have two Falconets each. Their two pound balls will do quite a job on these small boats. They can intersperse that with grape shot. Best of all, the Falconets are maneuverable. Weigh about 500 pounds each, but on swivels, two strong men can aim them fairly accurately." He thought for a minute, then added, "Don't forget the chain shot from the larger cannons. We can take their masts down with them." Chain shot were two cannon balls linked by chain. When shot from a cannon they whirled rapidly and were effective in taking down masts and sails.

"Good, good. I was counting on the chain shot, but I concentrated so much on the 8 and 12 and 24 pounders against the large ships, that I almost overlooked the falconets. Do any of the other ships have any small, maneuverable cannons?"

Dale was a big-picture man. He left details to his subordinates. Proctor had noticed this tendency when they first started working together. In Proctor's opinion his commanding officer showed too little interest in the details. He couldn't understand how a commanding officer could know if his subordinates were doing their job correctly if he didn't know the important details of the job himself.

Proctor looked away momentarily from Dale and into the harbor. As he did so he grimaced, astonished that the squadron leader was not more conversant with the armament of his own ships. Then he turned back to the commodore and said, "The *Enterprise* has two one-pounders. That should help, sir. I don't know about the other ships. No idea about the Swedish ships, either." As the captain of one ship, it wasn't Proctor's responsibility to know the armament capabilities of all the ships in the squadron. "We don't have time to check all the ships now. Let's just pray that their commanders have the good judgment to roll them out and use them when the time comes."

"Yes, yes, I agree. Best you get back to your ship now. The bloody Arab ships are getting closer."

Dale made the mistake a lot of the officers and crew members made in referring to the Tripolitans as Arabs. In fact, most Tripolitans, and for that matter, most North Africans, were Berbers, not Arabs. Certainly the Berbers and Arabs had much in common in Tripoli. Most of them spoke Arabic, though many of them also spoke one or more separate Berber languages. Many of them shared the same culture. Most of them lived together in relative harmony. But there were differences, too. Arabs tended to be light-brown skinned with dark hair and dark eyes. Berbers were lighter complexioned, often with blond hair and even blue eyes.

As Proctor rejoined Richard Hardy, his first mate at the helm of the *Trenton*, Hardy said, "Glad you're back sir. They're still coming at us, though fairly slowly."

"Not much wind this morning, Richard. They can't do much without wind. No forward movement and even less maneuverability. We have little to fear without wind." He paused soberly, then said, "But that could change at any moment. The commodore wants us to have our two Falconets ready to fire against those small boats that are sure to come around our stern to annoy us."

"I was assuming that, sir. We're ready with the falconets."

"Good man. If and when the wind kicks up they'll pick up the pace. Of course we'll be able to move, too, though I'm not sure we'll want to. We're well positioned now. We can always use our dories to pull us around to reposition our large cannons. I think we can handle an assault fairly well. Still, make sure the men don't underestimate these Tripolitans. They can be demons in a battle."

Chapter 45
The *Sabha*, Inner Tripoli Harbor 1801

Murad Rais was at the helm of the command ship *Sabha*. He turned to his second in command, a young sandy haired Tripolitan Berber named Rahim. With deep, penetrating eyes, a strong, prominent nose and a beard much darker than the color of his hair, his fierce countenance contrasted dramatically with his generally agreeable manner. He was taller than the average Tripolitan, and in many ways he reminded Rais of someone he'd known back in Boston. Except for language and dress, Rahim looked very much like the first seaman he'd met when he joined the crew of the *Betsey* 17 years ago. Rahim was a bright, talented seaman with the ability to lead. Rais liked to think that these were the reasons he had elevated the man to the position of second in command, but he sometimes wondered if Rahim's similarity to the only sailor on the *Betsey* he had any kind of a positive relation with might have contributed to his decision. Yes, that young sailor from 17 years ago had treated him like an equal. He saw that quality in Rahim.

Rahim waited expectantly for his admiral's words.

"Yes, Admiral Rais, you were about to say?"

"The wind is picking up slightly. Soon I expect we shall be able to get close enough to the Americans to do some damage. Now, pay close attention to this. I know we've been over this many times already, but I can't stress it enough. As soon as we are within range I want our dories and longboats to begin turning us so that our starboard sides are facing the enemy." This was because the heavy cannons on ships were arrayed in a line on both sides of the hulls. Sea battles were not waged by ships coming straight at each other, but by ships either passing alongside a few hundred feet from each other or lining up in a relatively stationary position with sides facing sides as would be the case now. The advantage was obvious. Side by side meant you could use the full firepower of your ship against your enemy. The cannons pointed out from the side, not forward. The disadvantage was that you exposed much more of your ship to damage. Nevertheless, with the limited accuracy of cannons being what it was, side by side was the only way to conduct sea battles.

"Yes, Admiral. Our men in dories and longboats have their orders. They know what to do."

"And our fustas and dhows are ready to circle their ships and pounce quickly? That is our big advantage, Rahim. If they fail to do their job, we are at a considerable disadvantage. You understand?"

"Yessir. I understand. If our small boats do a satisfactory job of diverting their crews and some of their fire, we can overwhelm the infidels." He then grinned archly, "Of course, we also have our little surprise. We cannot lose today."

Rais allowed himself a self-congratulatory smile. "We must never get overconfident, Rahim, but I agree, our little surprise should be the nail in their coffin."

Chapter 46
The *Trenton*, Outside Tripoli Harbor 1801

Twenty feet up the mainmast, Richard Hardy yelled down to Proctor at the helm. "There's more movement, captain. Moving faster now. Wind picking up. I can feel it up here. Some of their smaller craft are moving along the sides of the harbor. Almost like they think we won't notice them. Obviously hoping to slip out of the harbor and hit us from behind as you predicted, sir."

"Well we'll be ready for 'em, Richard." He allowed a few seconds to elapse before saying, "I'll never understand these Berbers. We've tried repeatedly to talk peace with them, but nothing ever comes of it. They want our money and blood more than they want our friendship."

"But wouldn't they get our money in trade if they made peace?"

"Their economy is based on taking things, not producing them. It's a criminal economy. They've convinced themselves that they're entitled to whatever they can take from nonbelievers. Not only are they entitled to it, they believe it's their obligation to take it and kill any nonbelievers in the process. Apparently they get their inspiration from certain parts of their Koran that they interpret as obligating them to commit these vicious acts. Maybe it's because that is what they truly believe. Maybe it just gives them a religious justification for pillaging anyone who is not a Muslim." He stopped talking for a minute, then said, "Forgive the lecture. I know I've said all this before. You must be tired of it."

"No, sir. I understand what you're saying. It's not as if we can ignore this."

"It is hard to avoid. They never let you."

The large Tripolitan ships were now within a quarter of a mile of the allied fleet. Suddenly Proctor saw a puff of smoke followed by a thump from one of the ships. It didn't make sense as the ships were coming at them head-on so the cannons on either side of the ships were facing away from the American ships. Must have been a nervous cannoneer. Even if the cannons were aimed properly it was unlikely the cannonball would have hit its target. A 12-pounder had a range of more than a half mile, but they were only accurate within a few hundred feet. Even then they were far from perfect.

"May have been a misfire, Richard, but let's consider it the start of the battle. They'll be more accurate the next time they fire."

A few minutes later Proctor said, "See, they're about two or three-hundred yards from us now, and they're turning their ships into firing position. I think they're still a little too far away to be accurate, but we shall see. We're already in position, so tell the men to begin firing as soon as the enemy presents a decent target. It'll give us a brief advantage. Hopefully we can do some damage before they're ready to begin firing."

"Aye, sir. I'm on my way."

"Quickly, Richard, quickly. I'll need you back here when the firing begins."

As soon as Hardy had left the side of Proctor a lookout yelled, "Unidentified vessels off to the east! Heading this way."

"How many?" yelled Proctor.

"Three."

"How far?"

"Two miles, sir. Maybe less." At that distance in a decent wind the enemy ships could be on them in 20 minutes or less.

Proctor's first reaction was annoyance verging on rage. How could the lookouts have not seen these unsuspected vessels sooner? As he looked off to the east at the oncoming ships, the answer was clear. At the break of dawn the region had been smothered with a blanket of fog. Gradually the fog had lifted, but a haze remained off to the horizon. It was understandable why the ships had not been visible until just now.

"Announce their country of origin as soon as you can," ordered Proctor up to the lookout. Maybe they were only merchant ships, though he doubted it. Unlikely that three merchant ships would be sailing together.

Hardy was now back at his side. "We're about to begin firing, sir."

As he said this the foremost cannon on the neighboring ship, the *President*, Dale's flagship, erupted in an orange-red flash with a thunderous boom. A half-second later it was followed by a cloud of grayish-white smoke. Seconds later the second in line followed. The noise was deafening. Soon all eleven cannons on the port side were firing as quickly as they could reload. The *Trenton's* cannons had joined the cacophony in earsplitting harmony. In between firings by the *Trenton* and the *President*, Proctor could hear the thump, thump, thump of cannons from nearby squadron ships. The battle was on.

Proctor noted unhappily that many of their shots were missing the enemy ships. It was to be expected—especially on the first volley. There was the occasional hit, of course. In most cases it was impossible to tell how much damage was sustained by the Tripolitan ships. It was clear, though, when a mast toppled that a ship was disabled. But losing a mast was a handicap only when sailing—not when at anchor fighting a battle.

There were two explosions on the Tripolitan ships. Explosions usually indicated that a ship's powder supply had been hit. Such a hit was almost always disabling. Both ship and crew could be out of commission or severely handicapped when their ammunition exploded.

On the second round of firing the American accuracy improved. Clearly they were doing damage. Unfortunately, the Tripolitans were also firing, and they were hitting their targets, too. A ball slammed into the hull of the *President*, splintering wood, but not endangering the crew.

Off in the distance, Proctor saw a flash on the deck of another squadron ship. Seconds later a ball scored a direct hit on the foredeck of the *Trenton*. There was a resounding crash, but no explosion. Screams pierced the morning air. Shrapnel and pieces of wood rained down on the gunners. Throughout his maritime career Proctor had heard tales about the terrible inaccuracy of Tripolitan cannoneers. After today he might change his opinion of their ability.

He told Hardy to stay at the helm. He was going forward to check on the crew and damage.

He approached a scene of utter horror. Before he could ask anyone how bad it was, his eyes told him all he needed to know. Lying on the deck in a pool of blood was a sight that even his battle-hardened soul could not accept. The partial body of a young seaman lay motionless. His head and upper torso were missing. Only a few feet away another young man lay screaming as he stared in agony at his left arm lying in its own pool of blood five feet away.

Proctor went up to the nearest sailor and asked, "Anyone else?"

The sailor was shaking. "No sir. Not as far as I can tell."

"All right, then. We can't afford to let this gun lay idle. Get another man to help you with a tourniquet for this man's arm. You need to stop the bleeding. When you finish with that, I need you to get back on the gun."

The sailor looked like he was going to faint, but nodded his understanding. Proctor patted him on the shoulder and said, "Good lad."

As he made his way back to the helm, Proctor ran to the side of the ship and threw up.

Chapter 47
The *Sabha*, Inner Tripoli Harbor 1801

Murad Rais shuddered as a ball hit the side of the *Sabha* with an earsplitting crash, not 20 feet from where he was standing. The damage was minimal, but the proximity made him wince. He was all too aware that he could die at any moment. Unlike most of the Tripolitans he knew, he had no expectation of Paradise and the virgins that supposedly awaited him after an heroic death in the *jihad* against infidels.

After giving the order to fire, he had not uttered a word for over two minutes to a grim Rahim standing silently beside him. Rais had commanded corsair vessels and crews in numerous assaults against infidel merchant ships and never once felt fear. This was different, though. Warships could fight back. The ships they were up against now were heavily armed and manned by trained fighting men. He knew days ago that it would come to this, but he'd been too involved in the preparations and too exhilarated by the opportunity to think about failure and death. The idea of defeating an entire American squadron led by a man he'd hated for over 15 years had excited him when the pasha told him he would have the honor to lead the assault. Ever since Proctor and his crew had mutinied back in '86 the hatred had grown and festered. Rais was not one to forgive and forget. The humiliation at the time had been galling. Now, though, in the midst of a fierce battle, he was face to face with a life and death reality. It was one thing to have the honor to lead the assault. It was quite another to complete the mission successfully and in one piece.

"Admiral? Admiral….," cried Rahim interrupting his thoughts.

"Yes, Rahim. What is it?"

"We've lost the xebec. Direct hit on the powder magazine."

"rrahim alllah Merciful Allah."

A dark cloud descended on Rais's spirits. Once again he fell silent, sending Rahim's already low spirits even lower. If his leader could not lead, where did that leave him?

"Give me instructions, Admiral. What shall I tell the the crew?

They are looking for direction. If we do nothing, all is lost."

Desperately Rais forced himself to think. He had to do something. He was the admiral after all. He had to say something. Finally he spoke. "All is not lost, Rahim. It was a lucky hit. Nothing more. We've hit them, too. It is not all one-sided."

"Yes, Admiral, but we have not disabled them. They are too much for us."

"They are not too much for us, Rahim. We will hit them where it hurts. It is only a matter of time. I know Americans. As soon as we hurt them, they will retreat," he lied. He then forced a smile. "Besides, Rahim. You have forgotten our secret weapons—the three brigs coming from Misrata. They are already within sight. Look, see for yourself. They are coming. They will distract fire from us by inflicting damage from the other side. You will see how quickly things will turn our way."

Chapter 48
The *President*, Outside Tripoli Harbor

Commodore Dale motioned for his first mate to come closer. "Elias, get the men prepared for a cease fire."

Elias Perry was not sure he'd heard correctly. A frown of disbelief transfixed his normally youthful features. "Did you say cease fire, sir?"

"Yes, I want the men to be ready to cease fire at my command."

Perry hated to challenge the great commodore, but he overcame his fear and asked, "But, sir, we're winning. Why stop now?"

"Our orders are to blockade the port, not destroy their navy. We're fighting now to defend ourselves, but once we have this under control, I have no intention to beat them into submission. Oh, before you make the announcement to the crew, signal the other ships to await orders. Don't signal about the cease fire yet."

Richard Hardy, aboard the *Trenton*, reported to Proctor. "Commodore Dale is signaling for all ships to be on the alert for new orders, Captain."

"New orders? What in the name of God could he have in mind?"

"Unclear, sir. Flags just said to be ready for new orders."

"I'm going over there, Richard. You're in charge till I return. You know what to do."

Minutes later Proctor stepped out of the dory into the stern of the *President* and made his way directly to the helm. The commodore was surprised to see him.

"What're you doing here, Proctor? Shouldn't you be manning your post?"

Proctor dispensed with the usual courtesies. Time was too important. "What new orders are we waiting for, commodore? I thought our orders were to defend ourselves against these savages?"

"I don't like your attitude, captain. What makes you think you can challenge my authority?" Why don't you wait like the other captains?"

"I didn't wait because once you give these new orders, it'll be too late. Besides, I'm not challenging your authority. Just asking for clarification, sir."

"I'll be ordering a cease fire just as soon as I'm convinced we have things under control."

"A cease fire! Good God, sir. We have them where we want them. We'll never have another opportunity like this. Shouldn't we finish the job?"

"We were sent here to blockade the Port of Tripoli, not to fight a war."

"But that was before they declared war on us, sir. Doesn't that change everything? They're attacking us at this very moment. If we can defeat them now, shouldn't we go ahead and do it? We'll never have a better chance."

"President Jefferson made it clear that we were to blockade Tripoli. He stressed that we not engage in war against these people, that we should defend ourselves if we are attacked, but that we are not to initiate military action. I am carrying out his orders. I expect you to do the same."

Proctor looked away and rolled his eyes. When he turned back to face Dale, he said, "Sir, conditions have changed. They've declared war on us. Attacked us. I can't believe the president would want us to stick to our original orders under these conditions. Surely you must see that?"

"You are a brazen one, Proctor. I suggest you go back to your ship and follow my orders. You seem to have forgotten who's in command here. Go back to your ship, or I'll have you replaced by a properly respectful officer."

Proctor shook his head in disgust, hesitated a moment, then stormed away. Minutes later he was back at the helm of the *Trenton*.

"Glad you're back, sir," said Hardy. "The three ships from the east are closing in. Everything all right, sir?"

"No, Richard, things are not all right. The commodore wants us to cease fire when he gives the order."

"I assume that'll be after we've whipped these bastards and they're begging for mercy?"

"No, that's not what he wants to do. He wants to stop firing as soon as he feels we have the battle well in hand. Sort of as a peace offering. He doesn't want to defeat the Tripolitans, just hit them hard

JIHAD AT SEA

enough so they stop attacking. He has no desire to beat them into submission."

"I know it's not my place, sir, but I think that's a mistake. These people will misinterpret that as a sign of weakness. They'll wait for an opportunity and attack us again when our guard is down."

"I couldn't agree with you more, Richard. Unfortunately, it's not our call. I'm afraid we'll have to follow the commodore's orders. I questioned him about it, and he is not open to discussion on the subject. Nearly took my head off."

"So we just fight until he tells us to stop?"

"That's about it, I'm afraid. Now let's take a look at these three mysterious ships from the east."

"They're not mysterious anymore, sir. We can see their colors. Tripolitan. They're trying a sneak attack from behind us. All three appear to be heavily armed brigs. Could be trouble."

"Between them and their smaller boats, we'll have our hands full. We'll be taking fire from both directions. Tell the lads to hold fire until I give the order. I want to make every shot count. We'll depend on the usual poor accuracy of Tripolitan cannoneers to keep us from harm until then."

"I understand what you're saying, sir, but I've noticed that they seem to be getting better with practice. Our ships have taken a few hits. I think the Swedes have been hit, too." As he said this a cannonball hit a neighboring ship near the foremast. A chilling scream was heard from the ship's deck. Hardy added, "We'll soon be taking hits from both sides, sir."

"All the more reason for us to hit them hard and often before these new enemy ships get in much practice. We let them get close; then we hit 'em hard. Our lads are good. I'm counting on their being better than these Berber fellows."

Minutes later the three ships from the east began firing. Hardy looked at Proctor wondering how long his captain would hold out before giving the order to fire. A ball fell just short of the ship splashing water on everyone on the deck. Hardy scanned the other American ships and saw a number of close hits. It was just a matter of time before they took a direct hit. As he wondered how much longer Proctor would delay the order to fire, he heard a resounding crash followed by the sound of splintering from the deck of the *Enterprise*, a hundred yards away. He was about to speak, when Proctor said, "Fire!"

Hardy relayed the word, and immediately the *Trenton's* guns began firing against the oncoming marauders. Within seconds the guns on the other American ships were firing, followed by the Swedish guns.

By now, the oncoming three Tripolitan ships were so close that Proctor could see the faces of their crew members. Proctor wondered whether he'd waited too long to give the order to fire. The acrid smell of smoke had turned the ship's deck cloudy. The air was punctuated by the crumps of distant explosions and occasional screams as the enemy guns began hitting their targets. Hardy looked at Proctor helplessly.

Suddenly they heard an explosion on one of the enemy ships. The bow was tilting at an angle, clearly separated from the rest of the hull. Men were leaping into the sea to get away from the fiery inferno. A minute later a second ship suffered a direct hit killing several crewmen and toppling a mainmast.

Proctor smiled at Hardy. "I told you our lads were better."

"Aye, sir, but we're still receiving fire from their main contingent in the harbor. We got their xebec, but the others are still firing. And don't forget their dhows and other little boats."

"You worry too much, Richard," said Proctor confidently. "If we stay with our plan, things will work out. My big fear is that the commodore will order us to stop before we finish the job."

As he said this a huge explosion could be heard off in the distance. From where Proctor was standing he couldn't tell which ship had been hit, but it clearly was one of the American vessels. Red-orange flames could be seen leaping into the air as black smoke made it hard to discern how badly the ship was damaged. Proctor turned to his first mate and said, "I may have spoken too soon, Richard. This isn't going to be easy. See if you can find out how badly she's been hit. Doesn't look good from here."

Chapter 49
The *Sabha*, Inner Tripoli Harbor

It was over two hours into the battle. "We've lost three ships, Admiral. The xebec and small frigates. They've also sunk two or three of our dhows."

"Yes, yes. I know, Rahim. It is not good, but they have sustained losses, too. We must keep in mind how we're hurting them. We have sunk one of their brigs and inflicted serious damage on several of their vessels. Our losses have been for the greater good. Allah will reward our men for their bravery. This battle is not over. You will see that they will not last much longer. We have taken our toll, and soon they will succumb."

Rahim squinted at Rais as if to question his sanity. Could the admiral be seeing what he was seeing? The Americans were winning, and they were losing. How could the admiral continue to exude optimism faced with these facts?

Rahim knew from past experience that Rais possessed a mercurial temper. Still, he felt obligated to speak out. "We are running out of supplies, sir. Our ammunition is low and many of the men are suffering from shrapnel injuries, burns and even lack of water. There's water on land, but we can't get it to the ships. They cannot hold out much longer."

"Bah! Listen, Rahim, the Americans suffer from the same things, and they are weaker. They cannot last much longer. Do not be so defeatist. We will prevail. Tripoli always prevails. It is Allah's will." Rais didn't really believe any of this, but felt he had to say it.

Chapter 50
The *Trenton*, Outer Tripoli Harbor 1801

Aboard the *Trenton* Captain Proctor was startled by a seaman rushing across the deck toward him. The crewman came to an abrupt halt and stood facing Proctor for a few seconds as he caught his breath.

"Yes, what is it sailor?" barked Proctor, knowing it couldn't be good.

"One of the dhows surrendered, sir. Five men aboard. How do you want us to handle it? Should we put them in the brig, take their guns, sink the boat?"

"Take their guns, sink the boat and hold the crew in irons for now. Bring one of them to me immediately. Let's see what we can find out."

"I don't know if they speak English, sir."

"I speak a little Arabic. From my days in a Moroccan prison," he explained at the surprised look on the sailor's face. "Bring me one of them, and let's see what transpires. Quickly now."

Minutes later the same sailor approached Proctor pushing his bearded prisoner ahead of him. The man approached reluctantly, constantly prodded by the American sailor. Coming to a halt in front of Proctor the prisoner glared defiantly at the captain, his coal-black eyes exuding hatred.

Proctor addressed him in broken Arabic. "Did your superiors really think your small boats could cause damage to large warships?"

The prisoner seemed surprised that an unbeliever could speak Arabic. "They believe we can distract you from firing at our large ships. I think we have done that."

"Does it concern you that you are fighting against people who meant you no harm? Who never wanted war with you." Proctor knew it was pointless to ask such a question of a common seaman, but he was interested in how the man would reply.

"By not believing in the Almighty Allah, you offend me and

JIHAD AT SEA

every Tripolitan. You could believe, but you choose not to. That is the greatest offense. If you reject Allah, you deserve to die."

Proctor could see that he would not get anywhere with this man.

"Who is your commanding officer?"

"Admiral Rais," snapped the prisoner. "A former infidel who, unlike you, saw the wisdom of belief in Allah and the prophet Muhammad."

Proctor was stunned. Could this Rais be the same Rais who was borne Peter Lisle? It had to be. It had to be the same Murad Rais Proctor had re-encountered 15 years ago when Rais was captain of a Tripolitan pirate ship. Somehow, despite Rais's defeat back then, he'd managed to become an admiral of the Tripolitan navy. Proctor shook his head at the improbability of it all.

"I'm going to release you in one of our dories. Go back and tell Admiral Rais that if he surrenders we will spare him and the rest of his navy." It was unlikely that Rais would surrender anyway, but if he did, everybody would win. America would no longer need to fear Tripolitan pirate raids, and Tripoli could salvage much of its remaining navy. Proctor would have to explain his going around Dale, but hopefully the satisfactory results would result only in a reprimand and not a demotion. If Rais declined to surrender, which was likely, Dale would never know.

The prisoner sneered, "I will tell him, but he will never surrender. He will fight on until your ships are at the bottom of the sea."

Chapter 51
The *President*, Outer Tripoli Harbor

After two more hours of brutal shelling the firing from both sides had receded dramatically because both sides were running out of ammunition, water and human endurance. The battle had been costly and exhausting for both sides. Tripoli had lost four warships and numerous small boats. Close to 100 Tripolitan men had been sent to Paradise. The Americans and Swedes had suffered losses, too: one American brig had been sunk, two disabled and nearly 50 lives had been lost.

It was obvious to Commodore Dale that the Tripolitans were no longer capable of waging an offensive. Coming to this conclusion, he brought all of his ship captains over to the *President* to discuss what he wanted to do next.

"It's quite clear that these rascals cannot continue much longer. If they do, they will only lose more lives and more ships. I would like to signal for a cease fire. If they agree, we can end all this without further bloodshed."

"But, sir,' said Proctor, "if they agree we've let them off the hook." He knew it was reckless to challenge the commodore, but felt he had to give it one more try.

Dale glowered at Proctor as if he were about to explode. He drew in a deep breath in an effort to control his temper and said, "We've had this discussion, Proctor. I have no desire to beat these fellows into submission if they're willing to agree to a cease fire now. I think they've learned that they can't trifle with the United States of America."

Proctor pursed his lips. In for a penny, in for a pound. "Sir, what if they haven't learned that? What if they conclude that we quit out of fear. Then the next time we face them they'll be more daunting than ever. It's already cost us too many men. Next time could be far costlier. Now we can finish them off at very little additional loss to our ships, or, for that matter, the Swedes."

Dale struggled to contain his emotions. He'd had it with Proctor. Still, if he demoted the man now he would have trouble with the other captains, as Proctor was looked up to by most of the officers in the squadron.

The commodore slowly made eye contact with the other ship captains waiting for some show of support. Finally, after a suspenseful period of silence, he said, "How do the rest of you feel about this. Should we do as Proctor here suggests and 'finish the job,' or should we cease fire now if the Tripolitans will accept our terms?"

Most of the captains, like their crews, were eager to return home as soon as possible. They were tired of living aboard ship, tired of no shore leave, tired of eating unappetizing food and tired of being away from their loved ones. Some were suffering from scurvy and damaged skin from overexposure to the sun. Yet most of them were loyal patriots who understood that they were at an historical point in American history. They realized that they had the opportunity to put an end to the Tripolitan scourge to merchant ships, seamen and their cargoes. Almost all of the captains sided with Proctor and saw the logic of continuing the battle until the Tripolitans were beaten into submission. One of them, however, agreed with Dale, and three others, while agreeing with Proctor, were afraid to voice their support for the captain of the *Trenton*. Dale's reputation as a harsh, unforgiving officer who didn't encourage challenges to his authority made them leery of going against his wishes. This left only two who had the courage to express their disagreement with Dale.

"It looks like only two of you agree with Proctor, so we will proceed as I originally intended. I will give this three more hours. If the Tripolitan guns remain dormant or nearly so, we will signal for a cease fire."

Proctor spoke up. "Then what, sir? Will we continue the blockade or leave the area?"

"It will depend on the terms of our settlement."

Chapter 52
The *Sabha*, Inner Tripoli Harbor 1801

"The Americans are signaling for a cease fire, admiral," said Rahim excitedly. "Will we accept?"

Rais beamed with self satisfaction. "It means we have defeated them. They no longer wish to continue because they know that we will destroy them. This way they can salvage some of their fleet and most of their crewmen."

"So we will accept?"

"I think we will. I must consult with the pasha first. It is his decision, but I will advise him that we should accept."

The Pasha Karamanli was surprised to see his admiral at the palace. He assumed Rais would be leading his forces against the infidels.

"What brings you here, admiral, in the middle of this conflict? Are you not neglecting your responsibilities?"

"The Americans are begging us for a cease fire, Your Excellency. I think they believe they are on the verge of defeat and want to save face, not to mention their remaining ships and crew members. I'm inclined to accept, but it is your decision."

"From what my associates tell me, the Americans are doing better than we are. How can you conclude that they are on the verge of defeat?"

"They have suffered the loss of one of their brigantines and severe damage to two other vessels." Rais then broke into a wide smile. "They are no doubt running out of water and other supplies. The biggest loss for them, though, is the death of more seamen. The loss of lives to the infidels is a far greater tragedy than it is for us, for they do not believe their fallen men go to Paradise."

The pasha said nothing as he considered what Rais had told him. Finally he said, "You know the minds of these infidels better than I do. If the Americans are in such dire straits as you describe them, why should we accept their offer of a cease fire? If what you say is true, they are vulnerable and can be defeated by our noble Tripolitan navy. We would be foolish to stop fighting now."

Rais swallowed hard. He had argued so persuasively that the enemy was incapable of fighting—knowing that it was not true—that he now found himself in a situation that he had wanted to avoid. Rais knew that his forces were on the verge of defeat. He knew that to continue to fight would only result in more losses of ships and more losses of men. Very likely his own life, too.

Based on what Rais had said to the pasha, the Tripolitan leader was right in expecting Rais to continue the fight. Rais could not suddenly argue that the enemy was still strong and capable of destroying the Tripolitan navy, for it would mean that he had lied to the pasha only minutes before. To hesitate now would be to disappoint the pasha. Something you didn't do if you valued your life.

Rais now found himself in a dilemma with two equally odious outcomes. If he refused to fight, it was almost certain the pasha would have him executed. If he did continue the conflict, there was a very good chance he would lose hundreds of men, himself included. Glumly he pondered his terrible choices as the pasha stared him in the face impatiently.

Chapter 53
The *President*, Outer Tripoli Harbor

"Their guns are more active, sir," said First Mate Perry. "I don't think they've accepted the cease fire."

"Damn!" cried Dale. "This is insane! They have to know that it's suicidal. Perhaps it's just some gun-happy hands violating the cease fire, and that will be the end of it."

"Maybe, sir, but it's more than one or two guns. They all seem to be firing."

Dale grimaced. This was the last thing he wanted to deal with. "All right. Tell the men to return fire. We can't just sit here and take their hits. Maybe if we give them another sound thrashing they'll see the error of their ways." He frowned and added acidly, "It's that damned Proctor."

Perry wrinkled his brow as he tried to grasp what the admiral meant. "Proctor, sir. I don't understand."

"He and Admiral Rais have had a long-standing feud. Many years ago they were crew mates on a merchant ship out of Boston. The ship was captured by Moroccan pirates, and the word is Rais, who was born Scottish, turned on his fellow crew mates to curry favor with the Moroccans. Proctor never forgave him. Can't say I blame him. Wouldn't be surprised if Rais is continuing the fight because he doesn't want to give Proctor the satisfaction of winning."

"It'd be pretty short-sighted of Admiral Rais to continue fighting just to spite an old enemy."

"Wouldn't be the first war fought out of a fit of pique. How many wars have rational causes?"

"But as you said, sir. It's suicidal for them to continue. By not accepting a graceful cease fire, Rais may die."

"I know I said that, Elias," snapped Dale, "but perhaps we should look at it from his perspective. It may be suicidal, but it may not be insane. If he accepts the cease fire, he may die anyway at the hands of the pasha. At least by continuing the fight he maintains a semblance of respectability in Tripoli. And if he's a convert to Islam, as I assume he is, he won't fear death as much as we would. Better to die in battle than in disgrace."

"If that is his thinking, sir, there's no point in reasoning with him. Shouldn't we just give him everything we've got and force him to surrender?"

"It is tempting, I'll admit, but that is not our mission. We are here to protect our merchant ships, not to attack Tripoli."

"But, sir. they've attacked us. Declared war on us. That *has* to change things."

"You're sounding more and more like Proctor," said Dale, showing his annoyance at the impertinence of his first mate. "I appreciate your opinions, Elias, but don't forget your rank. Enough on this matter. We will exchange fire with these people, but only until we have quieted them. We couldn't carry out a full-fledged assault on them even if it were our mandate. Our ammunition and supplies are low. You know that, Perry."

Soon Dale was forced to admit he may have been wrong. The incoming barrage was relentless, giving him no choice but to return fire. He had thought that the enemy was spent, but obviously they were far from it. The American and Swedish response to the stepped up assault by the Tripolitans would have to match or exceed the incoming assault or face defeat. Dale grudgingly ordered all ships to return fire. "Let's hope that we have enough ordnance to outlast these vermin, Elias. This is insane. They should have quit two hours ago. I don't know how they can continue."

"They've done a lot of damage, sir, in those two hours. We've lost more men and suffered too much damage to our ships. I fear it could be much worse in the next hour if they continue firing at this rate."

"I can't believe they have that much left, Elias. They must be losing men by the dozens. Our fire has been far more accurate than theirs. Thank God. We've made far more direct hits. How can they keep this up?" Dale thought for a moment, then said, "Best you check on the men. See how they're doing and report back to me.

Five minutes later, Elias came running to Dale with a hint of a smile on his face. "Their fire is slowing down, sir. The number and accuracy of the incoming fire has tapered off.

Dale allowed a small smile himself as he spoke to Elias.

"Yes, I can see that for myself. Listen, I have an idea. It's risky, but it just might work. Still, it depends on you, lad. If you don't want to do it, I can find someone else."

Chapter 54
The *Sabha*, Inner Tripoli Harbor 1801

Rahim did not want to broach the subject to Rais but he felt he had to. "Admiral, I fear we cannot continue much longer. They have overwhelming fire power, and only a few of our guns are capable of firing. We are losing men every minute. There is no hope."

The eyes of the admiral were now wild with anxiety. He felt trapped between two horrific inevitabilities. Rahim could see the fear in his eyes and knew then that all was lost. Finally, Rais managed to speak in a weak voice. "We cannot stop now, Rahim. It is Allah's will that we continue."

"But admiral, we can still accept their offer of a cease fire. A cease fire is not a defeat. We can still maintain our honor."

Rais began to tremble. He was finding it difficult to speak, both because of his emotional state and because he no longer knew what to say. The fear that had plagued him all his life had risen to the surface. He was in over his head. Rahim always sensed that his superior officer was somewhat unstable, but this was the first time he'd seen him actually lose control of himself.

Now Rahim felt panic. Probably he should assume the admiral's command, but to do that would be at great risk. One didn't challenge the authority of a Tripolitan admiral. It would be acceptable if the admiral were injured and disabled, but under these circumstances, Rahim would be putting his own life on the line. Still, if he did nothing, they would all perish.

Just as he was about to throw his hands up in despair Rahim noticed a dory slowly making its way toward the *Sabha*. One person was rowing, and another was holding a white flag. It meant that the Americans wanted to talk. This was good. This meant there was hope. Maybe Rahim would still get to see his wife and child again.

As the tiny boat neared the *Sabha*, the man holding the white flag signaled that he had a message for the admiral. Could he come aboard? Minutes later a nervous Elias Perry came aboard and was led to the helm and Admiral Rais. Rais collected himself enough to say, "Yes, what message do you bring from Commodore Dale?"

"Once again the commodore is willing to consider a cease fire."

"And if we don't accept?" challenged Rais halfheartedly.

"The commodore says that, reluctantly, he would be forced to consider further bombardment of your forces."

"If we accept the commodore's offer, will your ships leave the harbor?"

"If you agree that your navy vessels and your privateers will not attack and pillage our merchant vessels in the future."

Rais dearly wanted to accept this offer, but feared the wrath of the pasha. After all, Rais had brazenly told the Tripolitan leader that he would lead the navy to victory. Many would say that accepting a cease fire now would be admitting failure.

Suddenly an idea hit him. Maybe a cease fire didn't have to be considered a failure. In an instant his spirits went from dark depression to bright optimism. It all depended on how you looked at the situation. He could claim the cease fire as a victory. He would tell the pasha that he and his forces had forced the Americans and Swedes into the cease fire because they knew they couldn't prevail. By allowing the cease fire offer, he had forced the Americans to leave the harbor. Really a victory for him and his navy. A victory for Tripoli. As he mulled this over, Rais felt his confidence return. He couldn't wait to explain his success to the pasha himself. What just hours ago had seemed like the most wretched day of his life, now seemed like his greatest triumph.

He had gone from his funeral to his rebirth. All his life he'd gone from euphoria to depression and eventually back to euphoria depending on how he interpreted the facts in his life. A more introspective person would have been aware of these mood swings, but despite his above average intelligence, Rais had never come to grips with his condition.

Seeing that Rais seemed to be off somewhere in his own thoughts, Perry finally said, "Do you agree?"

Rais shook off his thoughts and said, "I must consult with the pasha first."

"What will you recommend to the pasha? Will you recommend that he agree to the cease fire?"

"What I recommend is between him and me. It is no concern of yours."

"Oh, but it is a concern of mine. If you intend not to recommend the cease fire, then I will return to the commodore, and I am sure he will resume the bombardment."

Rais expelled a breath in frustration. "Very well, I will recommend acceptance of the cease fire."

While Rais was happy with his new interpretation of the cease fire, he was not sure the pasha would be convinced that it was the victory Rais would claim it to be. As he entered the throne room of the palace, he faced the pasha with great trepidation. He could feel his hands sweating.

"What brings you to the palace, Admiral Rais, when you should be leading your navy against the infidels?" The pasha frowned grimly as he said this. Rais felt himself tremble, but tried not to show it as he stood nervously before the Tripolitan leader.

"I have good news for Your Excellency."

The pasha allowed himself a cold smile. "Then speak up, Admiral. Speak up. It is about time I heard good news from you.

"The Americans have offered a cease fire, and I'm inclined to accept. They don't know that, though. They think we prefer to continue our assault. I told them the only way we would agree was if they would immediately take the remnants of their squadron out of Tripolitan waters."

"I see," said Karamanli thoughtfully. "And are they willing to do this?"

"They are eager to do this Your Excellency. They know that they cannot take much more of our brutal bombardment. They are eager to leave while they still can."

"It is not the result I was counting on, Admiral, but it is not bad. May I ask why, since you are punishing them so brutally as you say, you decided to accept a cease fire when you could have utterly destroyed them?"

Rais feared this would come up. How could it not? He drew in a deep breath and said, "I have not accepted yet, Your Excellency. I leave it to you to decide. They don't know it, but we are nearly out of ammunition. If we had enough ammunition, I have no doubt we would send them to the bottom of the sea. They don't know we are low on powder and balls, though so I believe it's in our best interest to accept their offer and see the last of them. It is the equivalent of a victory without the loss of valuable ships and further loss of Tripolitan naval seamen. Without ammunition, we would not be able to protect the city. By accepting we turn a potential disaster into a victory."

The pasha squinted as he considered what Rais was telling him. "Then by all means, accept the cease fire. Your good news is not quite what I had hoped for, Admiral, but I suppose we must consider it more of a victory than a defeat. Let me be clear, though. If I learn that you have somehow not given me an accurate account of all this, you will pay."

Part 3

Chapter 55
The *Trenton*, Mediterranean Sea, Approaching Gibraltar 1801

More than a week had passed since the squadron had left Tripoli. The ships were low on ammunition, almost out of water and in dire need of food. All of the ships were in need of repair. All of the men were shaky from being at sea so long and living on substandard rations. Many of the crew had developed various stages of scurvy, including overwhelming fatigue, painful limbs, swollen bleeding gums, severe joint pain and lack of appetite. Before they could leave for America they intended to stop over in Gibraltar for supplies and the minimal repairs needed to make a safe crossing of the Atlantic.

It was a matter of opinion as to how successful the blockade and subsequent offensive had been: Admiral Dale believed that they had taught the Tripolitans a lesson. He was convinced that the pirates out of Tripoli and Derne and smaller Tripolitan ports would stay away from American and Swedish merchant ships in the future.

Proctor and most of his fellow officers weren't so sure. Proctor in particular, since he'd had personal experience at the hands of Barbary states. In his case it had been the Moroccans, but he knew that all the Barbary states viewed outsiders more or less the same way. Being attacked, imprisoned and forced into slave labor in Morocco was very personal for Proctor. In his opinion, you couldn't reason with the North African predators. The only thing they understood was force. Diplomacy was considered a sign of weakness—something to be disparaged and something to exploit. The U.S. had tried diplomacy more than once, and every time they'd ended up paying a monetary tribute. The only type of negotiations the Barbary states were willing to conduct was the type that meant the U.S. would pay them money. Proctor was sure that in the wake of their recent cease fire, the pasha would conclude that the U.S. had given the naval encounter its best effort. The U.S., by withdrawing from Tripoli when it could have conquered Tripoli, had only encouraged piracy in the future.

Proctor left Tripoli frustrated and angry that the squadron had not finished the job. As furious as he was, he was not a rebel or mutineer. He recognized the authority of Dale in his position as commodore, and was not about to attempt to challenge the chain of command. Besides, Dale was a respected naval man with a proud record. He and Proctor just didn't agree on certain things. Unfortunately they were important things.

In order to make the return trip to America as productive as possible, Proctor decided to approach Dale with a request. He would remind the commodore that Henry Orne, former captain of the *Betsey*, was still being held by the Sultan of Morocco for almost two decades. Proctor wasn't sure how Dale would react to his request, but he had to ask.

The morning Proctor approached the commodore was one of the finest days you could experience on the open water. Bright sun, calm seas and just enough wind to fill the sails to carry them toward Gibraltar and all the delights sailors dream of when they've been away at sea for far too long. They were still two or three days from Gibraltar, so Proctor figured the commodore would be free from the pressure he would feel as he was about to bring his squadron into the British port. Now the commodore should be as relaxed and receptive as he ever would be on the return voyage to the U.S.

"Commodore, I have a request," said Proctor.

"Yes, Captain, what is it?"

"I'm sure you remember when Henry Orne, captain of the merchant ship *Betsey,* was taken captive by the Sultan of Morocco."

"Yes, I remember. I'd lost track of it 'til you reminded me just now, but I remember. Sad thing."

"It's been 17 years, and as far as I know, he's still in Morocco."

"Never knew him, but I heard at the time that Orne was a good man." Dale furrowed his brows and squinted, as if struggling to dredge up old memories. "Yes, I remember. The entire crew was captured. You were one of them?"

"Indeed I was, sir."

"Eventually didn't you all escape with the ship when a tribute was paid?"

"Yes, yes. Exactly. Everyone got out of Rabat *except* Captain Orne. The sultan kept him on as some kind of advisor. As first mate it was left to me to take command of the ship."

"And you then returned to the States?"

"That was our intention, but things didn't quite work out that way. At least not right away." Proctor proceeded to remind Dale of how they'd first weathered a terrible storm only to be attacked by a Tripolitan ship commanded by Murad Rais, the very man they'd been up against little more than a week ago.

The commodore smiled. "Yes, I recall now what you went through with these barbarians. Glad to see you made it, Proctor. Ended well for you, didn't it?"

"Yes, I suppose it did, sir—and for most of the crew, too. But that's just the point, sir. We gained our freedom, but Captain Orne is still a prisoner. Seventeen years, and we as a country have done nothing to free him."

"Regretful. Truly regretful. One has to feel for the man and his family. Thank God you and the crew got out anyway."

Proctor saw that Dale wasn't going to make it easy for him. The man wasn't going to volunteer anything. Was it because freeing Orne hadn't occurred to the commodore, or was it because it was something he really wanted to avoid? Either way, it was clear to Proctor that Dale was not the sort of man who liked to go out on a limb. He didn't like to venture into anything that wasn't part of his official orders. This was puzzling to Proctor, as Dale had the reputation of being bold and even occasionally reckless when he was a young naval officer. What had happened to change the man so dramatically?

Proctor took a breath and said, "I was hoping, sir, that we could make a stop at Rabat and see if we can't free Captain Orne. We might not be successful, but at least we will have tried."

The commodore's normally ruddy features went white. Stopping at Rabat was the last thing he wanted to do. He wanted to get his squadron home in one piece without further risk or incident. What Proctor was proposing could result in a major naval confrontation. Lives could be lost, not to mention ships. Normally an articulate man, Dale was at a loss as to how to handle this. He didn't want to sound insensitive to the plight of an American held prisoner, but he didn't want to take on something that could end in disaster. Still, he had to say something. He was, after all, the commodore of the fleet.

"Captain, I can see that your heart is in the right place. You're loyal to your former commanding officer, and I admire that. I wish we could do what you propose, but we are not really equipped to carry out such a mission. We're a naval squadron. Our men are not trained to make land assaults."

"Henry Orne is not just my former commanding officer, sir, he's an American citizen abandoned by his own country. I'm not suggesting a military offensive. Just a contact with these people to see if they might be willing to grant Orne his freedom after his many years of service to the sultan."

"Why would the sultan give up a valuable advisor simply because we request it? That doesn't sound like an Arab potentate to me."

"He probably won't, but one thing I know about these people is they are unpredictable. On a bad day the sultan might lash out and threaten us. Yet on a good day there's no telling how he will react. At the very least he might demand something in return for Orne. Frankly, his reaction will probably depend on how relations are between Morocco and the United States at the time. As you know, relations between the countries seem to fluctuate from year to year."

Dale pursed his lips as he thought. "I agree, Captain, that it seems we have neglected Orne far too long. Something should be done. Some effort should be made. I'm just not sure that we're the ones who should do it."

Chapter 56
The *Trenton*, Mediterranean Sea, Approaching Gibraltar

Proctor sensed that Dale was torn between his conscience and his desire to bring his squadron home safely without incident. The very fact that Dale was torn meant that he could go either way. This was not the time for Proctor to back off.

"Would it not be worth it, sir, to at least give it a try? Think how good it would feel to return to America having freed a man who's been kept in captivity for so many years by the predatory Moroccans. It would be a boost for our country and justice for a man who served his country well in the past."

"I know what you're doing, Proctor, and it won't work. You want me to change our destination based on sentimental appeals."

"But sir, aren't many of our decisions based on the feelings we have for others?"

"Maybe they are for you, Proctor," said Dale scornfully, "but for me, decisions are based on facts and logic—not to mention following the orders of my superiors." After a brief pause he added sardonically, "Something you might think about." After another pause he added, "However—"

An agitated Proctor interrupted, "Then you're saying you have no interest in freeing an American citizen who's been kept prisoner for 17 years? He doesn't matter?"

"I did not say that. You have a nasty habit of interrupting, Proctor. What I'm saying, if you'd take the time to listen, is I'm willing to make a brief stopover in Rabat in order to ascertain Orne's condition. For God's sake, Captain, we don't even know if the man's alive. If he is alive, we don't know if he wants to leave Morocco. If, as you say, he's an advisor to the sultan, he may be treated very handsomely. He may not want to leave."

"I suppose it's possible, sir, but knowing Captain Orne I'm fairly certainly he'll want to leave. If he's happy there, at least we will have given him the opportunity to come home. However, it's very likely he'll jump at the chance to get back to Boston. I gather from what you just said that you're at least willing to give him the chance?"

"We'll inquire, but we're not going to go to war over the man. If the sultan is willing to let him go, we'll take him home. Seems rather unlikely to me, but we'll at least inquire."

"Thank you, sir. I think the show of force in their harbor might add weight to our inquiries, don't you, sir?"

Dale forced a smile. "I suspect such a show of force might help. Mind you, though, it will only be a show." After a momentary pause, Dale continued. "It will be a while, though, Captain, as there's no telling how long we'll be tied up in Gibraltar. These Brits are not easy to deal with, and it's hard to predict how long the repairs will take."

Chapter 57
Rabat, Morocco, Late 1801

It was his daily meeting with the sultan. The routine had not varied in 17 years. As was proper, Orne waited for the sultan to open the conversation. The wait was always a bit awkward for Orne, but he'd gradually accepted it as part of his life in Morocco serving the sultan. The sultan had grown noticeably grayer and considerably slower of movement over the past 17 years, but his mind was still quick and incisive. This observation made Orne aware of how he himself had changed during the years of service to the monarch. He was now approaching 60, and he felt every year of it. He'd long ago given up any hope of ever getting back to his wife and children in Boston. Fortunately, his crew had been able to escape, and he was happy about that. He would love to know how many of them were getting along.

Orne supposed that he was fortunate that at least his servitude in Morocco had not been as a slave laborer. True, in a very real sense he was a slave, in that he received no compensation for his efforts, but he was treated far better than most slaves. He had his own small, but private apartment, and he was provided with clothing and virtually any food that he wanted. Years ago he'd concluded that Moroccan food was fairly good once you got used to it. Different, but good. He could move about Rabat as he wished, though he sensed that the sultan had men keeping an eye on him most of the time when he was away from the palace.

The sultan smiled. In his own way, the sultan was capable of empathy. He could see things the way others saw them. His frame of reference was, of course, North African and Islamic. He was not a cruel man by the standards of his culture, though he could be harsh—even cruel by the standards of Europe and America. Still, he was capable of leniency and forgiveness. Orne often wondered if this leniency depended on the sultan's mood or on any doubts he might have had about Islam. He was not sure.

The smile was still there as the sultan spoke. "You are looking thoughtful this morning, Henry. Does something concern you?"

JIHAD AT SEA

"I was out in the streets earlier this morning, and as I was passing two men were having a conversation. I heard one of them say that there is a fleet of American warships approaching Rabat. Apparently they're coming from the east so they could be the same ships that have been blockading Tripoli this summer. They must be on their way back to the United States."

"Yet you say they are approaching Rabat?"

"Yes, your excellency, though it may mean nothing. I doubt that we have any reason for concern here in Morocco."

"But you don't know that, do you?"

"No, I don't. I suppose they *could* be visiting Rabat, though I can't imagine why."

"Of course you can," snapped the sultan impatiently. "Our corsairs continue to attack America's merchant vessels. America has not paid tribute to Morocco for years now. The ingrates. After we were the first nation to recognize the United States as an independent nation, they treat us like this. What could they expect? Now, instead of paying us a modest tribute, they wish to confront us with their warships. Do we have any idea how many?"

"Five or six according to the men on the street, though I don't think we should count on that. Who knows where they got their information? Could be fewer—could be more. For all I know, your excellency, all of this could be a wild rumor."

"There's always some truth to rumors. I will send some men out beyond the harbor on reconnaissance. In the meantime we must alert the navy and the army. If there is truth to this rumor, we must be prepared."

"Yes, of course, your excellency. We should be prepared for whatever the Americans have in mind."

Orne had never been so torn. After serving the sultan for 17 years and after being treated like a member of the sultan's inner circle, he felt a certain allegiance to the man—something he never would have imagined 17 years ago. Still, if the approaching U.S. fleet offered even the smallest chance at winning his freedom, he was not going to do anything to harm the Americans. The next 24 hours were going to be perilous indeed.

Chapter 58
The *Trenton*, Mediterranean Sea, Approaching Rabat

Commodore Dale beckoned for his first mate. "Perry, get yourself up here."

Perry appeared out of nowhere. "Yes, Commodore?"

"Get Captain Proctor over here. I need to talk to him."

Minutes later Proctor approached his commander. "Yes, Commodore, you wanted to see me?"

"I do. We're near Rabat now. Four or five miles at the most. We need a strategy if we're going to get Orne out of there. You said before that you'd come up with something. I assume you've done that or you wouldn't have talked me into this in the first place?"

"Yessir. Given a lot of thought to it. If you agree I'd like to see us line our ships up in the outer harbor, much as we did in Tripoli. No need to fire any guns, but the message should be clear."

"And that message is?"

"That we're not to be trifled with."

"Maybe so, but won't that be a bit provocative?"

"It may be, sir, but one thing I'm sure of is that we'll get their attention. If we anchor the squadron out of sight of the inner harbor, who's going to pay attention to anyone we send in to talk?"

"We don't know how receptive they'll be, Proctor. It'll probably depend on the current relations with our government."

"The last thing I remember, sir, is that the sultan reneged on the agreement we had when we paid them their tribute. The understanding was that the entire crew would be released upon payment, and as you know, that didn't happen. They kept Captain Orne."

"True, but that was a long time ago. We don't know what the current status is. A lot could have happened in the last 17 years. I know we paid them additional tributes for several years after you and your crew were freed, but whether that's continued or not, we don't know. We simply don't know how things are as of this moment."

"No, sir, we don't. There's only one way to find out. We send someone in to negotiate."

"We don't have the authority to negotiate with foreign governments, Proctor. We inquire. That's all we do. We have a simple conversation."

Proctor was not happy with this arrangement, but it was better than nothing. "Yessir. We inquire and talk. But if that's all we do, we don't have much to bargain with."

"Let's hope that the sultan or his authorities are able to see that allowing Captain Orne to return to his own country is the decent thing to do."

Proctor struggled to hide his disbelief. After taking a deep breath he said, "We view it that way, sir, but I doubt if the Moroccans do. I'm sure they can come up with a good reason why Captain Orne has been kept in the sultan's service. Dear Lord, sir, they probably think Orne considers it a great honor to serve the sultan."

Dale sneered. "I rather doubt, Proctor, that the high-ranking officials in Morocco are that credulous. They probably don't care what Orne thinks. They care only what the sultan thinks. I'm quite certain that they believe that the sultan gets what he wants."

"That may be true, sir, but they treat their sultan like a god. Any Moroccan would do anything to curry favor with the sultan. Since they consider nonbelievers inferior to Muslims, they could easily imagine an infidel being in awe of the very opportunity to serve the sultan."

"I suppose we shall see soon enough who's right about this. The important thing is to make the effort. Who do you propose that we send into Rabat to meet with the sultan or his minions?" He smiled. "As if I couldn't guess what your answer will be."

Proctor grinned back. "Of course you're right, sir. I think I'm the logical person to go in. I know Orne, I speak a little Arabic, and I know my way around Rabat. Or at least the part of Rabat near the palace."

"All right then. You can be the emissary, but I want you to take someone with you."

"Is that necessary, Commodore? I can do this myself."

"Yes, it's necessary. A two-person delegation should command more respect than a single individual."

"Do you have someone in mind, sir?"

"Yes, I think I should accompany you. If we're going to get your friend out of there we don't want to insult the sultan by not sending in the highest-ranking officer in our squadron."

Proctor's first reaction was disappointment. He and the commodore had never gotten along. How could they work as an effective team now? He looked at Dale, fearing that his disappointment was written on his face for the commodore to see. The commodore said nothing during this extended pause. Then it hit Proctor that maybe this was not such a bad idea. As he thought about it, it made sense. One thing he knew was that the sultan and all men wielding power in Morocco had a high opinion of their importance. One could easily offend them, and to show their importance they would not hesitate to punish you for the least little slight. If the commodore remained on his ship instead of meeting personally with the monarch, the sultan would be insulted and it would be more than a minor insult. The already slim chance of getting Orne out of Morocco would become zero.

"Yessir, it makes sense. The sultan would expect you to make the effort. He would be insulted if you didn't. I do have one concern though. If the sultan is in a particularly ugly mood there is no predicting what he might do. Who knows, he might take you captive, thinking he can command a generous blackmail from the United States."

"That's a chance we'll have to take. Pray to God it doesn't come to that." Ironic, thought Dale, that he would not only be willing to take this risk, but actually eager. He'd had a rich and colorful naval career, but had never met a monarch. The chance to meet with the sultan appealed to him. It could round out his career nicely when he got home. Especially if he could claim that he had persuaded the sultan to free an American long held in captivity. The irony was that, until now his only desire had been to get back to America and put in for a well-deserved retirement.

Proctor revised his opinion of Dale. The man was willing to take risks, risks that he didn't have to take. "Then I assume we'll take a dory in as soon as the ships are in place?"

"As soon as I've met with the other captains and given them their instructions for what they should do in my absence. More importantly, I want them to fire a warning shot into Rabat harbor if we haven't returned in 48 hours. If after another four hours we still haven't returned I want them to send a few broadsides at the ships in the harbor. Continue until we do return. We will not let these Moroccans treat us with disrespect."

Proctor was pleasantly surprised at the commodore's change of heart. Maybe there was still hope.

Chapter 59
Rabat, Morocco 1801

"Good God, Proctor, these people live in hovels," exclaimed Dale as he and Proctor made their way cautiously through the dusty streets of the Moroccan capital. "This has to be the most indigent place I've seen in all my travels."

"It's like this everywhere in North Africa, sir. World of difference from Europe and America. I used to think Spain, France and Italy were poor until I saw Morocco."

As they wended their way through the narrow, winding streets, Dale became aware of the stares of curiosity, bewilderment, and even fear. "They're looking at us like we are the strangest things they've ever seen."

"They don't get many visitors here. When they do, they're usually men who've been taken captive and are treated as subhuman slaves. They look with curiosity and suspicion at anyone who's different."

"The timid ones just stare," said Dale, "but the bold ones have their hands out."

"As I said, they see so few non-Moroccans, that they're not sure how to react to us."

"These poor buggers—look at their clothes. Most of them are moth-eaten rags. How do they survive?"

"From day to day, I suppose. You see how they live. Most of these places don't even have doors. Notice that a lot of these beggars are children."

"Who gives money to these mendicants? Everyone seems so poor I can't imagine them having enough money to share it with others."

"A few merchants and shopkeepers do better than the man on the street, but not many."

As they continued on, Proctor had the feeling that things were not going to go well for them. Their grim surroundings predisposed the normally optimistic Proctor toward a very pessimistic view of what they could expect in their immediate future.

Then, up ahead, they saw it. The palace. Clearly the grandest structure they'd seen. Definitely the grandest in the entire city. They slowed their approach now, taking in everything they could.

"I see the entrance is well guarded," said Dale. "Men with scimitars. We shall have to get by them if we want to see the sultan."

"Let's see what my limited Arabic gets us."

As they ascended the steep flight of steps leading up to the palace entrance, Proctor was well aware that the eyes of the guards were upon them. When they finally reached the top he approached a guard to the right of the large double doors.

"We wish to speak with the sultan," he said in Arabic.

"What business do you have with His Majesty?"

"We represent the United States government on official business."

"What business?"

"We are only permitted to discuss our business with His Majesty."

The guard considered this for a moment, then said, "You may enter."

Inside Proctor noticed that it was much cooler and much darker than outside. He and Dale stood for a while in order to adjust to the reduced light. Gradually they made out the stark figures of two more guards, one on each side of the large room. One of the guards approached and said, "What business do you have in the palace?"

"We would speak with the sultan," said Proctor in his limited Arabic. "We represent the United States government on official business."

"What business do you have?"

"We are under orders to speak only with the sultan."

"I must know the nature of your business to know if it is of concern to the sultan."

"I repeat, we are only permitted to speak of our business with the sultan. Surely you must be aware that a squadron of American and Swedish ships is at anchor in your outer harbor. If we leave without speaking with the sultan, you will have to explain to the sultan why you turned us away."

The guard looked across the room at his fellow guard, who nodded his 'go ahead'. Then he said, "Proceed, but do not speak until spoken to." After a brief hesitation he added under his breath, "I don't think you will be welcome."

Chapter 60
Sultan's Palace, Rabat, Morocco

As they entered the throne room Dale and Proctor noted that the sultan was not alone. Two attendants were hovering obsequiously around the seated monarch, clearly deferential as they bowed repeatedly. When the sultan saw the two Americans, he waved the two servants away. Dale was shocked at how quickly they scurried away and exited through a door just to the left of the throne. The throne, itself, was not as grand or elaborately adorned as he expected it to be. Rather it appeared to be nothing more than a large, carved wooden chair. The contrast between the simplicity of the throne and the hovering servants was fascinating. The sultan appeared to be a man of simple tastes who demanded constant attention.

The sultan waved them closer. As they made their way toward the throne, Proctor saw that he appeared to be in his early forties. He wore a neatly trimmed beard and mustache and was garbed in a white robe-like garment that Proctor recalled was known as a *dishdasha*. His head was wrapped with a white scarf called a *keffiyeh*.

As they drew within twenty feet of the monarch, a man materialized from the same door through which the two servants had just exited. The man appeared to be about the same age as the sultan. He, too, was wearing a white *dishdasha* and *keffiyeh*. He studied them for a minute, then said in a halting English, "I am Hussein, chief counselor to the sultan. So you represent the United States government?"

"Yes sir," said Dale, "we do."

"I understand that you cannot speak your business with anyone but His Majesty?"

"That is also true, sir."

"Then let me introduce you to the sultan. Do you understand that you do not speak until the sultan has spoken?"

"Yessir," said Dale and Proctor in unison.

Hussein then announced, "His Majesty, Sultan Suleiman of

JIHAD AT SEA

Morocco."

The sultan waved them closer. As they stood, not 12 feet from the monarch, Suleiman rested his chin between his thumb and forefinger as if pondering how to handle his two visitors. "What are your names and what is your business here?" Proctor was surprised to hear the sultan speaking in accented, but decent English.

Proctor glanced at Dale, who nodded. Proctor then said, "I am Captain Will Proctor and this is Richard Dale, Commodore of the United States Navy." He took a deep breath and continued, "We are here to see our friend, Captain Orne."

"Your friend Captain Orne exists no longer." The sultan smiled as he said this. Proctor swallowed hard and felt his heart skip a beat.

"He is dead? When did he pass away?" asked Dale.

"I did not say he was no longer among us," explained the sultan. "I said he longer exists as Captain Orne. He is now called Advisor to the Sultan. He has been called that for more than 17 years. My father, the great Mohammed III, gave him that designation when he was sultan. My brother, Yazid, kept him on when he was sultan, and I continue to benefit from Advisor Orne's services to this very day. Why do you wish to see him after all these years? No one from your little country has even made the effort until you two."

Proctor said, "I don't know why others have failed to make the effort. I find that surprising. Disappointing. Perhaps it has something to do with the rather tense relations between your country and mine. You did, after all, allow the attack on the merchant ship *Betsey*. You released her crew only after exacting a payment, but you still retain Captain Orne. Your ships continue to harass our merchant vessels. You have made no attempt to make peace with my country."

"Any tension between our countries has been caused by the United States and its unwillingness to cooperate with our requests. Requests that other states have willingly complied with."

Dale then said, "We are not here to negotiate treaties between the two countries. We wish Morocco no harm. We simply wish to meet with our friend to see if he would like to return to America after all these years."

The sultan pursed his lips, as if trying not to laugh. "You wish us no harm. It is difficult to believe you when my aides tell me that you have amassed a great number of warships outside our harbor."

"Our ships have been in the Mediterranean for much of the summer in an attempt to persuade Tripoli and its corsairs not to lay siege on our merchant ships," said Dale. "We are now on our return trip to America. It seemed a good opportunity to see Capt— er

Advisor Orne. If he wishes to return with us, we will be pleased to supply him with transportation."

The sultan squinted and placed his chin once again between his thumb and forefinger as he considered Dale's words. "Assume for the moment that your friend does not wish to return to America, or that we do not want him to return to your little country because he is too valuable to us here to part with him. What will you do then? Will you accept that and return home without him? Or will you use the fire power of your great fleet to extricate him and inflict great pain and suffering here in Rabat in the process?"

"Let us hope that it does not come to the use of force, Your Majesty. We will never forget that your great country was the first to recognize our newly liberated nation. We would prefer to have these discussions peacefully."

"As would I, Commodore, as would I. Those are encouraging words you have just spoken, but you will forgive my directness when I say that I didn't hear you assure me that you wouldn't resort to force under any circumstances."

"We would only resort to force if we were forced to defend ourselves or protect our ships or our merchant vessels."

"Hmm. I suppose I can understand such thinking even though I don't like it. Let me tell you why I find it hard to believe you. For centuries we have waged what we call *jihad at sea*. It is what you call piracy. It has served two purposes. For one thing it has provided revenue for a poor country that does not manufacture or produce goods that can be sold in other lands. Second, it has prevented the advance of the infidels' degenerate culture. Your culture, Commodore Dale.

"For centuries Europeans have claimed that they wanted to trade with us. We know that trade is their way of bringing their impure, corrupting influence to North African peoples. We wage *jihad at sea* to prevent this. Morocco and other countries in North Africa have been forced to resort to aggressive measures against nonbelievers like yourselves and the Europeans who have shown us little or no respect and treated us badly. Needless to say we do not forget the vicious Crusades Europeans waged against Arab and Muslim states centuries ago. We are convinced that nonbelievers are not now our friends and never have been our friends. If you were truly our friends you would become believers. When you say you come in peace you'll understand why I find it difficult to take you seriously."

JIHAD AT SEA

Chapter 61
Sultan's Palace, Rabat, Morocco 1801

Proctor tried not to let his face show his disappointment. The situation was deteriorating rapidly. He had to do something or their efforts would end in total failure.

With a feeling of desperation he said, "Your Majesty, it is true that during the Crusades Muslim people suffered greatly. That was many hundreds of years ago. European and American thinking and culture have changed over those centuries.

"As for what you call the corrupting influence of Americans and Europeans, it is true that many of our values are different from yours. I can assure you though, that if we could trade with you it would not be to change the way you go about your lives; it would be to exchange goods so that both cultures gain material benefit. Hopefully it would help your people as much as it would ours."

The sultan appeared to be in deep thought. A tense pause went on uncomfortably long. Finally, he said, "You Americans say good things, and I would like to believe you. At least you make some effort. Most Europeans seem willing to accept things as they are. No doubt because it is easier for them to do things as they always have in the past. For a number of years I have wondered what it would be like if we abandoned *jihad at sea* and engaged in trade with the Europeans. You'll forgive me if I didn't include you Americans. Frankly, until recently, you weren't worth mentioning. Anyway, as I said, I've been considering trying a new way to bring goods into Morocco."

"What's holding you back, Your Highness?" Asked Proctor boldly. Dale winced at this overly frank question.

"I have already told you," snapped the sultan. "I do not trust

Europeans or Americans. As much as I see the advantages of open trade, I still fear the corrupting influence of nonbelievers." Then he added, "And since we are being honest with each other, I will admit that I fear open trade because my country does not have much to trade. We do not manufacture things. We grow fruits and vegetables, barely enough for our own people. We raise sheep, goats and poultry. Again, barely enough for our own people. So you see, as attractive as open trade may appear to you, it would be of limited value to us."

"Would it not be worth a try?" ventured Dale. "You might be surprised at how many goods your people would produce if they saw profit in it."

The sultan offered a rare smile. "Who knows, Commodore, you might be right. I am, I suppose, prisoner of my own isolated culture. I know nothing of trade. Nearly all of our treasure has come via aljhad fi albahr or *jihad at sea* as it is in English. I must admit, your arrival today has forced me to think in ways that I have not thought in the past. I do not get such ideas from my own people. They do not venture to give their sultan suggestions."

"Not even from Orne?" asked Proctor.

The sultan smile again. "With the exception of Advisor Orne. He never ceases in his efforts to convince me that we should at least give trade a try. He gave my father many good ideas and he continues to this day to be a fount of ideas. Some, of course, I cannot implement either because of lack of funds or the danger of giving the masses ideas that could be troublesome. It is not easy to sit on the Moroccan throne. Oh, I know you must find that hard to believe, for I have much power and wealth. Yet you must also be aware of how over the years many sultans have been overthrown, even put to death. The man who sits on the Moroccan throne is never completely secure."

"Since I gather Advisor Orne has served the throne well over the past 17 years would it not be only fair to give him the opportunity to return to America to his family as a reward for his years of service? Perhaps he is happy here, but shouldn't he at least have the chance to decide after all these years of service to you and your predecessors?"

"I'm inclined to agree with you Captain Proctor, but I cannot allow this without a *quid pro quo*."

"Isn't 17 years of loyal service a reasonable *quid pro quo*?"

"I'm sure it is according to your American sense of values. However, you must understand that here in Morocco it would be considered a sign of weakness if I were to let Advisor Orne return to

America. My people would wonder why I would allow him to leave without getting something in return. I just reminded you of the vulnerability of the monarchy if the monarch shows the least bit of weakness. I have already explained that I'm inclined to believe that Advisor Orne has earned his freedom, but in order to make that happen I will need something from you or your country."

Chapter 62
Sultan's Palace, Rabat, Morocco

Dale had dreaded getting involved in horse trading. He was not a diplomat, he was a naval officer used to functioning within a chain of command. Besides, he was not authorized to negotiate with foreign leaders. Yet he couldn't walk away without at least some effort to bring back an American who'd been held captive for far too many years.

"We would like to see Captain Orne before we discuss an exchange. I'm sure you understand."

"I do understand, Commodore. I will have Hussein take you to his quarters where you may see for yourself that your friend is healthy and in good spirits. Then let us talk if there is reason to talk."

Suleiman snapped his fingers and one of the guards flanking the doors at the far end of the room came forward. The sultan said, "Bring Hussein here. I want to talk to him."

Minutes later Hussein appeared, bowing before the monarch. "Yes, Your Majesty. How may I be of service?"

"I want you to take Commodore Dale and Captain Proctor to Advisor Orne. Give them some time to talk. Then bring all three back to me. Do you have any questions?"

"No, Your Majesty. I understand." He then turned to the visitors and motioned for them to follow him.

The counselor led them out of the palace and into the streets. Soon they were on the street immediately behind the palace. The street was lined with modest two-story adobe structures. Hussein went up to the door of the third building from the corner and knocked loudly. It was only seconds before the door opened and Proctor got the surprise of his life.

"What is it, Hussein? It must be important for you to come to my quarters to summon me." Obviously Orne had not yet seen the other two visitors. But they saw him and were taken aback by what they saw. Proctor's former superior on the *Betsey* was garbed in a white *dishdasha*, much like most men Proctor had seen in Morocco. He

JIHAD AT SEA

knew that Orne was in service to the sultan, but it had never occurred to him that he would dress like a Moroccan.

"His Majesty would like you to speak with these two Americans."

Hussein stepped aside and Dale and Proctor came forward.

At first Orne did not recognize Proctor. Then, suddenly, it hit him. "Proctor! Will! My God it's good to see you. I'm sorry, I don't know your friend."

"Commodore Richard Dale of the U.S. Navy."

"Come in, come in. Please forgive me. The room is small, but you can find a seat." Then he looked at Hussein. "Counselor, do you want to come in, too?"

"Thank you. I will wait outside. I will give you a few minutes."

"Then we'd better get to it," Orne said as he closed the door. "My God, gentlemen. It's so good to see the face of Americans. Especially my good friend and former first mate on the *Betsey*. What brings you here?"

Proctor spoke first. "We have just returned from Tripoli where the commodore commanded a squadron of ships in a blockade of Tripoli harbor. We're now en route back to the United States, and we couldn't sail past Morocco without stopping in to see you. Hopefully to take you back to Boston."

Orne looked confused. "Take me back now? The U.S. has had 17 years to try to take me back. You're the first ones to actually make the effort. After all these years I've become comfortable here. I've been accepted, and have the respect not only of Sultan Suleiman, but most of the people here in Morocco."

"Are you saying you don't want to return?" asked Dale, incredulously.

"I honestly don't know. I gave up hope long ago and gradually accepted my life here. Strange isn't it? Now that I actually have the opportunity to return home, I'm not sure I want to. For a number of years I thought about my wife and children all the time. Gradually, though, I convinced myself that they would find a life for themselves and no longer need me. I had to think this way or I would have gone mad. You understand, don't you?"

"I suppose," said Proctor half-heartedly. "Look, Captain, I don't think we have much more time. You have to decide if you want to return. Even if you do, it's not certain that the sultan will let you go, but he said he'd be willing to talk about it."

"I've become a Muslim, you know."

Dale and Proctor were dumbstruck. "No, of course we didn't

know, Captain," said Dale numbly.

"Are you sure America will want me now?"

"I don't know, Captain," said Proctor, who felt as if the wind had been knocked out of him. Back home Muslims were people in strange, far-off lands. "I'm sure your wife and children will."

"I need to think about this. I hope the sultan will give me a little time. I hope you will, too."

Dale cleared his throat. He wanted to sound authoritative and commanding with his next statement. "I have a squadron that must be on its way no later than tomorrow. We'll need your decision today, Captain."

"What if the sultan says no?"

"Will that matter to you?" asked Proctor impatiently. "You don't seem eager to leave anyway. You don't seem like the commanding officer I respected 17 years ago."

Orne was obviously flustered, wrestling with his thoughts. After a few seconds he said, "I understand how it may seem, Will. It's just that, since I've been advisor to the sultan, I've found myself obeying orders, not giving them. Perhaps I have changed."

"If you go home, you can change again, sir."

"I still do think about my wife and children, who are no longer children. I might not even recognize them. Yes, I want to go back to Boston." As he considered what he'd said, the light in his eyes went dark and he frowned.

"If the sultan denies me this freedom and I remain here, I fear he will no longer treat me as well as he has up to now."

Proctor said, "He had to know from the beginning that you were being held against your wishes. Obviously it didn't bother him or he would have let you go free long ago."

"It was his father, Mohammed the third, who prevented my leaving 17 years ago. He was a hard man, but he could be charming when he wanted to. He had little concern for the feelings of others. His only concern was for his own security and comfort. I think security was uppermost in his mind. The Moroccan throne is and always has been precarious. When he died Suleiman's brother Yazid became sultan for two years. He was very much like his father. As long as I served him to his satisfaction, he cared little for my comfort or desires.

"Suleiman is somewhat different. While he does not think like Americans or Europeans, he is curious. He understands that his servants serve him better when they are well treated. He inherited me from Yazid and his father. As far as Suleiman's concerned, I'm a Moroccan who's always been in the royal court for the convenience of the sultans. If suddenly he thinks I've become ungrateful, how will he treat me in the future?"

Dale said, "We have just been with the sultan. He seems a reasonable man. I think you may be underestimating his ability to understand your situation. If you truly wish to return to your family, I think you should take the risk and request his permission. He will not release you if you don't ask for it. If you don't ask, you will remain in Morocco the rest of your life."

"I will ask."

Chapter 63
Orne's Quarters, Rabat, Morocco 1801

"I will ask, but first tell me what you can about America. I have been out of touch all these years. If the sultan does not grant my request for freedom, I may never have the chance to catch up on my homeland. Will, have you seen my wife and children?"

Proctor smiled. He was encouraged by Orne's show of interest. "I last saw them in the spring of this year. When I knew that I would have the honor of commanding a ship in Commodore Dale's squadron, I hoped that we might be able to visit Rabat to look into your wellbeing. Hence our being here now. Your dear wife Martha has made a life for herself and the children, though it is not an easy one, and she pines for you daily. She takes in sewing and laundry, which gives her some income. The children are now young adults. Your boy, James, has apprenticed himself to a local printer. Your daughter Felicity teaches at a nearby school. Both James and Felicity live at home with their mother and their combined income keeps them marginally comfortable, but with little to spare." As he related this Orne's eyes lighted up. His family became alive to him.

"You have awakened me, Will. Now I am eager to return to my dear Martha and the children. Before we go to the sultan, tell me briefly how our new country is faring?"

Dale spoke up now. "The nation is surviving, but we are finding that in some ways independence is more difficult than colonial existence. The national government struggles for money. The individual states, unwilling to grant too much power to the national government, are reluctant to contribute to the national treasury. Many of our soldiers who fought valiantly in the war of independence have still not been paid. Foreign governments are unwilling to grant us credit for fear that we will not pay them back."

"It sounds grim," said Orne. "Was it all worthwhile?"

Dale smiled. "There is much to be thankful for, too. I did not intend to make it sound grim. We are struggling, but we are making progress. We are free and freedom does not come cheap. Don't forget, it is barely 18 years since the end of the war. We are a young country, but we make progress every day. You will see for yourself when you get to Boston. Yes, in my opinion, it was worthwhile."

"That is encouraging news. I suppose I am ready now to meet with His Majesty."

Proctor now said, "Before we go, tell me whatever happened to Captain Habib, the source of all our troubles?"

Orne scowled. "I'm not surprised that you ask. His evil was rewarded by being inducted into the Moroccan navy. Mohammed III, Suleiman's father, and the sultan at the time, made him a commander in his navy in recognition of his capture of the *Betsey*. He is now second in command of the navy and just as dangerous as he ever was."

"Do you come in contact with him now in his capacity as a naval commander?"

"Unfortunately I do all too much. It is difficult for me because I cannot show my true feelings in the presence of Suleiman, who sees only his competence as a naval officer. As far as I know, Suleiman has no awareness of the brutality Habib inflicted or sanctioned when he was a corsair."

"Even as a naval commander," said Dale, "doesn't he still command ships to capture foreign merchant ships?"

"Yes, of course, but no one dares tell Suleiman of the brutal and often homicidal measure his commander takes when out at sea. Sixteen years ago, under Mohammed III, he would have been praised for such treatment. Suleiman, however, does not endorse such measures. Right now Habib is the favorite of Suleiman because the man is brilliant at depicting himself in a way that appeals to the sultan's sensitivities. Habib has many detractors, but they dare not talk against him. I cannot talk against him because the sultan loves him."

"I don't know how you stand it," said Proctor. "If I were in your shoes, I'd want to kill him."

"Don't think the thought hasn't occurred to me."

"I hope I don't see him while I'm here. I don't know what I'd do."

Chapter 64
Sultan's Palace, Rabat, Morocco

There was a loud knock on the door.
Orne opened it cautiously. When he saw the counselor he said, "Yes, Hussein, is it time for us to go?"

"I think His Majesty expects you. We should go to the palace."

"Yes, of course. Just one minute." Then Orne turned to his guests and said, "I suppose we should go. I never thought this moment would come. I shall say a little prayer."

"To the Muslim god or the Christian one?" asked Dale impertinently and regretting it as soon as he said it. "Sorry, that was not fair."

"Don't apologize. It's a reasonable question under the circumstances. I guess my answer is that there's only one God. Just between us I was never very religious back in America and I'm not now, though I keep that to myself here. I suppose some may say it was cowardly that I converted to Islam in the first place. Maybe it was. I know that if I hadn't, I wouldn't have survived long."

As they entered the relative coolness of the palace, Proctor heard Orne take a deep breath in preparation for what lay ahead. Hussein entered the throne room and announced the three visitors. Then he withdrew through a side door.

The sultan put down a quill that he had been writing with and looked up at his visitors. "Ah, Commodore Dale and Captain Proctor. I see that you have returned with my trusted advisor Henry. Henry, I believe your friends have discussed with you your status here at the palace."

"Yes, Your Majesty, they have."

"Have you made a decision?"

Orne pursued his lips and drew in another deep breath. "Yes,

Your Majesty. I have. I believe it is time for me to go back to my family. I make this decision with a heavy heart as I have grown to admire and respect you. I have come to love much about Morocco."

A smile devoid of any warmth transfused the sultan's face. "Come, now Henry. I have come to respect your honesty and frankness, a frankness lacking in most of my palace staff. Why do you spoil it all now with such nonsense? Admit it, you have tolerated me and tolerated Morocco, as you felt you had little alternative if you were to survive."

"Your Majesty, what I have just said is the truth. Let the Great Allah strike me down if it is not. I admit that when I was first forced to remain here in service to your father, I resented it. For many years it was hard for me serving him and serving your brother later on. When you took the throne I assumed things would not change, but that has not been the case. You have worked to improve the lot of your fellow Moroccans. You have treated me with respect. You are trying to bring Morocco into the modern world. Under you I have practically forgotten my desire to return to America, because my life here has meaning. It has been a privilege to serve you. We have not agreed on everything, but I have always considered you a man of good moral character."

"Then why do you now wish to return to America?"

"My family, Your Majesty. My family. I have not seen them in years. I hope that you will release me from my duties."

"Very well. You have served me and Morocco honorably and effectively. I will release you if your friends here or your government give me something so that my staff and the prominent families of Morocco do not see their monarch as weak. It cannot appear that I have been outmaneuvered by American unbelievers. It would be my undoing."

"What do you want, Your Majesty?" asked Dale cautiously.

"You could leave another educated man to serve as my advisor" He saw the resistance in their eyes and added, "He would only serve until the next time your navy sends ships to this region. It would be at least a year, though."

"There must be something else that would satisfy you, Your Majesty?"

"Then leave me a ship. My navy is small. We could use a well-equipped warship."

Dale frowned and closed his eyes in deep thought. It wouldn't be easy to explain to the navy department the giving away of an expensive warship. How would this affect his standing as a high-level officer? How would it affect his retirement? Proctor said nothing, but could imagine what his superior officer must be thinking. It was not an easy thing to decide, especially for a man like Dale who considered diplomacy and negotiation something that others did. Then Dale opened his eyes and made eye contact with Suleiman.

"Your Majesty, might we have a few hours to consider this? There is much to think about."

"Is your friend not worth such an exchange? I thought you Americans valued life above all else?"

"We do, Your Majesty, but since it is such a major decision, we must be sure it is the right decision. We must do what our government in America would approve of. I am not certain they would approve of the choices you have given us."

"I will give you three hours. You may deliberate in Henry's quarters. I expect to see the three of you again at the end of three hours. If you cannot agree on something, I'm afraid Henry will continue to be of service to me."

Chapter **65**
Orne's Quarters, Rabat, Morocco   1801

"I will not allow another man to be held here in exchange for me," said Orne forcefully. "I could never live with myself."

Dale said, "What if a man were to volunteer? What if someone welcomes the adventure, the challenge?"

"Respectfully, sir, I don't think the U.S. government or the American people would welcome such an exchange, even if a man did volunteer. Do we want it known that an American sailor voluntarily chose to help a despot like the Sultan of Morocco?"

"No, I suppose not. Then that leaves us with giving up a ship or saying no to the sultan and you, Captain Orne, remaining here in Morocco."

"We can't really consider the latter option as a choice, sir," said Proctor. "We must get Captain Orne home."

Orne spoke up. "If it puts you, one of your men or the interests of the navy in jeopardy, I'll understand if you have to leave me. I'm accustomed to things here. I'll survive."

Dale took on a doleful look. A tense moment passed before he spoke. "We will not leave you here, no matter what the cost. We will give them a ship. I'll deal with the admiralty when we return. It may cost me my rank, but It'll be worth it if we get you out of this hell hole." Proctor was surprised, but pleased to see the change in Dale's view of the matter. After all, the commodore hadn't even wanted to stop in Rabat in the first place. Clearly, faced with Orne's bleak situation, the humanitarian side of Dale came to the fore.

The sultan leaned back in his throne as the three Americans, followed by Hussein, entered the throne room. The sultan frowned as he considered what he was going to say. The suspense for the

Americans was building. Was the sultan going to go back on his word? Was he going to demand more than he'd agreed to? He had seemed gracious in his willingness to release Orne from his servitude, but was that all a façade? Was he really angered that his valuable servant wanted to leave him? All of these thoughts crossed the minds of the three Americans as they stood there waiting for the sovereign to speak.

"Have you decided on what you will give me if Henry returns to America?"

Then Dale surprised and shocked everyone by his next words. "I'm not so sure we need to give you anything, Your Majesty. I'm certain that you are well aware that we have a large squadron of powerful warships just outside your harbor. What's to stop us from simply walking out of here?" Proctor couldn't believe it. Could his commodore really have said that?

Suleiman scowled. "I'm disappointed in you, Commodore. I thought we had an agreement. I had hoped that the three of you were an exception to what we in Morocco have long believed. I had hoped that you were three nonbelievers that could be trusted. Apparently that isn't so. Apparently you are like all the others."

Chapter 66
Sultan's Palace, Rabat, Morocco 1801

All Proctor could think was that Dale's willingness to put everyone at risk appeared to have no bounds.

In response to the sultan's comments, Dale put his chin forward belligerently and said, "It is you Moroccans who can't be trusted. You're the ones who took our innocent merchant seamen into captivity. You're the one who's held Captain Orne prisoner for 17 years. Does that not give us the right to use whatever force we have at our disposal? We did not come here to be aggressive. We do not want war with Morocco. All we want is Captain Orne. Instead of willingly releasing him in accordance with all standards of decency, you make demands that further insult the United States. Do you have no shame?"

Proctor shook his head in disbelief at Dale's provocative words. There was no way they were going to get out of Morocco alive.

Surprisingly, Suleiman did not raise his voice in response to Dale's taunting. "Commodore Dale, I explained to you why I am making these demands. In my country a sultan does not make concessions to foreigners, especially infidels, without gaining something in return. If I were to do that my people would believe me unfit to be their sovereign. I cannot afford to take that risk. I understand that you may see it differently, but here in Morocco that is the reality."

"Your demands could be far more reasonable. You could ask for goods. We have a large cargo of cheese aboard. We have excellent French wine."

Suleiman sneered. "We do not drink alcohol in Morocco as do people in degenerate cultures."

Proctor glared at the commodore. Dale was adding salt to an already festering wound, and the sultan was throwing it right back at him. Unfortunately, the sultan held all the cards.

"All right, but you know what I mean. We could give you

something of value that would help you save face, but it shouldn't be a ship, for God's sake." Proctor winced at Dale's comeback.

"I am sorry Commodore, but I must stick to our agreement. I ask only that you do the same."

"Have you forgotten the ships in your harbor," asked Dale threateningly.

"No, I have not, Commodore, but I don't fear them as much as you want me to."

"Then you are not as smart as I figured you to be." Proctor groaned. Could the man be more tactless or provocative? Was he trying to get us all killed?

The sultan maintained his cool demeanor. "No doubt your ships will inflict damage to some of my vessels at anchor in the harbor. I think, however, if you examine the harbor you'll see that your ships are too large to approach the interior. Furthermore, the interior is not deep enough for your large vessels. You can injure us, but you cannot defeat us. Do you wish to spend precious powder and precious time on such an assault that is almost certainly destined to end in frustration for you? I can assure you, Commodore, that at the end of such an assault I will not be of a mind to release Henry Orne."

Chapter 67
Sultan's Palace, Rabat, Morocco

Proctor was desperate. Dale did not like to be second-guessed by his subordinates, but the stakes were too high for Will to hold back now. Dale's erratic, unpredictable behavior was baffling. Bad enough that it was confusing to the officers and anyone he dealt with. It was much worse than that now. That unpredictable behavior of Dale could have grave consequences for his American crew mates.

Proctor asked the sultan if he could have a word with the commodore. Suleiman nodded, presumably because he thought such a side discussion might lead to a resolution of their disagreement. Proctor then took Dale aside and in a low voice said, "Sir, don't you think we'd better stick to our original agreement? If we don't, we could end up with nothing, and Captain Orne could be held here forever. I know it's not fair, but we're not in control here. I think it's the best we can do under the circumstances. Frankly, I'm surprised that Suleiman agreed to let Captain Orne go. Obviously, the captain was a valuable aide to the sultan. It will almost certainly take some time to replace him. Suleiman can't just grab a foreign seaman at random. Orne is better educated and far more worldly than most sailors. I'm sure the sultan knows that, so I'm shocked, but pleased, that he agreed to let him go, even if he has demanded something in return."

Dale looked defeated. "You realize, don't you, that it means the something we're giving up is a proud ship in the U.S. Navy?"

"I know, sir, but it will gain well-deserved freedom for the captain. A man's life has to mean more than a ship."

"It means that arrogant son-of-a-bitch Suleiman wins."

"I suppose it does, in the short run. I'm surprised, though, that he's willing to free Orne under any conditions. Obviously, his father and his brother never did. In any event, sir, I'm mindful that, as you've said a number of times in the past, it's not part of your mandate to make war on Morocco or even to negotiate peace. You were not sent here to act as a diplomat. For that matter, you were not sent here at all. I'm sure I don't have to remind you that I'm the one who persuaded you to come here."

Dale sneered. "I'm well aware of that, Proctor."

"In any event, sir, we're here. I think we'll be lucky to pull off what we've agreed to."

Dale pursed his lips as he considered what he had to do. It was not easy, as he was having trouble taking advice from the upstart Proctor. He forced himself to recognize that the advice was sound, but it was a bitter pill to swallow coming from someone like Proctor.

At this point, Proctor noticed that the sultan seemed to be getting impatient, so he said, "Sir, I think we need to give the sultan an answer."

"Very well," said Dale loud enough for Suleiman to hear him and not hiding his exasperation. "We shall exchange one of our vessels for the release of Captain Orne." Proctor breathed a sigh of relief. Until Dale actually spoke those words, Will wasn't at all sure that Dale would give up a ship, even if it meant freeing a prisoner. Clearly, the commodore was not authorized to trade a ship for a prisoner. Dale kept surprising him.

The sultan smiled and said, "I am glad to hear that, Commodore, and since you have come to your senses I will overlook your insults, for I am a man of my word."

Dale then said, "Then, Your Majesty, will you also give your word that you will not send Moroccan corsairs to attack American merchant ships in the future?"

The sultan put on a sombre face. Slowly it mutated into a smile. "I would like to make that promise to you, Commodore. Really I would. But you see our economy depends on the efforts of our corsair warriors. It is perhaps not as productive as the manufacturing industry in Europe, but it is the foundation of much of our economy. If I made the promise that you request, I would be hurting the very economy that my country depends on. Of course, if your little country were willing to provide us with the courtesy of a monetary tribute, it would offset the loss of revenue, and then I could satisfy the promise you have requested. I'm sure you understand."

Proctor could see that Dale was steaming and wanted to say something in rebuttal. Will prayed that he would not. It was not their place to negotiate between the two countries. They had already negotiated for the return of Orne. That was enough.

After a moment in which Dale forced himself to remain under

control he said, "I am quite disappointed, Your Majesty. I had thought that we had a meeting of the minds. Since we don't, then we shall leave things as they are. We get Captain Orne. You get one of our ships."

Apparently unmoved by Dale's concerns, Suleiman asked, "I would like to know which vessel you propose to give to me?"

Dale glanced at Proctor, then said, "We will give you the *Trenton*. A fine frigate that has been under the command of Captain Proctor."

Proctor felt like he was going to explode. His heart beat rapidly. He had not felt such anger in years—not since Habib had captured the *Betsey*. Not since Habib had callously killed a fellow seaman. Under different circumstances, Proctor would have protested vehemently. Why his ship? Why not one of the others? Was Dale getting back at him for forcing the issue of Orne's release? No, that didn't make sense, not in view of the way Dale had resisted giving up a ship. As he thought about it, it probably did make sense that Dale chose the *Trenton*, since it was one of the smaller frigates that had been added to the squadron at the last minute. He found himself nodding slowly as the logic of the choice began to make a sort of sense. He wasn't happy losing his command, but he certainly couldn't argue about the choice. Not now anyway.

The sultan smiled in satisfaction. "Good, that is settled. We shall make the exchange tomorrow morning. Since I'll be losing the services of Henry, my able advisor, I would like to go over a few things with him this afternoon so that I know the status of various matters before he departs. In the morning I will send some of my naval officers to the *Trenton*. They will take Henry and the two of you along with them. As soon as your men have debarked from the ship and my men have taken command of it, Henry will be released into your custody. Are we in agreement?"

"Yes, I suppose that is acceptable," said Dale unenthusiastically.

"Good. I will have Hussein find you quarters in which you can pass the night. Tomorrow morning I will expect you to join my officers as they board the *Trenton* to take command. To avoid an unpleasant confrontation, you will need to inform your officers on the vessel that they will no longer be in command and must vacate the ship immediately. You will be given one hour to complete the task. At the end of that hour, my men will be in command of the *Trenton* and you and your other vessels will make your departure from Rabat. Commodore Dale, do you understand these terms?"

A crestfallen Dale nodded his assent.

Chapter **68**
Rabat, Morocco

Proctor awakened with a start as a brilliant orange sun was just making its presence known in the eastern sky. He and Dale had shared a modest, but comfortable room in a building overlooking the sea. Dale had awakened moments before him upon hearing a loud knock on the door. It was a servant carrying a tray of food. The servant had said that they should be ready to depart the room in one hour.

"I tell you, Proctor, I'm getting tired of being ordered around by a backward race that as far as I can tell hasn't made any progress since Biblical times."

Proctor wanted to say that it must be especially hard for Dale as he wasn't used to taking orders from anybody, but he held his tongue and said nothing.

Dale continued. "Here's what we'll do when we get to the *Trenton*. You will remain there to supervise the transition, but Orne and I will take a longboat with some seamen and return to the *President*. From there I'll inform the other senior officers of what is transpiring. They'll need to be notified that each of their ships will be assuming their share of the *Trenton* sailors. Good God, Proctor, this is hard to swallow."

An hour later the same servant rapped again and led them through the streets of the city toward the quay where they saw a group of naval men clustered around a small xebec. The xebec was perfect for the task ahead as it could be propelled by oars or sails. In the inner harbor they would need to rely on the oars, but as they approached open water the sails could be used to hasten the short voyage. As they stepped onto the quay, Proctor did a quick count and came up with twelve Moroccans. Enough to bring the *Trenton* under their control and even sail it, if necessary. Not nearly enough to conduct military operations, though. Just enough for a show of possession.

The quay appeared to be about two-hundred yards long. Nearing the xebec and the Moroccan sailors, Proctor squinted, not sure of what he was seeing. Could his eyes be deceiving him? No, unfortunately they weren't. As they came closer, there was no doubt as to what he was seeing. Good God, it was Captain Habib. The man looked older, but still had that demonic look and was no doubt just as prone to violence as the young Habib. He still wore a cutlass. No doubt the same vicious sword that 17 years ago had been thrust through the abdomen of Bosun James Cathcart.

Proctor looked at Orne and saw the recognition on the captain's face. There was a fire in Orne's eyes that scared him. Could the captain control himself at the sight of the man who'd ruined his life and caused the death of some of his crew members?

Proctor could only imagine what Orne must be feeling, for he, himself, was fighting to control his own thoughts, too. It would be satisfying to lunge at Habib, maybe even kill him, but would it be fair to the rest of the sailors in the squadron, for almost certainly it would mean an all-out conflict with the Moroccans. American sailors would be killed. Orne, himself, might die. The mission to free an American civilian would end in disaster and achieve nothing except to worsen the already bad relations with the Moroccans. As much as he wanted to strike out at the evil Habib, he convinced himself that he would resist the temptation.

They were now close enough to the Moroccans that Proctor could see the cold, cruel eyes of Habib. Memories of the nightmare 17 years ago came flooding back. It was going to be hard to stay in control.

Habib was the first to speak.

"Aha, Captain Orne. I see that you have somehow arranged to go home. In order to do that, your morally depraved country had to give up a handsome vessel. I think the sultan and the people of Morocco got the best of the exchange. Still, make no mistake, we will miss you around here. I'm told that the sultan has been entertained by your American peculiarities."

"I cannot believe that the sultan brought you into his navy, Habib. He should have put you into a jail cell, or better yet, sent you to the bottom of the sea."

Habib sneered. "I understand that you do not fancy me, Captain Orne. It is a known fact that infidels do not respect or appreciate Muslim warriors. It has ever been thus."

"You're not a warrior, Habib, you're a predator who preys on innocent merchant seamen. I notice that you don't take on armed navy vessels. If you had the courage of a true warrior you'd be in the outer harbor fighting our squadron."

"If His Majesty wanted me to do battle with your navy, I assure you I would, and it would be the end of the squadron. Since the sultan has not tasked me with destroying your inconsequential little squadron, you and your decadent comrades will be spared. I cannot tell you what a disappointment that is to me."

Proctor could contain himself no longer. "You talk a good story, Habib. You have never had the courage to attack anyone your equal, much less a powerful force like our squadron in the outer harbor. You know that Suleiman does not want you to attack the squadron, so it is easy to sound like the brave warrior. You are nothing but a cowardly worm, and now your men here know that."

Orne eyed Proctor and squinted toward Habib as if to say, "Let's not go too far. We don't need trouble."

Habib directed his words to Proctor. "Knowing that the sultan does not want me to destroy your squadron has given you a false courage, Proctor. Do not mock my courage when you need the support of others to give you a bravery you lack without that support."

Proctor wanted to respond, but took Orne's admonition to heart.

Habib then grinned malevolently. "Since the sultan has demanded one of your ships in exchange for you, Captain Orne, it's clear that he values a vessel more than he values your services. Once again, Morocco wins against the degenerate nonbelievers. But enough of that. Let us get on with our occupation of the *Trenton*."

Chapter 69
Rabat, Morocco 1801

Less than half an hour later the xebec pulled alongside the *Trenton*. Proctor looked up at the the rail of the warship where virtually all of the crew was peering down at the strange craft bearing a dozen or so Moroccans and three Americans. Clearly, the crewmen had no idea why the Moroccan vessel had pulled alongside. Proctor yelled up to First Mate Richard Hardy.

"We're coming aboard, Richard. I'll explain when I join you."

"What about the Moroccans?" Hardy yelled down.

"Let them board, too. I'll explain in a minute."

"I don't like it, sir."

"I don't either, Richard. Now drop the ladder so I can join you."

A rope ladder was thrown over the side. Proctor turned to Orne, Dale and Habib and said, "I'll go up first and explain about the transfer. Things should go better that way, once they understand what the boarding is all about."

Orne and Dale nodded their agreement, but Habib stiffened.

"I think I should go up with you."

"You can if you want," said Proctor, "but you could meet resistance. Don't forget, you're outnumbered. Let me go first. I'll explain about the exchange agreement, and things should go better."

"Very well, but if you resort to any trickery, remember that my men outnumber your colleagues here on the xebec. Instead of freeing Henry Orne, you may lose him and Commodore Dale."

"You're too suspicious, Habib. We're not Moroccan pirates. You can trust us."

"Yes, I can trust you to resort to deception."

"Look, it's your decision. Come with me if you want, but I'm telling you things will go better if I go first."

Habib scowled as he thought about this. Finally he gestured with his hand for Proctor to go ahead.

Proctor scurried up the rope ladder and was helped over the gunwale by Richard Hardy.

"What's going on, sir?"

"The sultan has released Captain Orne, but he's demanded something in return."

"'What does he want, sir?"

"This ship."

"Tell me you're joking, sir."

"I'm not joking, Richard. It was the only way we could extricate the captain. He's been held captive for 17 years, Richard. We had to get him out."

"But the *Trenton*, sir?"

"I know. I know. It's a huge loss."

"It's a slap in the face, sir. An insult to the United States Navy and a weapon that will most likely be used against us in the future."

"I agree, Richard, but we're going to have to live with it. We have to stick to our agreement. Now here's what we're going to do. We're going to divide up our crew and send a few to each of the other ships. Commodore Dale and Captain Orne will take some of the crew to the *President*. We need to start on that right now, as the Moroccans will be occupying the *Trenton* immediately. Once the crew has been dispersed and the Moroccans have taken command of the *Trenton*, you and I will go to the *President* with any remaining crew members."

Habib yelled up from the xebec deck. "We're coming aboard, Proctor. You've had long enough. Drop another ladder." With that Habib and his fellow Moroccans began boarding the *Trenton* two at a time. When the last of the Moroccans were aboard, Orne and Dale were allowed to come up. Then Habib surveyed the deck and noted that most of the American crew members were still on board. His nostrils flared at the perceived delaying tactic.

"Why are these men still aboard this ship?" he demanded.

Proctor glared at his hated enemy. "We just got here, Habib. We needed to explain about the transfer of command. You don't explain that instantaneously. The men had no advance warning that they were going to lose their ship. It came as quite a shock. Be patient. You will have your ship in due time."

"Due time, bah! We are not on your schedule, Proctor. I want these men off the ship immediately. Or we will remove them ourselves." Habib was not accustomed to negotiating. It was not in his nature to see the other side of an issue. He was used to giving orders and being obeyed without objection.

"You will do nothing of the kind, Habib. Our men are leaving as quickly as they can. It is not easy to leave a ship under such circumstances. Surely even you must understand how our men must feel about this."

"I am not concerned with the feelings of your degenerate crew members. Get them off now, or my men will throw them off," roared Habib. At this, several of the Moroccans were heard to yell *na'am! na'am! na'am! (yes! yes! yes!)*.

Proctor understood this and wished to avoid a confrontation so he yelled, "All right, men. Move lively."

Apparently the Americans were still not moving as quickly as the Moroccans wanted them to. As one of the American sailors began his descent down one of the ladders, a Moroccan launched himself at the seaman, shoving the man with the full force of his moving body. The American lost his grip on the ladder and fell into the sea. A different Moroccan flung himself at an American just about to descend the second ladder. Before he could make full contact with the American, a nearby sailor grabbed him and wrestled the Moroccan to the deck.

At this the Moroccans erupted into a pitched, full-scale assault, attacking the Americans with razor-sharp cutlasses. Clearly, taking the Americans by surprise had been the plan from the beginning. The Moroccans were outnumbered by the crewmen, but Habib and his lieutenants believed that the Americans were soft and would easily be overwhelmed by the superior fighting ability of the sultan's warriors. Especially with the element of surprise.

The startled Americans responded quickly, defending themselves with their own sabers and cutlasses. Meanwhile, Habib stood to the side of the melee, encouraging his men, but staying out of the fray.

The Moroccans savagely hacked away at the Americans. Proctor, who had not carried his sword into the sultan's palace, grabbed the cutlass of a fallen American and slashed and hacked his way into the fight. A wicked swipe of a Moroccan cutlass tore through his sleeve, fortunately just nicking his arm. Proctor saw blood, but felt nothing as he parried a second blow and quickly thrust his sword into the midsection of the attacking Moroccan. Proctor had barely withdrawn his bloody cutlass from the man's abdomen when he was confronted by a new and larger attacker. The man was indeed big, but slow, and Proctor was able to dispatch him with a single slice to the side of his neck.

The ferocious clash was punctuated by cries of pain and rage as men went at each other with a frenzied passion. A sword-wielding American slipped on the blood-soaked deck and fell with a resounding thud. A Moroccan took advantage of this and thrust his sword into the fallen seaman. Instantly Proctor slashed at the Moroccan before he could even withdraw his cutlass. The man would never kill another American.

Suddenly a gunshot was heard and a Moroccan toppled. Then another gunshot and another Moroccan fell. The battle ended as quickly as it had started. Habib had miscalculated the Americans' fighting ability. Between the ferocious response to the the Moroccan aggression and numerical superiority of the crew, Habib's forces had been decimated. Of the original twelve only three, including Habib, remained alive. The Americans had lost four. A few others were wounded, but expected to survive. The Moroccans had been roundly defeated.

Chapter 70
Rabat, Morocco   1801

Both Dale and Orne had survived the bloody battle, though both were injured. Dale had suffered a painful slash to his left rib cage. It was later determined that two ribs had been broken, but were expected to heal. Orne sustained a blow to his sword hand, nearly severing his index finger. The finger was later surgically removed out of necessity.

While Proctor and other sailors attended to Dale's and Orne's wounds, as well as the wounds of the other injured Americans, Habib moaned and whined that he wanted to be killed. Habib had escaped injury by hiding behind the foremast. His hope had been that his men would prevail and that he could then return to the palace to tell Suleiman that they not only had command of the ship, but they had also fought a valorous battle eliminating the American crew and officers.

The healthy American crewmen secured Habib and the two surviving Moroccans and attended to the injuries of the other seamen.

At some point, Dale noticed the cowering Habib and barked, "Sit and be quiet."

Habib said, "What are you going to do to me?"

"All in good time, Habib. All in good time. Now keep quiet, or I'll run you through right now."

"Please do that. Kill me, I beg of you. Kill me. Have your revenge. Kill me."

"You want to die?"

Orne interrupted, saying, "He does because he doesn't want to face the sultan. He failed, and the sultan doesn't tolerate failure. Even if the sultan spares him, he'll live in shame for the rest of his wretched life. From his perspective it's better to die."

When Dale and Orne were bandaged and given laudanum for their pain, Dale pulled Orne and Proctor aside for a quick conference.

"What do you propose we do with these three Moroccan devils?" asked the commodore.

An emotional Orne said, "Send these two wretches back with a message to the sultan telling him that his forces broke the agreement. Therefore we no longer feel morally, ethically or legally bound to honor our end of the bargain. Tell him that we're keeping the *Trenton* and have taken Habib into custody to stand trial when we get back to the States. You can also tell him that we're not impressed with the fighting abilities of his warriors."

With a grin, Proctor said, "I doubt, sir, that the two men we send back will convey that last sentiment."

"Orne returned the grin and said, "Probably not, but tell them that anyway." Then, as if it hadn't occurred to him until now, he said to Dale, "That is, sir, if you agree to what I've suggested?"

The normally flinty Dale forced a smile and said, "I like it a lot. Let's not delay. Let's send the two Moroccans on their way in their xebec straightaway."

"It'll take them a while to sail the xebec back into port, sir," said Proctor. "It's a big vessel for two men to handle. Still, they'll get back eventually."

"No hurry, captain," said Dale. "No hurry. I'm not concerned with that at all. I don't care if it takes them all day. What I do want to do is get this squadron underway quickly. Get the word out to all the ships that I want us to set sail within the hour. We're too far west to stock up on supplies in Gibraltar so we'll make harbor in Tenerife and then off to America." He beamed with satisfaction as he said this. The voyage appeared to be ending on a high note.

Part 4

Chapter 71
United States

After his return to Boston in late 1801, Will Proctor remained in the navy patrolling the coastal traffic up and down the East Coast of the rapidly growing young country. It was relatively easy duty dealing with smugglers and other illegal activities. It was not exciting, but a welcome relief after the conflicts in Tripoli and Morocco. Still, after a year he began to miss the adventure and challenge of facing off against America's Barbary enemies. He felt he could be doing more to defend his country. Commodore Dale had retired, but there had to be some way or somewhere he could serve again.

One day in November 1802 Proctor learned that Captain Habib had been tried and convicted of murder and was to be hanged in early December. On that same day Will also learned that the Navy Department had sent Commodore Richard Morris to the Med with a new squadron to replace Dale. American shipping interests were still being attacked by the Barbary pirates. To make matters worse, Sultan Suleiman of Morocco had recently declared war against the United States, no doubt a result of the defeat and humiliation his forces had suffered at the hands of Dale's forces in 1801. Morris was a respected naval officer whose father had signed the Declaration of Independence. Proctor was deflated. Maybe he could have been part of that new squadron.

Soon afterward Proctor was notified by his superiors that President Jefferson and Secretary of the Navy Stoddert were sending Commodore Edward Preble to lead yet another squadron to the Mediterranean in January of the coming year. Apparently the plan was to reinforce Commodore Morris's squadron. Because of Proctor's experience in the region, he was offered the command of one of the squadron's ships, the *Baltimore*. It wasn't a difficult decision for Will. He couldn't have asked for a better opportunity.

He knew the region, knew some Arabic and had plenty of command experience.

Preble was asked by the secretary of the navy to go to Boston and prepare the 44-gun *USS Constitution* for service in the Mediterranean. The *Constitution*, under the command of Preble, would lead the new squadron. In addition to the *Constitution*, the squadron consisted of seven other ships: The *Enterprise, Nautilus, Vixen, Argus, Philadelphia, Siren* and the *Baltimore*. The *Philadelphia* was the second largest frigate of the squadron with 38 guns. The other ships carried between 12 and 16 guns each.

The plan was for all eight vessels, which were departing from different American cities, to meet in Gibraltar. The last to arrive was the *Argus*, which didn't get there till November 1. The ships had been in various states of construction, which accounted for the difference in arrival time. As each one was completed and readied for the mission ahead, it set sail for Gibraltar.

Chapter 72
The Mediterranean, November 1803

After taking on supplies and resting the crews for a few days, Preble's squadron resumed sailing into the Mediterranean. On a dark night shortly after leaving Gibraltar, the *Constitution* found itself surprisingly close to a strange warship. It was too dark to determine what kind of warship it was. The *Constitution* hailed the other ship asking for its identity. The warship responded with its own question about the *Constitution*'s identity. The *Constitution* again asked the other ship to identify itself. Instead of answering, the other ship repeated its request for the American ship to identify itself. Preble, exasperated by the other ship's refusal to identify itself, next communicated the name of his ship and his country to the unidentified ship and demanded that ship respond in kind or he would send a broadside. The voice on the other ship responded that he would return broadside for broadside.

"What ship are you?" repeated Preble angrily.

"This is His Britannic Majesty's 74-gun ship *Donegal*, Sir Richard Strachan commanding. Heave to and send a boat."

Preble didn't believe him. The other ship did not appear to be large enough to carry 74 guns. He was not about to submit to the other ship by sending a boat. He grabbed a trumpet, scrambled up the mizen mast and called out in a loud voice, "This is the United States ship *Constitution*, 44 guns, Commodore Edward Preble in command. I am about to hail you for the last time. If you do not answer correctly, I shall give you a broadside. What ship is that? Blow your matches, boys!"

Minutes later a longboat was seen making its way to the *Constitution*. A British lieutenant came aboard and admitted that the British vessel wasn't a 74-gun ship, but rather a 32-gun frigate called the *HMS Maidstone*.

Preble's stand against a British ship earned him grudging respect from his officers and crew. Preble was known as a strict commander with a lightning temper. After this incident, though, it was said that "If the old man's temper is wrong, his heart is right."

American naval officers as well as those from European countries believed that Britain was mistress of the seas and one was wise not to challenge them. Because Preble had the confidence to stand his ground against the Brits he became a legend throughout the Mediterranean.

Meanwhile, Morris and his squadron had been in the Mediterranean for several months adhering to Morris's own schedule. Soon, Jefferson and the secretary of the navy learned that Morris, contrary to naval policy, had brought along his wife and child and was spending considerable time in Gibraltar enjoying the comforts of the local society. His orders from the secretary of the navy had been 'to subdue, seize and make prize of all vessels, goods and effects, belonging to the Pasha of Tripoli [Yusuf Karamanli]'. Instead, the squadron behaved more like a squadron leisurely touring the Mediterranean than an active naval force. The navy department became convinced that Morris had done virtually nothing to pursue the war against Tripoli and to counteract harassment by Barbary Pirates. Washington decided that Morris was not up to the job and recalled him to the United States. Preble was put in charge of Morris's squadron in addition to his own. In a matter of three years four squadrons had been sent to the Mediterranean Sea to fight Barbary piracy.

One of the frigates in Preble's squadron was the *Philadelphia* under the command of Captain William Bainbridge. The *Philadelphia* had preceded the *Constitution* to Gibraltar and had captured the Moroccan cruiser *Mirboha*.

Preble, with seven more ships under his command, sailed to Morocco and conducted negotiations with Sultan Suleiman. Faced with the overwhelming naval presence plus the knowledge that the Americans had already captured the *Mirboha*, Suleiman became convinced that it was in his best interest to reaffirm the Treaty of Peace of 1786 between the United States and Morocco. Thus far Preble's mission to the Mediterranean was a success. This was about to change, though.

As Preble and the squadron were finishing up in Morocco, Bainbridge took the *Philadelphia* eastward toward Tripoli. The ship came upon two Tripolitan corsair vessels and began chase. The 1200-ton *Philadelphia* was gaining on the two vessels when it ran aground on a reef. The corsair vessels were considerably smaller than the frigate *Philadelphia* and very likely had deliberately led the larger ship with its greater draft into shallow waters where they hoped it would be stranded on the reefs known to be in the area.

Captain Bainbridge was frantic. The bow of the ship seemed to be hung up on the reef. He needed to free the bow of as much weight as possible. He barked orders to his crew. "We need to haul all of the forward cannons toward the stern, lads. We've got to lighten her weight up front if we're going to get free of this sand bar or reef. Whatever the hell it is."

When the cannons had been loosened from their gun carriages and pulled slowly toward the stern by the sweating crew, his first mate reported the bad news.

"She's still holding tight, sir. We can't pull free."

"Then we need to jettison those guns into Davey Jones Locker, lads. Tis a sad thought, but we must do it."

The crew tied ropes to the 2,000 pound cannons and gradually through even greater effort were able to topple them into the sea. It still wasn't enough to free the ship so Bainbridge ordered all but two of the remaining cannons to be offloaded.

"Still holding firm, sir," said the first mate.

"Then dump the balls, powder and anything of weight you can find. We've got to get out of here before these damned Arab crazies learn that we're stranded."

Still the great frigate remained aground. Meanwhile, the Tripolitans in the nearby port city of Tripoli became aware of the stranded vessel and sent gunboats out to capture the ship and take its 307 crew members and officers into custody. As the gunboats neared the *Philadelphia*, they fired on the nearly defenseless stranded vessel. Bainbridge and his men returned minimal fire with the few remaining cannons still on the ship. The limited fire they could muster was ineffectual, and Bainbridge met with his officers to decide what to do. Since it was impossible to free the ship they agreed that to prevent loss of lives the only thing they could do was surrender the ship.

The crewmen were immediately put into slave labor, while the officers were confined to the abandoned American consulate in

Tripoli. Eventually the Tripolitans did free the *Philadelphia* from the reef and were able to salvage the cannons from the bottom of the sea. The now refitted *Philadelphia* was in Tripoli's possession in the inner harbor.

Preble's squadron cruised the Mediterranean for the next two months, during which time the commodore and his officers deliberated over what could be done to free the crew of the *Philadelphia* who had been taken prisoners. They couldn't afford to limit their attention to just the prisoners, though. They'd been sent to the Med to protect American interests at sea.

At one point not far from Tripoli the *Constitution* sighted the Tripolitan vessel *Mastico*. Preble ordered his crew to take possession of the Tripolitan warship. It turned out that the captain of the *Mastico* was none other than Murad Rais. The Americans also learned that the *Mastico* was one of the gunboats that had captured the *Philadelphia*. Rais and his crew members were put in chains while the *Mastico* was renamed the *Intrepid* and fitted out with better armament.

Toward the end of December a plan was taking shape. Preble had chosen the Sicilian port of Syracuse as their winter base. While in Sicily he conducted negotiations with Tripoli through the Tripolitan consulate. Since no American ports were available, and he couldn't keep prisoners aboard indefinitely, Preble reluctantly let the crew of the *Mastico* go free in Syracuse. However, he kept Murad Rais in chains to be returned to the United States to stand trial for treason.

In January a peace arrangement with the Tripolitans was agreed upon. It consisted of a ransom of $120,000 plus the exchange of the *Philadelphia* for a schooner.

The U.S. had been struggling to adhere to a no-ransom, no-tribute policy in the belief that such payments only begot more such payments. However, it was not easy to stick to such a policy when you knew that Americans were being held captive in dire conditions.

Still, Preble decided to try one more thing before accepting this hard-to-digest peace arrangement. He resolved to find a way to destroy the *Philadelphia*. If the U.S. Navy couldn't have the ship, they would deny it to Tripoli.

JIHAD AT SEA

Young Stephen Decatur, Captain of the *Argus*, suggested that an elite hand-picked team be sent in to accomplish the job. Decatur's father had fought in the Revolution, and Stephen had followed in his father's footsteps by joining the navy in 1798. Decatur's reputation as a smart, scrappy officer helped sway Preble into accepting his suggested team of bright, effective raiders.

Chapter 73
Tripoli, February 1804

When Proctor learned that the captured captain of the *Mastico* was Murad Rais, he was delighted. Finally his old nemesis would meet with proper justice. Now was not the time to worry about this, though. Now was the time to prepare for the attempt to destroy the *Philadelphia*. Proctor was glad to hear that Decatur had been put in charge of the small team of sailors that would carry out this dangerous mission. He liked Decatur and his reputation as an aggressive, efficient fighter made him right for the task in his opinion. Proctor understood why Decatur wanted to head up the team, as just a few years ago Decatur's father had commissioned the *Philadelphia*. What surprised and pleased Proctor was that Decatur wanted him on his team.

He was honored to be chosen for this mission—especially by a man he respected so much. Clearly the mission was risky. He told himself that he was not afraid. He smiled. If he were truly honest he'd admit that he was definitely more than a little nervous. Only a fool would not see the risk, but he wasn't terrified. Over the years he'd gone through so much in the Mediterranean, starting with being captured by Moroccan pirates and spending far too much time in Moroccan jails—not to mention the harrowing experience in the life or death mutiny against Rais and his *da Gama* crew of vicious pirates. No, he wasn't afraid to die for his country. Just not now. He had too much to live for. He and Elizabeth had plans for the future. They would marry and raise a family. At least five. Maybe more if they could manage.

He'd decided that if he received a promotion in the next year or two, he would make a career in the navy. If not, he would go to Harvard College and become an attorney. His teachers had told him that he had the ability. Either way he and Elizabeth would have a good life. He knew that Liz would rather he resign from the navy and go to Harvard, but she'd said that she'd support either decision. Whatever made him happy.

JIHAD AT SEA

He wondered what she was doing right now. Probably working in her mother's little bake shop. He could see her warm perky smile as she greeted townspeople when they entered the shop. It was that winsome smile that had won his heart and now made him yearn to be in her arms. He remembered yearningly the times that they had snuck off to their favorite secluded spot on the banks of the Charles River.

They had a lot in common. Both of their fathers had died leaving their mothers to fend for themselves. Liz's mother had fewer children to take care of so she was able to run a very successful bakery, while his mother had to remain at home with a brood of children. Fortunately, some of them worked to help out with the meager household expenses. He knew it wasn't easy for her. If he was home he could help out. Even after he and Elizabeth were married he'd help his mother.

The team was ready to go. The assault complement would consist of the *Intrepid* plus the *Siren*. The *Intrepid* would resume its identity as the *Mastico*. The Americans had brought along Sicilian port pilot Salvatore Catalano from Syracuse to act as interpreter as he spoke fluent Arabic. The idea was for the *Mastico* to sail slowly into the harbor as if it had business there. Hopefully the incoming *Mastico* would not arouse suspicion until it was too late. Of the 80 men in the assault team, only a few were above deck, and they appeared to be be unarmed.

The entrance into Tripoli harbor was about two miles long. Near the entrance to the port a fort overlooked the waterway. If they got past the fort, it would be one big hurdle behind them, and they'd be halfway to their destination. Their safety was still not assured, but they'd have passed a major obstacle. As they sailed past the fort the sailors waved to the men guarding the fort. Since they were flying the Tripolitan flag and were showing no weapons, they made it past with no problem. Now the next danger point was the inner harbor itself.

As they glided past smaller boats in the harbor they waved to the occasional boatsman, who returned the feigned courtesy. When they were within 200 feet of the anchored *Philadelphia*, a guard on one of the nearby piers yelled, "Where you going? There's no room in here for a boat your size."

Salvatore Catalano yelled back in Arabic, "We left here seven days ago for Constantinople, but we lost our anchor in a storm."

The guard on the pier seemed to be satisfied, then pointed to the *Siren* and asked, "What is that ship at the mouth of the harbor?"

"It's a vessel we purchased in Malta. She's dropped anchor out there till we can find a better mooring for her." This seemed to satisfy the man, and he returned his attention to his own boat.

Decatur turned to his small team and said in a low voice, "So far, so good. We're almost there. We'll pull alongside the *Philadelphia* and pray there's not too many guards aboard. Remember, if we encounter anyone, use your swords, pikes and knives, not your pistols. We need to keep the noise to a minimum."

"What if *they* shoot?" asked a sailor.

He smiled a wry grin, "Then we shoot back. But only if they shoot first."

As they approached the *Philadelphia*, Decatur could see only three men on the deck of the larger ship. He knew there could be more because the *Philadelphia's* deck was ten feet higher than that of the *Mastico* so it was impossible to see anyone on the far side of the huge frigate's deck. So far the port was quiet. Only one of the three men on the *Philadelphia* even glanced at the *Mastico* as it came nearer. So far, so good.

Just as the *Mastico* was easing close to the *Philadelphia*, the guard on the pier noticed the anchor at the stern of the *Mastico* and yelled, "Infidels!"

Immediately Decatur said, "Prepare to board as soon as we come alongside."

The Americans could hear confusion on the deck of the *Philadelphia*. Apparently they were arguing about what they'd just heard from the guard on the pier.

When the *Mastico* bumped up against the hull of the larger ship Decatur gave the order to board. In less than ten seconds, a half dozen grappling hooks attached to rope ladders were thrown over the gunnel of the *Philadelphia*. Decatur led the boarding party, followed by Proctor and 16 or so more sailors. Proctor was amazed at how fast the men climbed the rope ladders and chains. One of the boarding crew later described the scene as a cluster of bees busily scurrying up the side of the ship. The boarding was surprisingly fast. By the time Proctor was aboard many of the raiding party were already slashing away at the Tripolitan guards. He was impressed by the fighting ability of his teammates, especially Decatur, who seemed a herculean combatant against ordinary mortals.

It was all over in a matter of minutes. The Tripolitan guards had been taken completely by surprise and soon had no heart for continuing an obviously losing battle. A number of them were seen rowing away in a small boat. Others jumped overboard and began swimming for shore or a nearby pier. Twenty or so guards had been cut down in the fray. Their bodies were thrown overboard into the stagnant harbor. One survivor was taken prisoner. Amazingly only one American suffered a wound, and that was not serious.

Now they had to get on with what they came to do before more Tripolitans arrived on the scene. Decatur ordered his men to distribute combustibles from the hold of the *Mastico* throughout the *Philadelphia*. They made sure to include the storerooms, cockpit, gun room and munitions room. When Decatur was sure that every part of the ship was covered, he walked along the deck from hatchway to hatchway shouting, "Fire!" Sailors then lit spermaceti candles soaked in turpentine and threw them onto the combustibles.

The fires spread rapidly. Decatur remained on the burning ship until every last man had made it to the deck of the *Mastico*. When the last man was off the *Philadelphia*, Decatur jumped down onto the deck of the *Mastico*.

The *Mastico* now resumed using its *Intrepid* name and attempted to escape free of the burning *Philadelphia*. As they were pulling away, one of the seaman shouted that the main boom had somehow run afoul of the *Philadelphia's* anchor chain. Decatur looked around and said, "I need a man with good balance to climb out there and free us."

Proctor volunteered. He'd done a lot of mast climbing and work on spars and felt confident in positions other men avoided. It was not an easy task to maneuver one's body along an eight-inch thick boom with nothing to hold onto but the boom itself, since the mainsail had not yet been raised. A man could easily lose his balance and topple into the harbor.

Proctor straddled the boom, which was swaying ever so slightly. Slowly he pulled himself along, catching himself more than once when the boat swayed more than normal. All the while the rest of the team on the *Intrepid* waited tensely, knowing that if Proctor fell into the water, they would have to fish him out, losing valuable time. Worse, it would mean that they still had not gotten free from the anchor chain. They knew that it was only a matter of time before angry Tripolitans showed up to stop them. There would be no getting away then.

Proctor was finally at the end of the boom where it was entangled with the *Philadelphia's* anchor chain. He struggled frantically to free the boom so that they could be on their way. The American raiders watched as his struggles were frustratingly unsuccessful.

Just when it seemed as if all hope of success was doomed,

Proctor gave the thumbs up. Decatur and the other men gave a sigh of relief. Their relief was to be short-lived, though, for they now heard angry yelling as guards and other Tripolitan sailors came running toward the nearby pier. There was not much time left if they were to get out of the port alive. Proctor decided that it would be better to drop into the water than inch his way back on the boom. He was just about to let go and swim to the side of the ship to be pulled to safety when he felt the ball hit his neck. Images of Elizabeth and his mother flashed through his fading consciousness. His last thoughts were of hopes that his fellow raiders would make it out safely.

Decatur froze. He found his heart racing and he struggled to catch his breath. He liked Proctor. Just when it looked as if they were going to make it this happened. He shook his head in resignation.

"All right men," he said, "we've lost Will. Let's not lose anyone else. Man the oars and get the sails up. Let's get out of here. Have your weapons ready to return fire." The ketch slowly inched away from the *Philadelphia* toward the outer harbor, taking small arms fire the entire way.

They were perhaps no more than 100 feet away from the end of the pier when they began taking cannon fire in addition to the small arms. The *Intrepid* returned fire with small arms, but couldn't use its cannons because their stern was facing the Tripolitans. They were clearly outgunned because of this. Fortunately, the enemy fire was inaccurate and they were able to rejoin the *Siren* with only one other raider taking a hit, and that wasn't fatal.

Meanwhile the fires on the *Philadelphia* had grown into a raging inferno. The American raiders broke into a cheer, but immediately cut it off as they remembered Proctor. Denying the Philadelphia to the Tripolitan predators was a major victory, but like many victories, it had come at great cost.

THE END

Writer's Notes

Jihad at Sea is a work of fiction based on a little known period in American history called the Barbary Wars. The Barbary Wars were our first encounter with radical Islamic terrorism. From the end of the American Revolution in 1783 until the end of the War of 1812 in 1815, American shipping in the Mediterranean Sea and off the coast of North Africa was subjected to brutal attacks by pirates from four North African countries known as the Barbary coast: Morocco, Algeria, Tunis and Tripoli (Now Libya). The cost to American shipping was great. Worse than the loss of cargoes was the loss of lives and ships. The Barbary pirates not only took vast quantities of merchandise, they enslaved the crews and took possession of the ships. *Jihad at Sea* is a story that tries to portray realistically and accurately the Barbary Wars. Much of the story is historically accurate, but in some cases I have taken liberties to make the story flow better as a work of fiction.

The Barbary Wars began in 1783 at the end of the American Revolution when Americans were no longer protected by British treaties with the pirate states. The Barbary Wars went on for another ten years after the 1805 Battle of Derne as the four predatory North African states continued their practice of attacking unarmed merchant vessels. The four Barbary states continued to exact payments from the United States and European countries. Often, when one of these countries agreed to accept a certain amount for tribute, it would increase the amount previously agreed on before carrying out the terms of the agreement. Treaties would be signed and broken at the whim of the Barbary monarchs.

From the end of the American Revolution in 1783 until 1789 when President Washington was elected, the Continental Congress paid tributes to the Barbary states in order to carry out trade in the Mediterranean sea. When Washington took office he continued the practice of paying tributes because he had no navy to protect American shipping.

When Thomas Jefferson became president in 1801 he struggled with the matter of how to deal with the Barbary pirates. It had become apparent that the U.S. could not afford to continue to pay tributes and ransoms to the Barbary states. In 1800 tributes and ransom to the pirate states came to 20 percent of the nation's total budget. Something had to be done.

When it came to a choice between peace or war, Jefferson always came down on the side of peace, but he knew that a strong military was necessary to attain that peace. He believed that a nation needed to have the capability of punishing countries that did us wrong. Further, he believed that it was important that such countries had to beware that we had that capability. It was not enough to merely ask for peace, for the Barbary states would view such a plea as weakness. Jefferson believed that a strong navy was an absolute necessity if the U.S. was to put the fear of Allah into the Barbary states. He hoped that merely having sufficient might to threaten the Barbary states would be enough to attain a peaceful resolution with those states. In 1785 he wrote to Secretary of State John Jay saying,

> "Justice . . . on our part, will save us from those wars which would have been produced by a contrary disposition. But how to prevent those produced by the wrongs of other nations? By putting ourselves in a condition to punish them. Weakness provokes insult and injury, while a condition to punish it often prevents it. This reasoning leads to the necessity of some naval force, that being the only weapon with which we can reach an enemy. I think it to our interest to punish the first insult: because **an insult unpunished is the parent of many others**. We are not at this moment in a condition to do it, but we should put ourselves into it as soon as possible."

Obviously, Jefferson understood that the mere threat of punishment might not always be enough. Unfortunately, this policy of punishing the insults was not always followed. Much of the time when Jefferson and John Adams before him sent squadrons off to the Mediterranean to protect our merchant ships at sea and occasionally to blockade Barbary ports, they gave strict orders to fire only when fired upon. This policy of firing only when fired upon meant that Barbary pirates that attacked American merchant ships didn't get punished if U.S. Navy ships were not nearby when the attack occurred.

In the late 18th century it was understandable that American forces did not take an aggressive stance against Barbary pirates, as the U.S. army and navy were almost nonexistent. After the turn of the century, though, with Jefferson's help, America began to build a serious navy. Despite this new strength, the government was often unwilling to push the Barbary states too hard, hoping against illogical hope that negotiation would win peaceful agreements and force would not be necessary. It took a great many years for our leaders to understand that the Barbary monarchs had no interest in compromise, that they thought differently and their belief system argued against compromise. Negotiation to them meant *how much* tribute or ransom they could get, not whether such payments should be exacted at all.

The actions and words of the real people in *Jihad at Sea* are for the most part portrayed as accurately as I could make them based on my research. Except for when I quote their exact words from historical documents, the words I have given them are mine. However, I tried to make their speech consistent with what my research revealed they believed at the time. Commodore Richard Dale's actions were accurately portrayed except for the battle in Tripoli Harbor in 1801. Dale actually ended the blockade and pulled his squadron out of Tripoli without fighting.

Timothy Pickering did not play the role he did in this book, though his behavior is not inconsistent with the kind of person he was.

Sultan Suleiman's somewhat enlightened mentality was purely the creation of the writer's mind. I could not find anything in my research about his personality or thinking. However, put in context with his predecessors, it is likely that his thinking about exacting tributes from western nations was fairly accurate.

The crew of the *Betsey* was actually released several months after its capture when a ransom was paid by the U.S. government. Murad Rais, (nee Peter Lisle) did turn traitor while in captivity and did convert to Islam and become a pirate for Morocco and later admiral in the Tripolitan navy. Rais was never tried for treason in the U.S. He actually married the daughter of Yusuf Karamanli and died a natural death in Tripoli.

It was not until the end of the War of 1812 that Barbary piracy finally ended. In 1815, when The U.S. and Britain signed the Treaty of Ghent ending the war, England and several other European countries began to put pressure on the Barbary states demanding the end of piratical attacks on merchant ships. Finally, after decades of paying tribute, the Europeans adopted the American philosophy of using naval and other military strength to force the predator states to allow free trade in the Mediterranean Sea. At the same time merchant ships grew larger and better equipped to fend off pirate attacks.

RICHARD SCOTT

Richard Scott is a retired editor, writer, and publisher, having been president and publisher of the David McKay Company and president and publisher of Fodor's Travel Publications. He's also been managing editor of *American Bookseller* and *Bookselling this Week*. In the 70s Mr. Scott was co-host with Isaac Asimov, Brendan Gill and Nat Hentoff of a nationally syndicated radio talk show called 'In Conversation.' He lives with his wife Jeanne in Salem, Massachusetts.

Made in the USA
Middletown, DE
08 October 2016